Irish War

Irish War

Book 16 in the Anarchy series
By Griff Hosker

Contents

Irish War 1
William, Earl of Cleveland 5
Part One Scotland 5
Prologue 5
Chapter 1 8
Chapter 2 19
Chapter 3 29
Chapter 4 45
Chapter 5 60
The Warlord 68
Part Two 68
Stockton 68
Chapter 6 68
Chapter 7 81
Chapter 8 94
Part Three -Wales 105
Chapter 9 105
Chapter 10 118
Part Four- Ireland 131
Chapter 11 131
Chapter 12 142
Chapter 13 156
Chapter 14 167
Chapter 15 179
Chapter 16 193
Epilogue 209
Glossary 212
Historical Notes 214
Other books by Griff Hosker 218

Irish War

Published by Sword Books Ltd 2017

Copyright © Griff Hosker First Edition

The author has asserted their moral right under the Copyright, Designs and Patents Act, 1988, to be identified as the author of this work.

All Rights reserved. No part of this publication may be reproduced, copied, stored in a retrieval system, or transmitted, in any form or by any means, without the prior written consent of the copyright holder, nor be otherwise circulated in any form of binding or cover other than that in which it is published and without a similar condition being imposed on the subsequent purchaser.
A CIP catalogue record for this title is available from the British Library.
Thanks to Design for Writers for the cover and logo.

Dedicated to Hilary Springgay; a lovely lady taken far too soon.

Irish War

William, Earl of Cleveland

The northern borders are still filled with danger and we need a strong hand here to control it. I hereby appoint William of Stockton to be Earl of Cleveland and I charge him with the protection of the border.
Henry II- The Welsh Marches

Part One Scotland

Prologue

My father and I had barely had moments with each other before he was whisked off with King Henry. He was going to war in Anjou. It seemed that our destiny was to be apart. Yet he had spent some little time with my wife, son and daughter. They had met and seen each other. For that I was grateful. More than that the four of them got on so well that it was as though they had always known each other. Even now, just five days after they had left, Samuel still pined for the grandfather he had just met. Each night he would ask me to tell him tales of his deeds. I found that I did not know them all. I sought out Aiden one day. He had been with my father the longest of any of those who lived in the castle and the valley. He had been bought as a slave. Now he led my father's hunters, scouts and gamekeepers. I rode with him around the manor and he told me the stories I did not know. Aiden was the one who knew them all. Now that I knew them I could pass them on to my son. My father had done great deeds. They were the kind of deeds which shape kingdoms and gain thrones. They were tales filled with my father's honour fighting the treachery of others. I discovered that my father was a very modest and noble man.

Aiden was plain-spoken and simple of speech. I heard the stories devoid of hyperbole and exaggeration. "I know not how he did most of what he did do, my lord. My task is easy. I find the enemy but your father, why he seems to read the minds of whichever foe he fights and makes their plans look like nonsense. He makes men do that which seems impossible and yet they do it. In all the time I have known him he has never been foresworn. He sleeps alongside his men and shares their food. He does not take all, he shares." He shook his head, "I know that I am lucky to have him as my lord."

He had filled in the gaps by the time we reached Stockton again. "Thank you, Aiden, what you have told me is most helpful."

Aiden reined in and looked at me earnestly, "But lord, he is not becoming any younger. He still fights in the fore. He still risks his life. I wish that he were here, lord, for then he would be safe. You would look after your father."

I shook my head. "I am a shadow of that great man."

"You are wrong, lord, for I spoke with Masood and know that the Warlord's blood courses through your veins too. You are young. Young men make mistakes but you have atoned. Your father told me of the Crusades. You have been reborn and here you can be the new Warlord and let your father enjoy his autumn years."

"I thank you for the stories, Aiden, and I will try to make him stay at home, but the King seems to need him."

"He has served the King, the King's mother and the King's grandfather. Surely that is enough for any man."

Aiden was right. The royal family owed him more than they could ever pay. I was now, even more saddened by my father's departure and I went to his solar. Aiden was right. The Warlord had done enough. The talk with Aiden had focussed me. I had a job to do. My father and the king had entrusted me with the peace of the north and my first task was to meet with the King of Scotland. King Malcolm was young. I had been given clear instructions by King Henry. In return for the prisoners we had taken I was to demand the return of both Northumbria and Cumbria. As compensation, I was to offer King Malcolm the County of Huntingdon and the title of Earl. It was a clever move for it would mean that the King of Scotland had to pay homage to the King of England. Just as important was that Malcolm could not be a knight until King Henry knighted him. I knew that young King Malcolm was passionate about knighthood.

The King had asked me to use the offices of the Bishop of Durham. I had sent a message to de Puiset asking him to visit with me to discuss my visit to Scotland. Despite using the king's name, the refusal had been perfunctory bordering on the downright rude. I would have to do this alone but, when I had done with the Scottish King, then I would turn my attention to the Bishop.

I planned on travelling to Carlisle to give my demands, personally, to King Malcolm. I would not use a letter. I had a wax tablet and a stylus. I had used them in the Holy Land. I made a list of the knights and men I would take on my visit. I chose them carefully. Sir Wulfric and Dick were the first names I wrote. They had served my father longer than any and were doughty warriors. Sir John of Stockton, Sir Harold of Hartburn and Sir Gilles of Norton would also come with me along with their retinues. I would take Brother Peter too. He was a priest and that might aid the negotiations but he was also a warrior and who knew when that skill might be needed. Now that Ralph of Bowness was my castellan I knew that my family would be safe in my father's castle. I would be accompanied by a little over a hundred men but they were the finest warriors to be found in the land and I was not worried. If I needed it I had Hugh of Gainford still holding on to Barnard Castle for me. It would be enough. I would take my servants and a baggage train. I was representing a king. I needed to look as powerful as one.

Chapter 1

I left clear instructions with my wife, the Steward and Ralph of Bowness. My father had told me how he had left the valley once and raiders had almost destroyed it. That would not happen while I was in command. I sent riders to have the knights who remained to ride long patrols to the borders. I had left Sir Phillip at Piercebridge. That was the main route south.

It was hard to say goodbye to my wife but I left her in good hands. Alice, my father's housekeeper, viewed my family as the one she had never had. She took the children to the kitchen for some sweet treats the cook had made while I said goodbye to my wife.

"Be careful, husband."

"This is not the Holy Land and I do not go to war. I go to barter with a king. I will return before the month is out." I held her at arm's length. "What think you to your husband now? I am advanced by a king to speak with a king. I am the lord of the whole of the north!"

She leaned forward and kissed me, "You are always the same man to me. I have seen your greatness and know that many kings could learn much from you but I am pleased that you have been rewarded."

I shook my head, "I think the cold of England has affected you. I am lucky and I know it. I will have Alice light a hot fire tonight."

She stepped on her toes to kiss me goodbye, "You are a fool. But you are my fool. While you are gone I will get to know the people of Stockton and perhaps some of the other ladies of the valley."

"Visit the town but do not venture beyond it. With so many knights and men at arms with me, I would be happier with you safe in my castle. Besides, I shall have a feast when I return and we are rid of these prisoners; then you shall meet the other ladies and they will all be awed by your beauty."

"And you, my husband, have been affected by the sun of the Holy Land!"

Irish War

I took Edward and Edgar as my scouts. Aiden had earned the right to stay at home along with Masood. They were both teaching Samuel how to use a bow and a sling. Knights did not need to use those skills but my father believed that a warrior needed to be able to use anything to defend himself. I could use a bow and a sling. I had rarely needed to. One day I might. The other reason I did so was that it would give Samuel discipline. When he began to train as a knight then he would have to exercise during every waking hour. He would practise, first with a wooden sword, and then with a spear. He would work up to a metal sword and a lance. I had asked my two scouts to keep him working. It would stop him getting into mischief while preparing him for the rigour of the training involved in becoming a knight.

We rode first to Piercebridge where I spoke with Sir Phillip. Satisfied that he knew my mind we pushed on to Barnard Castle. Sir Hugh of Gainford held it for my father. We had captured it from the Scots and it was a thorn in their side for the mighty castle guarded the western approach to the valley. The Scots had tried to take it many times but it was even more difficult to take than Stockton. The men at arms and archers stayed in the town. The knights and squires, along with our servants stayed in the castle. I had brought my four servants. All had been warriors and they could double as guards if we needed them.

I had been a squire at the same time as Sir Hugh and we got on well. His family had all been slaughtered by the Scots and my father had raised him. It made us more like brothers. He had four knights in the castle. My father had knighted them all. One was Sir Richard who had recently been his squire. He would be given a manor closer to home but he had wanted to learn from Sir Hugh. He had the greatest responsibility of any knight in the valley. If Barnard Castle fell then the whole of the valley could be ravaged.

With Hugh's wife Anne as mistress, we ate well in the huge hall. Wulfric and Dick sat together and looked like our grandfathers. They were almost twice the age of any of us. Both had seen us when we had been young. Both had helped to train us and yet I was now commanding them.

I sat next to Hugh. He knew the border like no other. It was one reason why Sir Richard had asked to serve in the castle. He wished to be where the danger was the greatest. I noticed him crane his head to catch every word that was said between the two of us. He was keen to learn.

"So, Hugh, how is the border?"

"It is quiet at present. When the Scots change kings there are always disputes and pretenders who seek to take the throne by force. That means our life is a little easier for a while. King Malcolm is young. He is but fifteen years old. He wishes to be a great warrior but he is a mere pawn. The sons of Máel Coluim mac Alaxandair seek to undermine him. He is beset by raids from Orkney and there are others who claim the throne. He knows not whom to trust."

"Then that is good news."

"It would be except that he has no control over his own lands. Banditry and brigandage are rife. Petty lords seek to create empires. Since his grandfather died we have had more skirmishes with them than before. And the Bishop of Durham, de Puiset, plays a dangerous game. He flirts with some of the Scots and, I believe, encourages them to raid."

"How do you know?"

"Some of the Scots we have had to deal with were coming west from the valley of the Wear. That is the Palatinate."

"Then when I have spoken with this boy I will ride to Durham and tell him of my new title and authority."

"I am sorry, Earl, I forgot to use your title!"

I laughed, "Like my father, I believe that titles are there to impress our enemies. I need them not with friends."

"Do you wish all of my knights and men?"

I shook my head, "You need to leave a good garrison and knights here to defend the castle but I would have you with me. You know the Scots better than any. I am new to them. You will have a better idea if they are trying to deceive me."

"Then I will bring just one knight with me; Sir Richard. He is keen to learn how a knight should conduct himself."

I saw, out of the corner of my eye, the relief on the face of Sir Richard.

"Who are they that represent a threat to King Malcolm?"

"There are foreign enemies but domestically it is Ferchar, Mormaer of Strathearn, Fergus Of Galloway and his son Uhtred and Walter Fitzalan. If the three parties ever decided to join with the sons of Máel Coluim mac Alaxandair then King Malcolm would fall and we would have a mighty host to face."

"Could we defeat them?" I smiled, "Without my father?"

"We could but with or without your father it would be bloody and we would lose many men. More than that, we would lose crops and people would starve. Better that we did not have to fight them."

"Your advice sounds good. Then when we ride have all the knights ensure that we look regal. Every banner and standard must flutter as we ride. I know that the Scots will feel stronger not having to face the Warlord but we have enough men who have fought them to make an impression. If the king is as young as you say then this should be a simple task."

Things were never simple on the border. We would have a hard ride the next day and I retired early. These days I did not need to tell my squire, Alf, son of Morgan, what to do. He had developed into one of the best squires in the valley. He had been helped by knights such as John of Stockton who had been my father's squire. His deficiencies had been in horsemanship and now he was as accomplished as any. He woke me before dawn and brought me water to bathe and clothes for travelling. When I had donned my mail, he strapped on my sword and followed me to the Great Hall. Cold food was laid out and other knights were there eating already. Wulfric and Dick were old campaigners They had taught me, when young, to eat when you could and to eat as much as you could for you never knew when supplies would run out.

Wulfric was a big gruff warrior. He was more like a bear than a man. Yet there was none, save Dick, who was more loyal to my family. That was because neither had ever married. My father's family was as close to a family as they would get.

"So, Earl William, will we get to fight the Scots?"

"The king wishes us to make a peace but we need to ride in strength for we wish the return of Cumbria and Northumbria."

He beamed, "Then we will fight for the Scots will not give up those two jewels. That bastard Stephen gave them away! I still recall Northallerton! Had the knights of the north heeded your father we could have taken the whole of Scotland! We sent them packing that day!" I saw Sir Richard's eyes light up. He had not been there but, along with the battle of Lincoln, that had been one of my father's greatest triumphs. It had been a great victory. It was the pinnacle of my father's career as a commander.

Dick nodded, "I was speaking with some of Hugh's knights. King Malcolm is young but we will be travelling in dangerous territory. I will keep my archers ahead of the column. Edward and Edgar are good. They can warn us of danger."

"I rely on you two to help me make the right decisions."

Wulfric laughed, "A battle is where I make my best decisions! Dick here is your man for strategy!"

"Do not disparage yourself, Wulfric. I need you to use those battle-hardened eyes which can detect threat and weakness in battle to do the same when we negotiate. I do not doubt that they will not allow all of my knights to accompany me. You two will be amongst those that do."

Dick laughed, "And we are the lowest born, save Harold! There is an irony! The low born are equal to the high born!"

"You have earned your place at the high table by your deeds in battle." Dick had been an outlaw when my father had met him. He was right. He had had a remarkable journey. We finished our food. "Let us ride, we have many leagues to cover this day."

Sir Hugh had two of his scouts with Edgar and Edward. Alan and Carl were local men who knew the road west. The four of them left first and we headed towards Bowes. One of Sir Hugh's knights, Sir John of Bowes, had a fortified hall there. It was not a castle for, if danger threatened, then the people of Bowes could easily flee to Sir Hugh's castle. After passing the hall we followed the old Roman Road over Stainmore. It was a bleak road. Few people lived there. That made it more dangerous for us. It meant no one could give us a warning of danger. There were many places where we could be ambushed. Of course, for an ambush to take place then an enemy would have to know, in advance, of your plans. I had acted swiftly following the king's commands and I hoped that no one could take advantage of our journey. We had chosen the longer route as it was easier on the horses and had less opportunity for attack.

We passed a number of small castles as we headed west. Not all were occupied. English knights had had them until Stephen gave them away. There were many men serving my father who had fled to Stockton when the Scots had taken them. The Scots who held them now had a small garrison. There might be, perhaps, twelve men in each one. We could have taken any of them but my orders were to talk. We passed the occupied castles with just baleful looks. If my negotiations went well then soon they would have English lords in them. Appleby Castle was the newest of the castles. Built by the Earl of Chester it commanded the road. We made certain that we skirted the castle. The Scots did not use the war bow but if they had crossbows then they could hit one of us.

It became obvious that we would not make Carlisle before nightfall and we would have to make camp. Our four scouts constantly returned to give us information on the road ahead. We stayed the night at Brougham Castle. It had not been invested by the Scots. Instead, they had a lord at Penrith. That was just a few miles up the road. The Scots had taken the gates from the castle. No doubt they had been used to build something but the hall remained and we were able to sleep dry. Our horses had somewhere to graze and access to water. We would arrive at Carlisle fresher than I had expected.

The fact that we had passed Appleby and spent the night at Brougham meant that King Malcolm was apprised of our imminent arrival. Riders had been sent ahead of us to warn him. We were not at war and we were not attempting to hide. We knew that we had been seen when Edgar rode back to tell us after we had passed Penrith, that riders were heading our way.

I needed no words to order the experienced men I led. They prepared for battle without a word of command. Shields were pulled a little higher so that they could be used in a heartbeat. Swords were slid in and out of scabbards. Archers strung bows and readied arrows. Our helmets hung from our cantles but could be donned in an instant. We all wore a mail coif upon our heads.

When the Scots came I almost laughed. There were four mailed men on large horses and the other twenty who came with them had no mail and rode on the small horses favoured by the Scots. With round shields and short swords, they were not a threat. I saw Dick's archers unstring their bows. We would not be fighting this day.

The leader was an older warrior with a grey beard. He had a surly manner. There was a distinct similarity between him and the young warrior next to him.

"I am Fergus, Mormaer of Galloway! What are you doing in King Malcolm's lands?"

"I am here as an emissary of King Henry of England and Duke of Normandy and Anjou. What I have to say is for the king's ears alone."

They did not move. I saw the younger warrior grinning, "You bar our way, mormaer."

The younger warrior spat to the side and began to scratch his armpit, "Norman, you are not passing us."

I nudged Alciades forward, "What is your name?"

"Uhtred son of Fergus." He frowned, "Why do you ask?"

"I prefer to know the name of the men I kill. Now out of my way. The men I lead have killed more Scotsmen than those who squat like toads in

Carlisle Castle. The twenty-four who bar our way will not bother us." I turned to the mormaer. "Control your whelp and learn manners or I will have blood spilt here this day."

I spurred my horse. The horses of Fergus and Uhtred moved out of the way and when Wulfric and the rest of my knights followed the Scots were forced into the ditch. One of the mailed warriors could not control his horse and he was thrown, heavily to the ground.

Wulfric rode next to me. "You should have bloodied them, Earl."

"There may be a time for that but King Henry impressed upon me the need to secure the land peacefully."

I heard hooves a short while later and saw half a dozen of the riders on ponies. They were galloping across the valley sides to reach Carlisle before we did. It was to be expected. The castle was triangular in shape with two bridges over the moat. It had a solid keep. As we neared the castle I saw that the King's standard flew from the tallest tower and that the walls were lined with men. The gates were, however, open. I turned in the saddle, "Brother Peter, Sir Wulfric, Dick and Sir Hugh bring your squires and come with me. Sir Harold take charge and make camp here by the Eden."

Sir Harold nodded, "Yes, Earl William."

It still sounded strange to hear my father's title given to me. I nudged Alciades and the nine of us entered across the bridge over the moat. The armed guards who looked up at us bowed their heads as we passed. My standard was known. Once we reached the bailey servants were waiting to hold our horses.

"Alf, you and the other squires stay here. Keep your ears and eyes open."

Carrying our helmets, we walked towards the gate to the keep. It was a large square keep. This would be the first time I had entered. A pair of guards stood at the door. I wondered if we would be stopped from entering but they stood apart and bowed to allow the five of us to enter. Once inside we were greeted by a priest. "I am the Canon of Carlisle, Henry Murdach. The King asks if your intentions here are peaceful?"

I smiled, "Does the king fear five men and one a priest? We do not come here to hurt his majesty."

The canon nodded, "Then follow me, my lord."

The Great Hall had been prepared for our visit. The King was seated on a throne on a raised dais. Next to him were two huge warriors. They were the chamberlains who would lie next to his door each night. He was flanked by two knights. I later discovered that they were Ferchar, Mormaer of Strathearn and Walter Fitzalan. Both were much older than the king. They glowered and glared at me. Next to them were two huge bodyguards. There were two tables set out at right angles to the dais. Scottish lords, ten of them, sat on one table while the other was empty. I gestured for my knights and Brother Peter to sit at the empty table. I strode up to the dais. I took from my surcoat the letter written and signed by the king. I flourished it.

"King Malcolm, King Henry has sent me as his representative to discuss certain matters appertaining to the border. This is my licence to do so." I unrolled it so that he could see the signature and the seal. I made no attempt to hand it over.

I saw King Malcolm open his mouth to speak. The knight to his right spoke. "You speak to a king. Show more manners!"

"I speak for a king and you speak to an earl. I would have more respect in your tone if I were you."

King Malcolm stood, "This is a bad start to peace talks! You are now the Earl of Cleveland I believe?"

"I am, your majesty."

"And your father?"

"He is now elevated to Earl Marshal. He is with the king."

He came down from the dais and clasped my arm. "I have spoken with knights who knew of you in the Holy Land. They say that there was no nobler knight in the whole of Christendom. I envy you your reputation."

I smiled. I found myself liking this earnest young man. "You would be a knight?"

"I would but as my father died when I was too young I must await a king to dub me."

I spied hope here. "I am sure that will happen."

I saw him chew his lip and then look over his shoulder, "The Earl and I will walk the walls and talk."

The knight who had spoken to me said, "I like not that, majesty. I do not trust Normans!"

"Lord Fitzalan, I will be quite safe but if it makes you feel better we will take the Earl's priest and Canon Henry with us."

The two priests rose and followed us leaving the Scottish lords looking annoyed and my knights bemused at the turn of events. Carlisle was unusual. It was a triangular castle. The king led me up the stairs and we left the keep to walk along the fighting platform. I saw that the men who had lined it as we had arrived were now moving to their warrior hall. They had been ready for a fight. King Malcolm was no coward.

"What does my cousin want, Earl? Speak plainly for I am new to the world of negotiations."

"As am I, your majesty. I am a warrior. I will state it simply for you. King Henry would have returned to him Northumbria and Cumbria. The lands given by King Stephen will become English once more. They were signed away and King Henry would have you sign them back to him."

I heard an intake of breath from Canon Henry.

"I like this castle."

"I am certain there are better castles in Scotland."

"My grandfather gave estates to knights."

"Then give them other estates in Scotland."

"They will not be happy."

"I will speak bluntly, for that is my way. King Henry has sent me to negotiate. If my negotiations fail then he and my father will bring the full force of the English army to bear on Scotland to impose his will. How many times has a Scottish army defeated an English one?" He said nothing. "He does not want to take them by force but he could." We had reached the wall closest to where my men were setting up camp. "I have brought but a handful of knights. Look there at the men who accompany my knights. They ride palfreys. They are all mailed. The archers are the finest in England and all are mounted. If I brought all of my men then this castle would be totally surrounded. Could you stand? How many archers do you have? How many crossbows?"

"My people are not afraid to defend their land."

"Yet this land is English. It was given away in my lifetime. You say you are new to negotiations. How many battles have you fought?" His head dropped. "I have been fighting since I was but ten years old. That was twenty-four years ago. I have fought in England, Normandy, Anjou, Provence and the Holy Land. I know how to war and I know how to win." I was not boasting, I was speaking the truth. "I am like my father; I never lie. Believe me when I say that if you refuse this offer then you will lose the flower of Scotland and we will still end up with Cumbria and Northumbria."

"I am not sure."

"You are threatened from the north and the isles are you not?"

He looked up in surprise. "How did you know?"

"I know. The men you might lose to us would be better employed fighting the Vikings and rebels in the north and the west."

I saw him thinking.

"The Irish raid your lands and take slaves. Think how the men you use to defend castles from us might be better used to defend your people."

We reached the gatehouse and walked through. He said nothing along the whole length of the second wall. Then he stopped and looked at me. "And in return?"

I had won, "You would be granted the County of Huntingdon in England. It is worth far more than Cumbria and Northumbria. They grow wheat in the land and the manors yield an income more than Cumbria and Northumbria combined. It is a rich county and it would be yours." What I did not say was that he would have to pay homage to King Henry. I saw that he was still not convinced, "And of course it would allow, in time, King Henry to knight you."

His eyes lit up and in that instant the deal was sealed. "My lords will not be happy."

"And you are king. As king you make difficult decisions but you make them for your country."

"Would you agree if you were in my position?"

"I am never foresworn. I never lie and so I will answer truly. I am not you. I am the son of the Warlord. The Warlord chased your father and grandfather back to the New Castle and here after Northallerton. Our castle held out against Scots and King Stephen so the simple answer is that I would fight to hold on to what I deemed valuable because I have the men and the skills to do so. Look around, King Malcolm, do you? Do you have lords that you can trust as I trust the ones who follow me? Do you have mailed men who are skilled in war?"

"Thank you for your honesty. And I, too, do not lie. We would lose. That will change when I have made my army the equal of my cousin Henry. We will fight England but I need to become a warrior first. I need the skills which will help me to do so." He turned, "Canon Henry, I would have your support in this."

The canon held the king's stare and then bowed his head, "As you wish, majesty."

I later discovered that the Canon hoped to be the next Bishop of Carlisle. By agreeing to help the king he stood a chance of being advanced to another Bishopric. When we entered the Great Hall again everyone stood expectantly. I gave King Malcolm a slight bow and I saw a smirk appear on the face of Lord Fitzalan. He thought he had won. I sat between Wulfric and Dick. Brother Peter stood behind me.

King Malcolm went to the throne. He waved over his steward, William mac David. "We have decided to relinquish our claim to Cumbria and Northumbria. They will revert to the English crown. Have it so written."

There was the briefest of pauses and then all hell broke loose amongst the Scottish lords. My men remained stoically silent with expressionless faces. They knew, better than any, that the slightest of smiles would be seen as an insult and blood would be spilled. We had achieved what we had come here to do peacefully and I did not intend to start a fight. When Lord Fitzalan approached the king then the two bodyguards intervened. They drew their swords and stepped between the king and his lords.

The Steward took his staff and banged on the wooden floor. "Silence! I demand silence!"

Gradually the room quietened. King Malcolm said, "If you cannot behave as gentlemen then leave. I am ashamed of you all. Look at how the English behave. Are we animals?"

Ferchar, Mormaer of Strathearn, pointed an accusing finger at me, "I see the Warlord's evil fingers all over this! You will rue the day you ever came here, Norman!"

I said nothing. King Malcolm spoke in his Steward's ear. The Steward pointed at the mormaer, "Ferchar, Mormaer of Strathearn, leave Carlisle and return to your estates. You are banished from court until King Malcolm says other."

The Scottish lord was not happy. I thought, for a moment that he would draw his sword and blood would be spilt but he thought better of it and stormed out. Four other lords followed him.

King Malcolm said, "We will keep alone until the feast this night. I have documents to write. Earl Cleveland, I pray you to bring your knights and squires. We will show you that Scotsmen can behave like true knights."

I stood and gave a slight bow, "I never doubted it for a moment."

As we headed back to our squires and the horses Wulfric said, "Well I doubt it all the time!"

Just then Ferchar, Mormaer of Strathearn and his followers galloped from the stables and swept out of the castle. They headed north.

Dick said, "That does not bode well, lord. I will make sure my archers keep a good watch this night."

Chapter 2

Sir Harold and the other knights were anxious to know what had happened. They had seen and heard the Scots as they had left and wondered what it meant. "We are invited to a feast this night. Make sure that our men are on their guard. I agree with Dick that this does not bode well."

I trusted the king. I had met enough men with ulterior motives to be able to detect someone who was speaking truthfully. His lords, on the other hand, were definitely both belligerent and antagonistic. I could see why. King David had given them all lands and estates in Cumbria and Northumbria. Although not as rich or as rewarding as estates further south in England they were still more valuable than anything in Scotland. They were all going to become poorer. As I had discovered in the Holy Land, knights who were used to a certain standard were loath to lose it. They would fight to retain their new-found wealth. When we returned for the feast we all wore our surcoats but we did not wear mail. I could not see us being murdered in the castle. We would not be staying in the castle, instead, we would be sleeping in the tents we had brought. My servants would ensure that I slept both comfortably and safely.

Alf helped me to groom. My father had instilled in me certain values. One was to be both clean and well-groomed. That came from living in the East. I had combs and oils. Alf had been born in the east and he understood the rituals. My squire combed my hair and beard. He trimmed the ends of my beard and then nodded. He was still clean-shaven. "Have you any instructions for me, lord?"

"Just do as you did this morning and listen. Did you learn anything?"

"Just that there are many enemies of the king. He has few lords who support him from what the other squires and servants were saying. If I was King Malcolm I would surround myself with many warriors."

That had been my fear. The sooner we had the agreement the better. If Malcolm was deposed it would not make much difference if King Henry had the parchment. We had the men to take and hold both counties by force. The worst thing which could happen would be if he died without signing the precious document. He was a young king without experience. Had he been older then the squires and servants would not have been so free with their criticism.

I was eager to get to the feast. We had, however, to wait until we were summoned. Before we left I summoned John of Chester. He was my sergeant at arms. "Keep a good watch and make sure that none of our men is tempted to speak with the garrison. I fear either treachery or a trap."

"Do not worry, lord. As soon as we neared the Scots our men became careful."

We walked to the castle. Our horses would be able to graze and we did not need them. There were more of us this time and I felt safer amongst them. I noticed that Wulfric and Dick flanked me and I knew, without looking, that Harold would be behind me. It was ingrained in their nature to protect me.

Just as there were more of us so there were more of the Scots. Although Ferchar, Mormaer of Strathearn and his men had left they had been replaced. I noticed that Fergus and Uhtred of Galloway were present. The only smile we saw was on the face of the king. My knights and men at arms could smile now. They were almost relaxed but none of them would drink too much. They would wait until we were back in England for that.

"Earl, you and your men put us to shame." I noticed then that the Scottish lords had not made any effort to dress for the feast. My men all wore clean surcoats and they too were well-groomed. The ones who had been present earlier had not bothered to change and most of the ones we passed whom we had not seen smelled of horses.

"My king and my father would be disappointed if it were not so."

He led me to the head of the table and waved his other hand. The Canon appeared with a parchment in his hand. "All it requires, Earl, is your seal and the signatures of the Canon and your priest. We have wax."

The priest unrolled it and held it flat. I read it but I knew that the king would be true to his word. When the wax was dropped I used the seal King Henry had given me and then my own seal. That made it unique. Brother Peter and the Canon dipped the goose quill into the ink and signed. The Canon's signature was very flowery while Brother Peter's was quite simple. When the wax had hardened it was rolled up.

I handed it to Brother Peter. "Keep this safe, Brother."

I saw the malevolent looks from the leading Scottish nobles. They had not accepted this loss of so much land, stolen from us, with as much equanimity as the king. They would want the parchment. It was evidence of the agreement. They would destroy the document if they could. Without it, they could dispute the agreement. The king and I sat next to each other but other than that there was no mixing. The Scottish were on one side and the Normans on the other.

King Malcolm seemed genuinely interested in the Crusades. "I should like to have gone on one, Earl, to fight for Christ against the infidels. What greater glory is there!"

"I fear, your majesty, that the Seljuk Turks have won. The Crusaders I met, Hospitallers apart, were out for one thing, riches. The Muslims have religion at their heart. They care not for riches as do the Frankish and English knights who are there. They care not for power, which is all that the kings and princes seek, they want one thing. They want the world to be Islamic! You cannot defeat that. We can stop them encroaching on our land, as they have done in Spain but we can do nothing about the Holy Land. Christians will bleed but they will never recover that which we once had. There are too many fanatics who are willing to die for what they believe."

"I believe you, Earl, but it is a depressing thought. Are their warriors better than ours?"

I shook my head, "No, your majesty, man for man, we are better but they are like fleas on a dog. No matter how many you kill there will a dozen or more to take their place. They are fanatics. They believe that dying for their religion guarantees them a place in heaven."

"I was born too late."

"You could still go to the Holy Land, majesty. It is a remarkable land. My wife is a Jewess and I lived with her family. It is a pity that we cannot all live there in peace."

"With the killers of Christ and Muslims?"

I heard the outrage in his voice. My argument was wasted. "Perhaps not, your majesty and it is a perilously long journey to get there."

"I may go." He glanced around at his lords. They were loud and they were drunk. They did not eat their food, they tore it. They were not happy. "Then again, I may have to gain control of my own country first."

He ate a piece of venison but I am not even certain he tasted it. He washed it down with a wine which was not as good as the wine from Anjou which my father kept in his cellars at Stockton.

"I fear I will have to grow up quickly. Perhaps I shall live in Huntingdon. It sounds like a more civilised place than here. I fear the daggers in men's eyes. You know that others claim the crown?"

I nodded. "I fear you will always have enemies." I liked Malcolm. I knew that I was disobeying King Henry but I would not have been my father's son if I had not spoken. "You understand that you will owe obeisance to King Henry as Earl of Huntingdon?"

He nodded, "I am not a fool and I know that he will be my liege for my English land, but it will gain me a knighthood. Once I am a knight then I can look my lords in the eye. I see it in their faces. Why should they be commanded by a milksop?"

I lowered my voice, "To be fair, your majesty, none of them have covered themselves in glory. My father has trounced them more than enough. You were wise to sign the document. With the men I have now, I could sweep these lords from any field they chose. That is not arrogance. I know my men and I know what I can achieve. My father is with King Henry now in Aquitaine and Anjou. The rebels there are lost and do not know it."

"How have you and your father managed to get to such a position? I pray you to tell me for I genuinely wish to know."

"Both of us surrounded ourselves with men we chose and who chose us. They fight for us and we treat them as equals. King Henry himself was my father's squire. He was trained by men like Wulfric and Dick here. You must immerse yourself in your men.... if you can trust them."

He pushed away his food and quaffed some wine. "Aye, there's the rub. They all wish my throne. Whom can I trust?"

I felt sorry for King Malcolm. He was a king without loyal supporters. Dick had been listening and he leaned forward to speak, quietly, to the king. "Seek out those who are good warriors and who wish to follow your banner. Ignore those who seek power and glory. Make those men whom you choose as your heart. Make them the heart of Scotland. It may be a small heart but it will beat in time with yours and it will grow. It does not happen overnight." He drank some wine. "When the Warlord found me, I was an outlaw in Sherwood. I saw in him someone I could follow, as is Sir Harold. I have never regretted that decision for one moment."

I nodded, "Wulfric was a man at arms whom my father hired. He treated him well and knighted him. From those beginnings, my father built the legend that terrifies Scotland still."

King Malcolm nodded, "You are right. There are mothers who threaten their naughty children with the Warlord. My own father would visibly shake when his name was mentioned."

"Your county and your estates are vacant. You may take possession whenever you wish."

"Where is the king now?"

"As I said, he is in Anjou. Like you, he has enemies who seek to undermine him. He and my father are teaching them the error of their ways. He will be back soon enough." He nodded and I saw the relief on his face. He had land in England. He had somewhere secure should his rivals oust him.

I saw that the food had finished but, more than that, I sensed that the Scots were becoming more than boisterous, they were becoming belligerent. I rose, "I fear it is time we were abed. I thank your majesty for your hospitality."

He stood and clasped my arm. "We will have your castles emptied within two months. Grant me that, I beg of you. I have allies and they will help me enforce my will." I felt his fingers bite. "And no matter what happens I am glad that I both met and spoke with you. You have shown me more kindness and respect than any of my countrymen. Go with God."

We left together and I made certain that Brother Peter and the precious parchment were surrounded by the rest of us. Every shadow was a threat, as we headed through the castle and across the bridge to our camp. If I had thought that all I had to do was ride here, negotiate and leave then I was wrong. I had only just begun to perform the task set for me by King Henry.

John of Chester greeted me, "Good evening, my lord."

"Is all quiet?"

"All is quiet, lord, and now that you are here we will put more traps around the entrance to the camp."

"Traps?"

I saw his teeth in the dark. He was grinning, "These are Scots, lord. They would steal the pennies from a corpses' eyes. They will not get past our men this night. You can sleep safely."

"Good." I turned to face my knights and Brother Peter. "I thank you for this night. You showed great forbearance in the face of insults from the Scots. They will pay for that should they try to harm us. Brother Peter, you may keep hold of the parchment. I will assign two of my men to act as chamberlains and they will ride with you on the morrow. I would try to make Barnard Castle. The road twixt here and there may be fraught with danger. Whatever happens that parchment must reach Stockton."

The former Knight Hospitaller nodded, "Aye lord. You are right to fear treachery. I was not in my cups this night and I watched the Scots. They plot and they plan. The king is surrounded by snakes!"

I retired to my tent. Alf followed me. "Fetch me a light, Alf. My work is not yet complete." I was tired but I needed to get a message to Queen Eleanor informing her of the treaty. When King Henry returned he had to know quickly. He had planned on coming north to deal with the Scots. Now he did not need to. However, I needed the Queen to know that there were castles which required their lawful lords. I would also need to send a letter to the Countess of Chester. Carlisle and Cumbria had been part of her husband's land. It was the men of Chester who would have to invest the castle with a castellan and a garrison. The Earl had died and his son was under ten years old. I had confidence in Maud, Countess of Chester. She would appoint a lord to hold Carlisle. I had walked its walls and I would not have wanted to take it by force. I could see how lucky the Scots had been when Stephen had given it to them.

After finishing the letters, I managed an hour of sleep before I woke and roused Alf. "Fetch me Edgar and Edward."

I had not been disturbed in the night. Either the Scots had not come to do me harm or my men had thwarted them. As I stepped out and walked towards the fire Henry son of Will approached me, "Morning lord."

"All quiet?"

He nodded, "It is now, lord. Two assassins or thieves came in the night. They were good, just not good enough. We caught them near Brother Peter's tent. They put up a fight. I am sorry we could not keep them alive for questioning."

"Where are their bodies?"

"We took all of value and slipped them into the moat. They will rise, eventually, lord but by then we will have gone."

They had tried something. My men had done well but I wished they had not disposed of the bodies. I might have recognised them. "Fetch me their goods." He hurried off as Edgar and Edward arrived. I handed them the two letters. "I want you to ride to Stockton with these letters. They are addressed. My Steward will send one, by ship, to London. I want you two to take fresh horses and ride to Chester and deliver the other, personally, to the Earl of Chester. Take a spare horse and change them at Barnard Castle. I need you to reach Stockton with all haste."

"Aye lord."

"I know that it would be a shorter journey to ride to Chester from here but the news you carry is secret. I need two of you. There will be Scots who will seek to find these letters and take them. Do not let that happen."

They both grinned and Edward said, "If we let Scots get them then Aiden would skin us alive. He trained us better than that. We will do as you command, lord."

"And tell my wife that I am safe. I will be home 'ere long."

They hurried off.

Henry returned with the assassins' belongings. There was little to identify them save one thing. One of them had attached to his dagger, a circular piece of metal. On it was the sign of a boar. I had seen it before. It belonged to the men from Galloway. I had seen it on Uhtred's shield. I knew one of my enemies now.

We left before dawn. We rode as though to war with Sir Hugh's scouts ahead of us and Dick's archers flanking the column. Brother Peter rode in the centre with John of Chester and Henry son of Will on either side of him. We were helmed as we rode and, this time, we carried spears.

We were passing Penrith when the scouts rode back. "Lord, there are Scots waiting close by Brougham Castle. They are hiding in the walls and on the other side of the river too."

"Did they see you?"

Alan of Bowes looked offended but he just shook his head, "No, lord. We did not use the road."

"How many men are there?"

"Their numbers were hard to estimate, lord, but I would say there were sixty or more in the castle and another fifty in the woods. The ones in the woods were mounted."

I tried to picture the place we had camped. There was a bridge over the Eamont which led to the castle. The road then continued east to our home. They would attack us once we were on the bridge. It was a clever move. I turned to speak to Dick. "They mean to attack us on the bridge." He nodded his agreement. "I would have you and all of our archers ride ahead and secure the bridge. I will lead the knights and men at arms to the woods where the horsemen wait. Can you hold those who will come from the castle?"

"We can and if they get too close we can mount and ride as though heading east."

"Good. Brother Peter, you and your bodyguards will go with the archers. Dick will keep you safe." I turned to Alf, "Go and tell Harold One Eye to take charge of the baggage train and keep on the road. They are to follow the archers." As he rode off I shouted, "The rest of you prepare for war! We are going to upset some Scots!"

My men cheered. I wondered if the Scots would hear us. The woods in which they hid was just a mile and a half away. I decided that I didn't care. If they heard and were prepared it would not save them. Dick and the archers galloped towards the bridge with Brother Peter and my two men with them. Harold One Eye and the other servants, with swords drawn, led the baggage after the archers. I raised my spear and spurred Alciades up the slope across the open ground towards the woods in the distance. I knew we would be seen but that did not matter. The leader of the horse would have a dilemma; which of our two bodies would they attack or would they realise that their trap had failed and withdraw? Indecision is the worst of faults in a leader. They delayed and in that time, we approached to within four hundred paces of the woods above the small farm.

They decided to charge us. We were not, as we normally were, boot to boot. The ground did not suit that. We were one loose line. The Scots were on smaller horses than ours. Some were armed with spears and others javelins, Only the four knights who led them had mail. I recognised the banner as that of Fitzalan but I could not see him. He was a large and distinctive warrior who wore a full helm. This knight had an open helmet. That meant it was one of his knights. I rested my spear on my cantle and I pulled my shield a little higher. Most of the Scots had the round shield their forebears had borne. They were easy to carry and very useful when on foot. On a horse, they offered little protection.

I chose the man I would hit. Their mailed men were to my right and I could not reach them. It seemed to me that they were trying to get at my archers. Sir Hugh and his men at arms held the right. He and Sir Harold would deal with them. I spied a Sergeant at Arms. He had a mail vest and open helmet. He was leading some men who had no mail. He had a spear. The Scots were always brave, not say reckless warriors. This one was no exception. He came at me eagerly. Perhaps he saw my mail and horse as prizes worth the risk. He had momentum for he was coming down the slope. I lifted and couched my spear. He held his overhand. We were approaching spear to spear. I pulled back my right arm as I spurred on Alciades. I began to move my long shield across my middle. My full-face helmet restricted my view but it also meant that I would only be hurt with a very lucky blow through the eyepiece. A long spear, wavering up and down is hard to control. I was aiming for his middle. Timing was everything and I pulled back and punched it at him when he was five paces from me. As I had expected his spear came for my head and clanked off the side of my helmet. It shook my head. I felt my spear strike metal and then tear through into his middle. He screamed in pain. As my spear was torn from my hand I drew my sword.

I ignored the Sergeant at Arms. He was dead, badly wounded or unhorsed. I was just in time to bring up my shield and block the blow from my left. A Scot had seen my victory and tried to strike me unawares. Helped by the slope I wheeled Alciades around and swung my sword across the Scot's back. My blade bit through to the bone. He threw his arms up as his spine was severed and his lifeless body tumbled to the ground. I used the slope to continue down towards the mailed men who had been fighting Sir Hugh and Sir Harold. I saw that two of them, with the banner of Fitzalan, were heading west to Carlisle. Their followers galloped after them.

Ahead I saw that the men in Brougham Castle had sallied forth and were charging towards Dick and his archers. They had dismounted. I saw Brother Peter, my men and the servants with the baggage heading west. Dick and his archers lay between them. I turned to Alf, "Signal reform!"

He took the horn and sounded it twice. I spurred my horse down the slope. Sir Gilles and Wulfric flanked me. I saw that Wulfric's war axe was bloody. "These Scots are brave but they are no opposition."

I said nothing. I was watching Dick and his archers as they calmly mounted and headed west. The Scots were so intent on pursuing them that they had not seen us. Dick was riding slowly to encourage them. He would be able to stop any time he chose and send arrows at them. We crossed the bridge three abreast and then, on the other side, I slowed to allow the rest of my men to form a line.

There was a wail as the Scots realised their fellows had not managed to stop us. This time I recognised the banner of Galloway. A cow's horn sounded and most of the Scots stopped and then began to head back across the Eamont. I wheeled my horse and the line of mailed and mounted men I led hurtled down towards the river. My sword was the best weapon to use. I leaned from my saddle to sweep it across unprotected backs. It bit into flesh and hacked into skulls. Even helmets could not stop my sword from killing. Even when a helmet did not break the iron bar that was my sword fractured their skulls. The river took many of the survivors. I saw Fergus and his son, along with their mounted men, swim the river and clamber up towards Brougham Castle. They had survived but thirty of their men lay dead.

I reined in, "Alf, sound halt."

I waved over Gurth son of Garth, "Take my men at arms and bring our dead and wounded. Collect the horses and any arms from the dead."

"Aye lord. That was an easy victory! We had a harder time in Provence!"

"We are not home yet." I dismounted Alciades and led him to the river to drink. The bodies had all been swept downstream and the water was clear. I knew two of my enemies: Galloway and Fitzalan. However, I suspected that the Mormaer of Strathearn had not yet done with me.

Irish War

Chapter 3

We had lost but three men at arms although Brother Peter had five others who had wounds needed tending. My archers and those of Dick had escaped totally unscathed. That was good for archers were the hardest of warriors to replace. The horses we had captured were only fit for carrying baggage. Two of the wounded were carried on litters. We buried our dead by the chapel in the castle. There was no chance of us reaching Barnard Castle before dark and so we headed for the deserted Roman fort of Stainmore. The ditches and the earth ramparts remained. It was defensible. We were still close enough to Carlisle for another of the Scottish lords to try to take the precious parchment.

We lit fires and boiled water to have some hot food. Brother Peter saw to the wounded. Wulfric was in bullish mood. "I told you we would have to fight. How will King Henry be able to control the land? I cannot see the Scots giving up without a fight!"

"King Malcolm said he would need two months. That gives us enough time to recruit an army to take north and eject any Scots who are foolish enough to try to hang on to our castles. The men of Chester can deal with the ones in the west and we can deal with those in the east. The New Castle, Warkworth, Bamburgh and Alnwick are the only castles which might give us a problem."

Wulfric persisted, "But if they defend them, what then?"

I smiled, "King Malcolm is not as naïve as you might think. The two months deadline expires when winter begins. Would you wish to be besieged in a castle during winter? We have ships which can supply us from Hartness and Stockton."

Sir Hugh said, "And the Bishop of Durham?"

I nodded, "Hugh de Puiset and I will need to have words. When we leave you at your castle I intend to travel home along the Durham road."

The next day we parted at Barnard Castle and I led my depleted force of men towards Durham. There were a number of reasons for my decision. The Bishop had refused to accompany me. I needed to exert my authority. Secondly, I needed him to know that King Malcolm had freely agreed to the handover. Thirdly, I wanted to use him and his knights to help me to retake the estates and manors which would be vacated by the Scots. King Henry had given me a task of Herculean proportions! I had told Sir Hugh that I would not need him when we headed north. I wanted him as a bastion for the Earl of Chester in case the Scots tried anything untoward.

It was getting on for dusk as we approached the castle. I had allowed Sir Harold, Sir Wulfric, Dick and the rest of my knights, archers and men at arms to return home. I kept my squire and my handful of archers and men at arms, along with Brother Peter. I did not fear the Bishop and I did not want him to think I did. By arriving with so few men it would be my authority and not the weight of numbers which would be used to persuade him to obey my orders. I had the threat of my father and his men behind me.

The sentries recognised my banner. There was a debate amongst them which I ended, "I am the Earl of Cleveland. I am an emissary of King Henry of England. Open the gate and admit me!"

The gates swung open and we entered the outer bailey. I glared at the sergeant at arms who shuffled as I reined in Alciades next to him. "A little tardy there, sergeant."

"Sorry my lord. I was not certain…"

"Not certain about what?" He hung his head. I spurred Alciades to the next gate and the inner bailey. This time I was admitted immediately.

A Canon hurried out to greet me. "You have caught us unawares, my lord."

I gave him a scathing look, "Really? I asked the Bishop to accompany me to Carlisle and he refused. Did he think I would ignore the insult?"

"No insult was intended, lord. He was busy."

I nodded, "Ah, too busy to obey the orders of his liege lord. Take me to him and I want accommodation for all of my men and hot food. We have travelled far this day!" I was not normally this brusque but the Bishop was a cunning and devious man. I needed him to know that I was not a young knight. I had spoken with Kings and Princes and I knew how to conduct myself.

I swept into the keep and headed for the Great Hall. Hugh de Puiset was a two-faced man. He was a hypocrite and he smiled as he greeted me, "My lord, this is a most pleasant and unexpected surprise."

"Bishop, I asked you to come with me to Carlisle and you refused. Why?"

I could see that he was taken aback at my direct statement. He did not know what to say. He had no lie ready. "I er, I."

"King Henry is now the ruler of this land. The Pope has to sanction King Henry's appointments but he can dismiss you."

He looked shocked. I saw the senior priests around him looking equally shocked. If he lost his post then all of them would lose the most lucrative post in the whole of England. "Lord! What have we done wrong?"

I sat in a chair and waved for the servant who hovered nearby to bring me wine. I pointed to a different finger as I enumerated them, "Let me see: refused to accompany me to Carlisle, allowed Scots to raid Durham and my valley, failed to care for your flock... need I go on?"

He was silent, "You know not what it is like, lord, to be so close to the Scots. I do not have enough men!"

"The Palatinate is richer than Cleveland and yet we maintain a larger army than you."

"Your father does not pay me taxes."

I smiled as I sipped the wine. "And King Henry has told me that we are exempt from any future taxes to Durham!"

He sat down, "But..."

I held up my hand, "The days of the civil war are over, Bishop. You can no longer play off the Scots against the English, Stephen against Henry and the Empress. You are accountable... to me! King Henry has made me Warlord of the North in my father's absence." I waved a hand and Brother Peter took out the parchment. "Read this!"

He opened it and began to read. He read it twice. I waved my hand for more wine.

"Then you have regained Northumbria and Cumbria?" He seemed in shock that a lord so young had achieved this.

"Without, it seems, you doing anything to help. Northumbria will no longer raid Durham. You will have no further excuse to withhold taxes for the king. I will expect you to furnish knights and sergeants at arms, as well as the fyrd, for my campaigns to recover Northumbria and Cumbria. We have this document but that does not mean the Scots will go quietly. You have a month to prepare men to follow me."

He nodded. I had shaken him to his core. He had thought himself an island who could carry on ruling his land as though a king, unaccountable to any. His eyes glared hatred. I did not care. I was not worried about a Bishop who was worldlier than any merchant I had ever met.

"I have asked your canon for food and accommodation. We have fought a battle to reach here. This document was bought at a price."

"Of course, Earl."

In contrast to many meals, I had had this one was a tedious and unpleasant experience. The food was good but the Bishop spent the whole of it trying to explain why he could not supply men and knights. He was attempting to avoid the service which he owed as Prince of the Palatinate.

Finally, I put down my knife, "Bishop, you are aware of your obligations? You should have knights appointed to manors who are available for service to the crown. Each knight has an obligation to provide archers and men at arms. If they do not then take their land from them and give it to a knight who will do so."

"You do not understand. I have my own obligations."

I became immediately suspicious. He was squirming and I suspected he had done something of which King Henry would disapprove. "What obligations?"

"There are men who have done service to me and I owe them. They are the lords of many of my manors."

"And they are not knights?"

"Of course, they are knights. They are just not warriors. They are farmers and they are merchants. They bring in revenue to the Palatinate."

"Then if they are lords of the manor they will be summoned to follow me. Before I leave I want a list of every lord of the manor. If you cannot command them then I will. I have the King's authority." I stood, "And now, I will retire. I hope the writing of the list does not keep you awake overlong."

From his angry face, I suspected it would. Now I knew why he had acted in the way he had. He had sold manors to rich men who wished to become richer. It explained why he had been so tardy in responding to requests for help. He did not have knights. It was so clear that I knew when I told my father he would be equally angry. A young priest took us to our room. My archers and men at arms were in the warrior hall. Brother Peter slept with the other priests. When we entered the room we had been allocated I said, "Alf, place the chair behind the door." He looked at me in surprise. "It will give us warning if any come to do us harm."

Irish War

As events turned out we were not disturbed by any. We left the next day and Brother Peter gave me the information he had discovered. "There is a division in the Bishop's people. Many of his priests are as venal and self-serving as he is but there are others who adhere to the teachings of St. Cuthbert."

"Is there anything I can do?"

"The Bishop of Durham has to be approved by the Pope himself. King Henry would need a good candidate to oust the Bishop. He has friends in Rome. There is a new Pope. Perhaps he will be less antagonistic towards our king."

"Then I will leave that Gordian knot for my father or the King himself. I will spend the next month doing as I was ordered. We will have men ready to move north and retake Northumbria."

"I pray that it will be peaceful, lord."

"As do I but I doubt that it will. You are a priest and you are unlike the Bishop. If you were a lord of a rich manor in Northumbria then you might choose to hang on to it."

It was good to be home. I indulged myself and played with my children and doted on my wife for two days. When Edgar and Edward returned with the message from Chester then I turned to work once more. The Countess was delighted and assured me that she would deal with Cumbria. I knew that her husband, Ranulf, had been very bitter about the loss of the lands. His wife, who was the regent for he son, was made of different metal; steel. With that out of the way I had my steward write letters to all of my lords asking them to present themselves and their men six weeks from the receipt of the letter.

King Henry had made monies available to me and, as the Bishop knew, we paid no taxes. I had John of Craven and Ralph of Bowness begin to make siege engines. They would be made in Stockton and carried north on wagons. We would assemble them close to the places we would need them. I ordered vast quantities of arrows. We had many archers and they could be the difference between success and failure. I sent Sir John down to Beverley to buy more horses. We would need many remounts. I sought out Alf and had him make more suits of mail.

He nodded at my request. "Lord, have you thought of a new helmet?"

"This one has served me well."

"It has but there is another one. It is called a great helm. When King Henry was here I saw some of his knights sporting one."

"I have seen them. They look to be too big and heavy to be of any use."

Alf nodded. "So I thought until I began to make one. The first one I tried was far too heavy. I discarded it. I applied myself and began to design another."

He went to a sack and brought out a helmet. It had a bronze cross running down the centre and across the brow. The same bronze ran around the top but it was the part below the eye holes which was most intriguing. He had placed many holes there.

"You see, lord, it struck me that I could lighten the helmet without damaging its integrity. The holes make it lighter and less hot. Yet the helmet is as strong as the one you wear. I would say stronger for there is no hinge to be damaged. The bronze is rivetted to the helmet and it has a leather skull cap which you wear beneath. Try it."

I placed the leather cap on my head and then pulled up the mail coif. Alf lowered the helmet onto my head. I had better vision than my full-face helmet and it was cooler. More importantly it was no heavier than the one I usually wore.

I took it off, "Alf, I am indebted to you. How much do I owe you?"

He shook his head. "You owe me nothing. But for your father and yourself I would still be a poor blacksmith. As it is I am one of the two richest men in Stockton. Besides as soon as the other knights see what I have made I will have commissions from all of them." I knew that he was right. After he had handed it over he paused, "However, lord, there is a boon I would have from you."

"Ask anything, my father and I owe you much."

"The only church we have is your father's chapel. When it was first built it was big enough for the people who lived in Stockton. Over the years our numbers have grown. Many have to listen to services outside the walls. It is not right, lord."

I nodded, "I agree. What do you suggest?"

"Ethelred and I have made much coin. We will provide the stone and the mason if you would give us land to build a church."

"Of course. I think that is a good idea. Where were you thinking of as a site for the church?"

"The high ground above St. John's well. Even if the river floods it will be dry and we would like a tower for a bell. That way when we look up, beyond our walls, we shall see our church. It will give us peace of mind and there is land for a cemetery. The chapel does not have enough room."

"And I will pay for a third of the church too. I know that if he were here then my father would do the same."

I felt much happier after my conversation with Alf. By the end of the next week the war machines were coming on well and I had a missive from London. Queen Eleanor had received my letter and thanked me for my actions. She told me that the revolt in Anjou was over and her husband and my father were returning home. Perhaps my father would be allowed some time to see his family.

Alf was proved correct. A week after I had been given the helmet he was inundated with work as my knights all asked for a new helmet. The exception, of course, was Wulfric who was more than happy to use his old helmet.

We also found men who wished to serve us. Some came with William of Kingston's ship. He had been approached while in London. Some of them were men who had served with my father in Oxford and the West Country. Released by lords and having no employment they sought the knight whose word they could trust, the Warlord. I had been acutely aware that I had too few men at arms and archers and I took them all on. As my father had warned me, William, the Steward, complained at the expense for all needed a horse, mail and a surcoat. I was strong, as my father had advised me. We had to build another warrior hall. This one was just outside the walls. We had filled the inner bailey. I had John of Chester and Robin Hawkeye begin to train the new men. They had all served before and it did not take long. It was just the signals and calls that we used which were different. The formations and standing orders were the same as my father had used. We had but twenty-eight days for then we would be heading north to ensure that the Scots complied with the document signed by King Malcolm.

I made sure that I spent time with my children. I spent more time with Samuel than Ruth. I did not love my daughter any less but there always seemed more that I could do with Samuel. She was younger and, well softer and gentler. Samuel was keen to show me the skills he had acquired from Aiden and Masood. He took great pleasure in taking me into the woods which abutted the river and showing me how he could track through the leaf covered trails.

"And I hunted rabbit! Aiden showed me how to skin it." He wrinkled his nose. "Father, it stunk! I would not have thought that such a small creature could contain such a smell!"

"You have done well but you have not neglected your studies while I have been away, have you? "

"No father, I have practised my reading and my writing." His voice told me that he had not enjoyed it. I had been the same.

I put my arm around his shoulders and led him back to St John's well and the castle. I sympathised with him. I had hated the lessons but I had endured them and now I appreciated the skill. As we neared the gate I was greeted by people entering and leaving my castle. With winter approaching they were all stocking up with what they might need for the winter. Sometimes the winters on the Tees were benign. At other times the cold would be so severe that you could drive a wagon over the ice on the Tees. Wolf winters were, thankfully, rare but there were still wolves in the remote places. I remembered one such winter and the howling of the wolves still sent shivers up my spine.

"Good to see you returned, lord."

"Your son is the image of you, lord."

"Another Warlord eh, lord?

Every man wished to speak with me. Most had fought alongside my father. One or two had fought alongside me. Old Tom, with the one hand knuckled his stump as he had passed. My father had rescued him from a life of a beggar in the far south of the land on the road to Oxford. He had been a former man at arms who had been wounded. My father had given him a horse and money and he had come home. Now he lived, once more, in the town in which he grew up.

"Lord, I heard you sent the Scots packing."

"I did, Tom. How goes it with you?"

"Your father gave me a second life. It was as though I was reborn. A man should return to his roots. When I die it will be in the land in which I was born."

"Hopefully you will be spared that."

"God willing, lord."

Samuel and I entered the castle. "How did he become wounded, father?"

"I know not but my father would. There were many battles during the civil war."

"And grandfather fights now?"

"He does. He and the king have just subdued the rebels in Anjou and he is heading home."

Samuel became excited, "Grandfather comes here?"

I did not want to raise his hopes. "Perhaps. As you know it is not a short journey to England from Anjou and the king may have need of your grandfather."

He nodded, "You and the king look like brothers."

I laughed, "That is only because we are of an age." That was not true, of course, Henry was ten years my junior but others had commented that we had a similar gait and build. Perhaps because we had both been raised by father we had both learned them from him. I knew that I looked very much like my father when he was younger. Old Alf the blacksmith and Ethelred the merchant always commented on the similarities. I thought it sad that there appeared to be no trace of my mother in me. She had died when I had been young and I had barely known her. At least my son and daughter had their mother to raise them. There had been no woman in my life when I had been growing up. Alice had come when I was a man grown. As we entered the hall and I heard Ruth squealing as she played with my wife I smiled. My children had their mother.

The time to leave came all too quickly. I received two letters, by ship, from the King and my father. The King's told me which lords should have their lands returned to them and which were for me to appoint. It was a great honour. We had to delay our departure to await the five returning lords and their retinues. I was not certain they would live in their northern manors but I guessed King Henry had insisted that they help to retake them. I did not mind the delay. I had more time with my family and the extra men would make my task much easier.

The letter from my father was much more personal. He asked after my family and explained that the king wished him to go to Wales and help to retake the land lost to the Welsh. He promised to return north as soon as he could.

While we awaited the last two lords I dined with Henry de Percy, Roger de Mowbray and Richard fitz Roger. The Percy family had lands around Topcliffe and in Sussex but there was also an estate on the Aln which belong to them. It was called Alnwick. It had a motte and bailey castle but Henry de Percy was keen to build a stone one. His family was wealthy and King Henry had granted him permission to build a castle. Roger de Mowbray had come all the way from Anjou. King Henry wished him to have Bamburgh as his home and to build a keep there. The young knight was castellan only. The king had decided that Bamburgh would be a royal castle. As we spoke I heard my father's words for he had maintained that a strong Bamburgh would keep Northumbria safe.

Richard fitz Roger was a little younger than me and had impressed the king. He was to be given the castle at Warkworth. That too was a simple castle but King Henry wished a stone one to be built. As we spoke I saw the King's strategy. Bamburgh and Warkworth could both be supplied by sea. Warkworth could control the Coquet valley while the castle on the Aln would dominate the valley of the Aln.

Henry de Percy said, "King Henry has appointed Richard de Braose to the New Castle. He wants a strong castle building there. Have you seen the site, lord?"

"I have and I applaud the King's strategy. With your three castles and the New Castle strengthened then we have a line of bastions along the east coast."

"What is the land like to the north, Earl? My family has estates in Anjou. Is it similar here?"

I laughed, "No, my young friend. You will find it cold and inhospitable in winter."

"That is what I feared. There was a rumour that wheat cannot be grown there."

"It is not a rumour; it is the truth. Your bread will be oat or barley bread."

Roger fitz Richard shook his head, "Then what is there of value there?"

The young knight disappointed me slightly but then he had come from a land so different as to explain his views. "It has land for sheep and cattle. There is a great trade in wool. The seas teem with fish. I do not think you will be poor, living on the Coquet."

When the last three lords arrived, we headed north. I rode towards Durham. My riders had warned the Bishop that our arrival would be imminent. We did not enter Durham. I was keen to head north but I made sure that all the men I had asked for were there. I allocated them to the siege and baggage train. It was an insult but I knew most of the other knights who rode with me. I assumed that those appointed by King Henry would have been examined by my father first. As Earl Marshal, he wielded power which was second only to the king.

We rode north and our army snaked along the great road built by the Romans. The bridge the Romans had built still spanned the river. The gatehouses on either end had been added by King William. They were made of wood. This would be our first test. If they contested the crossing of the Tyne then it would be a marker that the Scots were unwilling to obey their king. I had the document with me. Brother Peter carried it. This time he was escorted by four of my new men.

When I saw the gates at the end of the bridge open I knew that they had decided to allow us to reclaim the castle unopposed. As my horse clattered over the stone bridge I saw why. The castle just had a curtain wall and the old Roman gates. It would not have withstood a siege. I turned to Richard de Braose who would be the new lord, "You and your men will have your work cut out to build a strong castle here."

He nodded, "King Henry promised me stone. The first thing we will do will be to improve the quay so that they can tie up safely. I do not envy you your task, lord. I fear taking the north will be harder."

Wulfric said, "If they are all as easy as this then it will be a pleasant winter ride."

I hoped that we would not rue Wulfric's words. We spent the night at the castle and, leaving Braose and his men, we left at dawn to head north to Morthpath on the Wansbeck. This time the motte and bailey were occupied. I waved forward Ranulf de Merlay whose family had built the castle. "Come, Sir Ranulf, let us go and speak with your tenants. Brother Peter, Alf!"

With my banner and my priest, I rode bareheaded towards the bridge over the dry moat. There were men on the walls. "I am the Earl of Cleveland." I held out my hand and Brother Peter thrust the parchment into it. "This is a treaty signed by King Malcolm of Scotland. He relinquishes his title as Earl of Northumbria and the county. This land now belongs to Sir Ranulf de Merlay who holds it for King Henry of England. Open your gates and admit your lawful lord."

Suddenly I saw a head appear above the gate and a crossbow. Before it could release a bolt, a pair of arrows flew over from behind me and the crossbowman plummeted to his death. I did not turn around. That would have been either Dick or Robin Hawkeye.

I handed the parchment to Brother Peter. "If I draw my sword then all hell will be unleashed and every living thing in the castle will be slaughtered. Open the gates!" I put my hand on my pommel. There was a pause and I heard heated words. Then the gates creaked open and we entered. I saw the lord, he was dressed in mail but the rest of his retinue were poorly armed. We would have been able to take the castle with little loss.

"For the attempt on my life I could have every man blinded! Instead I give you your lives, leave!"

"But our belongings!"

"Take what you can carry and be grateful that I give you your lives. You should have left when King Malcolm ordered you."

"King Malcolm!" There was derision in every syllable.

"He is still your liege lord. Go!"

"Where to?"

"Scotland begins north of the Tweed!" They hurried back inside the hall. "Sir Ranulf, take your men and make sure that they do leave."

We camped by the river. It was a cold night. I could have stayed in the hall with Sir Ranulf but if my men suffered then so would I. As we sat around a fire Sir Wulfric said, "This will be an easy campaign, lord. You were right. The two months delay has helped us. Sir Ranulf said they had few supplies laid in for winter."

I nodded, "I am guessing that the lords with the bigger castles have taken the supplies. Warkworth may prove to be more difficult."

We had just fourteen miles to travel the next day. It became obvious, as we neared the castle, that it would be defended. All of the farms which lay in our path had been abandoned. The animals had been taken from the fields. When I spied the banner of the Fitzalan family fluttering from the wooden keep then I knew that Walther Fitzalan had decided where he would make his first stand. Dick and Wulfric nudged their horses next to mine. "That is a mighty site for a castle."

I nodded. The River Coquet flowed around the castle and they had dug a moat across the neck. The drawbridge was up. The only place we could attack was across the two hundred and fifty paces of the moat. "Set up camp here. I will ride and see if they are willing to negotiate."

Dick said, "I will send your archers to watch your back. We do not want a repeat of Morthpath."

"You are right. Alf, Brother Peter, let us go and see if these will surrender too!"

We had to stop two hundred paces from the gatehouse. There was a wooden palisade next to the moat. The gatehouse was made of wood too. I began to work out how we would take it even as we rode up.

"I am the Earl of Cleveland." I held out my hand and Brother Peter thrust the parchment into it. "This is a treaty signed by King Malcolm of Scotland. He relinquishes his title as Earl of Northumbria and the county. This land now belongs to Sir Richard fitz Roger. Surrender the castle to me."

Irish War

This time it was a knight who spoke to me but I saw, next to him, the lord I had evicted from Morthpath.

"I am Angus Fitzalan. My uncle has made me lord of this land. We hold it the castle and you will bleed your lives away if you try to take it." He gestured to his left, "My cousin James lost all to you, son of the Warlord. We will not! The ones south of here were as spineless as King Malcolm. You will now find Scotsmen who have iron in their backbone."

"That is your last word?"

"It is!"

I turned and led my men back. "Unpack the war engines. We need a ram and two onagers. Sir Harold, take your men and have them cut down logs to make a bridge over the moat."

Sir Wulfric shook his head, "They are wooden walls! They are fools."

"Aye they are. Sir Richard, you too will need to build in stone as quickly as you can!"

"I have the stone sailing north already, lord. We can land it next to the castle. I beg you let my men lead the attack."

"Aye, for it is your home for which you fight."

We only had one wall to watch. While men began to build the machines, others erected our tents. Dick led my archers west to find a crossing of the Wansbeck. I dismounted and walked to the shore. I wished to enjoy the peace of the waves breaking on the beach, Brother Peter joined me.

He shook his head, "The lord is foolish. If he had stone walls behind which to fight then I would understand it."

"You are right. This castle was built by Lord Alexander. Had he not been killed at the battle of the New Castle then I fear he would have begun to build in stone and we would have struggled to reduce it."

He pulled up his habit and tucked it under his belt. He waded into the river and began to pick shellfish. I watched him for a while. He made a pile of them before stepping ashore. "This is what I missed in the Holy Land. England is such a rich land. A man can pick greens all year. He can forage in the river for shellfish or fish for eels and river fish. I know not why lords seek a home in that inhospitable land."

"You are right. My wife does not like the cold but she cannot believe how well fed the people are." I pointed to the castle. "I will wager they will not have enough supplies."

Brother Peter shook his head, "Lord, it will not come to that. You will reduce this before the end of the week."

I hoped he was right. I planned on reaching Norham before Christmas. I wished Sir John of Stockton to be Castellan there. He had shown that he could act as one when he had done so in Stockton. One of my father's first squires, he was reliable as Sir Leofric and Sir Wulfric. Technically the castle belonged to Bishop Puiset. His predecessor had built it but as he had done nothing to aid me I had decided to use my powers to benefit Sir John.

Dick and some of his archers returned and Brother Peter and I headed back to the main camp. "There is a ford just a mile or so upstream. I sent half of my archers under Aelric. They will watch the north bank of the river."

"Good. We may have to resort to fire arrows. The keep and the walls are made of wood."

Dick was as confident as Brother Peter. "We will not need fire although that might aid Sir Richard. He intends to build in stone. If the wooden walls are burned down then it will speed the building."

"Aye but he will need a roof over his head. Fire will be my last resort."

By the middle of the next day the onagers and the ram had been constructed. Logs had been cut and split into planks. Using ropes, they were made into bridges. We had three of them. Our men at arms advanced to the moat with their shields held before them. Behind them came the archers. The men at arms would be human shields and allow the archers to loose over their heads. Once in position the ram, manned by Sir Richard and his men, accompanied by the two mangonels, moved closer.

Crossbow bolts began to rattle off our shields. Dick was in command and he let the crossbows shower the men at arms. I could not help smiling. Dick knew that the worst enemy of the crossbow was constant use. There were mechanical parts which could go wrong. A bow was simple. If the bowstring broke or became too slack then an archer would simply replace it. He was waiting until they had used many of their bolts and until some of the machines of the devil broke down.

I heard his calm voice command and I waited. "Draw!"

We had a hundred archers. There was an audible creak as a hundred bows were pulled back by the most powerful men in my army.

"Release!" From my vantage point I saw crossbowmen and other warriors fall as the arrows fell amongst them.

"Release!" A second shower had a similar effect. Shields were raised. I shouted, "Bridges!"

My men picked up the bridges and ran to the ditch. They overlapped the ditch by a pace on each side. One of Sir Roger's men was hit in the leg by a bolt but the rest escaped injury.

Dick shouted, "Ralph of Wales, take your men across!"

Thirty archers and their men at arms raced across one bridge while the other two sections kept down the heads of those on the walls.

Ralph of Wales shouted, "Ready, lord!"

"Henry Warbow, take your men across."

This time Ralph of Wales' men, closer to the walls, added their arrows.

"Long Tom, take your men across!"

With my archers and men at arms now in position it was time to send the three war machines over. The ram used the centre bridge while the two onagers flanked it. Once again two men were struck by missiles. This time, as they were closer, it was stones.

Dick shouted, "Archers, draw!" There was a creak, "Release." They repeated their actions for twelve arrows.

During that time the onagers, with men at arms protecting them began to loose rocks at the walls adjacent to the gate. The cracks sounded like thunder. I saw the walls actually shake. The ram rumbled towards the gate. As soon as it neared it the two onagers switched targets and began to drop stones inside the castle. Those who were sheltering would have no warning as the rocks crashed and cracked through flimsy wood and shingle. Sir Richard and his men pulled back the ram's head and it thundered into the wooden gate. I saw the walls adjacent shaking. The onagers had damaged them.

I turned, "Sir Wulfric, prepare your wedge!"

"Aye lord."

He turned and began marshalling his men. They would be five men wide. That was determined by the width of the bridges. As soon as Sir Richard broke through then Sir Wulfric would assault the gatehouse. With his war axe, he was a terrifying sight. I saw parts of the wall, where the onagers struck, break. If the Scots had surrendered then they might have avoided the slaughter which was to follow. My archers were now conserving their strength and their arrows. The walls had no targets. I was guessing that they were waiting behind the gate.

When the gate shattered it took with it two sections of wall. There was a huge gap. As Sir Richard and his men left the ram Sir Wulfric led his column at a run through the gap. I heard the clash of steel and the cries of the first men dying. I raised my sword, "Men of Cleveland, follow me!"

We marched across the three bridges. Alf carried my standard in one hand and his sword in the other. He was a brave man. Without a shield, he was a target for any with a sling, a bow or a crossbow. I stepped around the abandoned ram and over the bodies of the first of the dead. Most were Scots but Sir Richard had lost two men. The defenders were racing across the inner ward towards the keep. Sir Richard and his men were keen to avenge their two losses and they hurtled after them. There were crossbows on the top of the keep but too few of them. Archers sent their arrows to pluck them from the fighting platform.

I could hear screams from inside the keep. They had women and children with them. As we raced up the mound I saw that there were many bodies littering its side. There were few of our men. They were simply outclassed. Sir Richard and his squire threw themselves at the door as the last Scot raced inside and they tried to close it. They failed and the two of them burst in. I saw weapons hacking at them but the two wore mail and had good swords.

Wulfric led his men to crash through after them. I could hear Wulfric's roar as he hacked his way through the defenders on the ground floor. It was now a matter of time. My men knew their business. They would not rush. They would take their time and slowly chop and hack their way to the fighting platform. Wulfric was leading them. If they surrendered he would accept it. If not then they were as good as dead. When I saw the standard flutter to the ground then I knew that it was all over. We had taken what would become a pivotal castle in King Henry's east coast defences against the Scots. I wrote another letter to my wife and sent it back with Edward. I began to spy a hope that I might be home before Christmas.

Irish War

Chapter 4

Dick and his archers rode to the Aln and reported that the motte and bailey there was empty. I sent Henry de Percy and his men to take the castle and make it Henry's. He was keen to begin work on a solid stone structure. With the Aln, Coquet, Wansbeck and Tyne secured we could control the land south of the Coquet. We left the next morning for Bamburgh. I had no doubt that they would defend this one and there was a stone gate with a wall at this castle. The castle of Bamburgh, the ancient home of the Bernicians, would not be easy.

We had twenty miles to travel and the land was flat. We could, however, be seen from a great distance. They would know we were coming. We could not avoid it. The castle was large and would have an impressive garrison. I believed that, although we had garrisoned four castles and sent prisoners back under escort, we still had our war machines on the wagons and more than enough men for the task. We would have to lay siege to the castle. The castle was in the heartland of the land stolen by the Scots. It was cold, especially at night, but winter was not yet upon us. We needed to capture Bamburgh and to get to Norham as soon as we could. We could not afford a long siege at Bamburgh. If the castle was too well defended and looked too strong then I would leave a holding force and head to Norham. I wanted the border closed! If we had to sit around Bamburgh all winter then we would do so.

The banners flew from the walls. It was Fitzalan again. He had not been at Warkworth. Would he be here? I suspected not. We had questioned the captives. They were loyal to their leader whom they felt should be King of Scotland. Malcolm was seen as a milksop. They gave us no indication of the Scottish lord's whereabouts. Bamburgh was a hard place to take but, unless the Scots had ships to keep it resupplied, it was an easy castle to besiege. They had a wall but had they supplies? All of the places we had captured had not had the supplies a garrison would need to stave off hunger.

"Dick, Sir Harold, take your men and secure the settlement. Make sure that no one can enter or leave from the north." There were houses and a church around the small harbour of Bamburgh. "If they are English in the houses then leave them be. If they are Scots evict them and send them north. It is not yet winter. They can find their kin and live off them." This was a cruel war. I had been ordered to look after the English. We had given the Scots more than enough time to vacate and return to their northern homes. If they had chosen to defy King Henry they would discover that his Warlord was no milksop!

This time there was no ditch. The castle stood on top of a mighty rock. There were two entrances. One was only accessible at low tide. That one was on the small harbourside. The other involved a climb up a steep, twisting path. A wall allowed the defenders to assault any attacker as they laboured up the slope. At the top of the path, the gatehouse was set at right angles to the path. This would not be easy. I led my war machines, knights, men at arms, archers and baggage train to the south gate. That would be where we would make our main assault.

I rode my horse towards the flat area to the south of the castle. More than four hundred paces from the impressive castle walls we would be safe from missiles and sheltered by the dunes from the wind. It was set amongst grass held sand and would be dry. The dunes would also help to disguise our camp both from the walls and any ships which came to resupply the castle. What we did not have ready access to was fresh water. I realised that the settlement had to have a well and I sent Sir John and his men to find it. They could then join Sir Harold and Dick. We had more than enough men at the south gate.

I waved John of Chester over. "Begin to build the onagers and ram. We will just need one of each."

He nodded, "It looks a perilous hard place to take, lord."

I nodded. "And this time we will not have wooden walls to destroy. We will have to destroy stone."

He pointed, "They only have a wooden keep."

"True and it is surrounded by a wooden palisade. It is this stone wall and gatehouse we need to worry about." I walked to the beach and stared at the sea wall. The huge stones had been there for centuries. They not only defended the castle from man but nature too. I could see that winter high tides had battered the seaward walls. I headed back to the camp.

Brother Peter wandered over. He was rubbing his chin. I watched him staring at the walls. He saw me staring and smiled, "When I was in the Holy Land I spoke with some Muslim warriors we had captured. Unlike the Templars, we did not slay them on sight. They were interesting fellows. They told me that you can destroy castle walls, even if they are made of stone, by digging a hole beneath them and packing them with timber supports. When you burn them, then the wall will collapse."

I pointed, "That, however, is built on solid stone."

He nodded, "I know but do you see the mortar between the stones? It is old and crumbling. In places, weeds have grown there. I am wagering that on the east side, the seaward side, it is even worse for the action of the wind and the waves will weaken it."

I could not see where he was going with this but he had my interest, "Go on."

"If you had men fill woven baskets with kindling and a candle then, at night, you could have them scale the dunes and place the slow fires at the base of the walls. They would burn slowly. You might have to repeat this four or five times but I believe it would work. The mortar would crumble and we could then try to lever out stones. Who knows they might fall of their own accord. If it did not work then you have lost a little kindling and candles. You could do it while you batter the walls with the siege machines."

"You may be right and, at the very least it will worry the defenders. I do not think that they will have many sentries on the sea wall. This way we force them to increase their vigilance and we can then use the onager to batter the wall and seek weaknesses. Thank you, Brother Peter."

"So long as I save men's lives then I am happy."

It was getting on to dark by the time we had the castle surrounded and the camp ready. We had taken all of the supplies from the village and we slaughtered two pigs and four sheep. They would be added to the dried rations we had brought. The wind was from the south and it took the appetising smell into the castle. It was a small thing but it would add to the discomfort of the defenders. We had to break their will as well as their bodies. We were like the tide on a stone. It would take time to reduce it to pebbles and then sand.

I left Wulfric to begin the assault with the onager. I went with Brother Peter and John of Chester to examine the sea wall. I told him about the plan. "What do you think, John of Chester?"

"Aye, lord, it could work. If we had archers who could see well at night then it would stop us being attacked while we worked." He turned to Brother Peter. "Will it work?"

Brother Peter shrugged, "I see no reason why it should not."

I waved to the two men, "You get the baskets and candles organised. I will go and see how the attack goes."

As with Warkworth, the archers were protected so that they could close with the walls. The difference at Bamburgh was that the walls were much higher and they had stone behind which to shelter. We would not see as many men pitching over the walls. On the other hand, the crossbowmen had to lean out to hit our men. The onager was protected by planks of wood. It was being directed at the wall next to the gate. The second onager was being prepared but it would not be used until the first one suffered damage. Alf handed me my shield as soon as I came within range of the crossbows. I was a tempting target. A bolt thudded into my shield. Then there was a cry as one of the archers hit the crossbowman.

I went behind the onager where there was some protection. "How long before we have a breach?"

Wulfric rubbed his beard, "Two days and we should be able to use the ram. We can then switch the onager to the walls at the side of the gatehouse."

"Good. I will ride and see Dick and Harold." I wrapped my cloak closer about me. The wind was icy. I had forgotten just how cold this Northumbrian coast could be.

Alf and I mounted our horses and rode beyond crossbow range before joining the track which led from the south. We were able to ride along the length of the castle. In size, it reminded me of Chinon although the stone work was nowhere near as good. The wooden keep looked old fashioned. I also knew that it would be vulnerable to fire. If we had the chance we would use fire for Roger de Mowbray had been ordered by King Henry to build a stone keep. We would need to destroy the wooden one.

The tide was in and so there was no action at the sea gate. My men were eating when I arrived. As we dismounted we heard, from the south, the crack of the onager as it sent its stones at the gate.

Dick had some bread and cheese in his hand as he rose to greet me. He said, "It has started, lord."

"Aye, it has. And here?"

"I have sent men up the coast to capture a couple of fishing boats. We can do little when the tide is in and that is when the Scots will try to bring ships with supplies. I want boats of our own so that we can discourage them." My Captain of Archers pointed to the gate, "See how they have a narrow shelf on which to land. There are bollards there to tie up ships but, looking at the height, they can only do that at high tide. None came this morning and the tide is on the ebb."

"Good, then they have had no supplies today."

"I am guessing not."

I told my knights of our plan. "Have your archers prepare fire arrows. I will send Alf with word when we attack. If you send fire arrows and my archers at the south gate do the same then the fire by the walls may be dismissed as arrows which missed their targets. They have wooden buildings within."

Dick said, "If the wind is right we may set fire to the keep, the warrior hall or the stables. All are made of wood."

Sir Harold nodded, "There were five English families here. They had endured much at the hands of the Scots. They have helped us greatly. They showed us where the Scots hid their food and their treasure. They showed us a second well too. They hate the Scots. Some villagers were killed by the barbarians!"

"And the Scottish families?"

"There were ten of those here and another eight had farms. We spent this morning evicting them. Sir John and his men are now scouring the land to make sure that they are gone and to ensure that they are not being reinforced."

"Good."

We rode back to the south gate. I saw that the first onager was being repaired and the second one was being used. With tighter ropes, it was more powerful. I could see damage to the gatehouse already. One stone had been dislodged. They had built a thick wall at this most vulnerable part of their defences but we had only been attacking for half a day and we had evidence that we were winning. We needed patience. Most of the men were in camp. We could rotate those protecting archers and the onagers. We were wearing down not only the walls of the gatehouse but the will of the defenders.

I withdrew half of the archers and set them to making fire arrows. William of Lincoln led them. Alf said, "Lord, you need to eat."

"Aye."

Men had been along the shore collecting shellfish. My servants and guards were also cooks and they had made a stew with the fish and greens collected in the fields. There were still some bones and meat from the animals we had slaughtered. They had been added. It was tasty.

Harry One Eye, who had taken charge of my guards, nodded towards the settlement, "Do they have ale there, lord?"

"I saw none, why?"

"There is little water close by."

I saw Sir Tristan practising with his men, "Sir Tristan."

He hurried over. "Aye lord."

"There is a fishing village which is ten miles or so south of here. Take a wagon and see if they have ale."

"Do we take or buy?"

"If it is Scots then take and send them hence. If it is English then buy."

As I ate the stew I realised that, thanks to King Stephen, it would take many years to rid the land of the Scots. Worse, they would be keen to retake the rich land. Having enjoyed the riches of England after the poverty of Scotland they would fight hard to retake it. We would have war for years. We would need strong knights to hold it and make certain that we had secure borders. We were north of the Roman Wall here and that made the land harder to hold on to.

As darkness fell we withdrew the onager so that it could be repaired. Leaving a guard on the gate to prevent a sortie from the castle my men ate. John of Chester and Brother Peter had made their slow fires. "We will have to wait until low tide, lord. If we risk it at any other time then the spray may douse the flames."

I nodded, "Alf, ride to Dick and tell him that we will attack at low tide. Ask Sir John to return with you."

"Aye lord."

Harry One Eye came up with a beaker of foaming ale, "Here lord. Sir Tristan found some beer. We have enough for a couple of days."

I drank it. It was not as good as that we had in Stockton but it was better than nothing. I would have other knights scour the land for other alewives. The reduction of Bamburgh was well underway but we still had some way to go.

It was later when Alf and Sir John rode in. "Sit. On the morrow, I would have you take your men and scout the road to Norham. I need to know if it is occupied and what defences it has. Are there Scots twixt here and there?"

Sir John took the ale proffered by Harry, "We rode as far as Belford. There were five Scottish families. We did not need to evict them. We approached slowly and they fled."

"Did you ride north to Norham or to Berwick?"

"Norham."

"Then it may end up being a refuge for the families that we have sent north."

Alf asked, "Is that a good thing or a bad thing, lord?"

"It could be good, Alf, for they will have many more mouths to feed and Norham is not a large castle. Women and children may well become distressed when we attack."

He nodded, finished his ale and stood, "I will ride back and prepare my men."

I stayed at the gate while John of Chester led my men down to the sea wall, just before low tide. I saw lights in the sky as Dick and his archers began to send fire arrows into the castle. As it was nearly low tide they could get much closer and I realised that my captain of archers was sending his arrows towards the keep.

I nodded to Robin Hawkeye, "Begin our arrows."

The two attacks, at opposite ends of the castle, would distract the defenders. It gave John of Chester's attack more chance of success. I saw why Dick had chosen to attack the keep; the wind was from the north and east. Robin and the rest of my archers concentrated upon the roof of the gatehouse. Although the gatehouse itself was made of stone, they had a wooden roof to protect the defenders from arrows. The wind fanned the flames and soon the gatehouse was on fire. I saw that the keep was blazing too. They would be unable to haul up seawater to douse the flames as it was low tide. They would have to use water from the well. That would diminish their supply of freshwater. Brother Peter's plan was working.

Once we had used the last of the fire arrows my archers switched to ordinary arrows and they sent them at any shadow they saw on the walls. The fire in the keep was contained but it was badly damaged. Brother Peter, John and the others returned and I looked at them, expectantly. Brother Peter shrugged, "The fire burned but we will not see the results until the morning." He pointed to the glow from the keep. "Your archers did well."

I nodded, "It went better than I had expected. Well done to all of you, now rest. Let us see what daylight brings."

Daylight brought good news. There was now no roof on the gatehouse. I had the onager begin to lob stones there before we risked the ram. The keep was useless as a place to defend. The top had burned and although they had put out the fire the blackened timbers showed that it would be much weaker. Once we breached their gate then the castle would be ours. When we looked at the sea wall we saw that four of the stones from the base of the wall had fallen into the sea. Had we been able to attack from that side then we could have broken through.

"We will try the same thing again tonight."

"They will be ready this time."

"I know."

We had two onagers sending rocks at the walls. I knew that it was risky but I saw the chance to break the deadlock. Fate determined that we would not. As the sun began to set Ralph of the Ox Bridge galloped in, "Lord, Sir John has sent me. There is a Scottish army assembling at Norham. They are heading south! He says they will be here by tomorrow morning."

Wulfric was the only one of my knights who was not put out by that. "I would rather meet them on the open field than wait outside the walls."

I said, "How many men are there, Ralph?"

"Thirty knights and more than two hundred others. They were beneath the banner of Fitzalan. Half are mounted. There were others coming from the west to join them."

"Roger de Mowbray, you stay here and maintain the siege. I will take the rest of the army around to the north. That is where the attack will come from."

"And if they sortie, lord? I have but forty men."

"Then you will resist them. Use the servants from the camp if you have to. This is your castle, Sir Roger. Use the onagers to discourage them. Have your men move around. They will be busy repairing the damage to their keep. They cannot know that there is a relief force on its way. We will leave after dark so that we can be in position when Fitzalan arrives."

"Aye lord."

"Sir Wulfric, I will go and speak with Dick now. As soon as it is dark then bring the men, as quietly as you can, to the north camp."

"Aye lord."

"Warn Harry One Eye and the guards that they may be called into service as warriors again."

Sir Tristan laughed, "They will enjoy that. All of them think they are twice the warriors that whole men are!"

Alf and I mounted. My squire had also brought Alciades and Remus. We would not need them until the battle but, in the battle, they might make all the difference. Dick and Sir John were awaiting me. "Do you have any firmer ideas on numbers, Sir John?"

"No lord. I counted thirty banners but you know the Scots. A single could mean one lord and five men or a mighty lord and fifty men. There were banners coming from the west."

"Then perhaps the Countess' man has scoured the lands to the west sooner than us."

Dick snorted, "They have no castles to subdue. King Malcolm was in the west. He would have ensured that they complied with his agreement. All of the rats scurried east. It is why we have had to fight so hard."

I wondered who commanded for the Countess. "Did you make more fire arrows?"

"We have, perhaps thirty but no more."

"Then we will send them at their keep. It will distract them from Sir Roger. I do not want them to know he has so few men."

"Aye lord."

"Come, the two of you, ride with me and let us see if we can find somewhere to defend."

With our squires, we headed north until we came to Budle Bay. We followed the high ground which overlooked the bay until we came to Waren Burn. We were just over two miles from Bamburgh. We had high ground and the burn. Although shallow, it would act as a defensive ditch before us. "What think you, Dick?"

"Perfect. My archers can stand behind us. I am guessing that it is, perhaps a hundred and fifty paces to the burn. With our elevation, we could make that a killing ground."

Sir John pointed to the south. "The further south you go the burn becomes less of an obstacle."

"Then we shall place some men at arms there and have them placed obliquely to stop us being flanked. Were there many fyrd with them?"

"Aye lord. I would say a third to a half. The ones who came from the west were largely armed with hand weapons."

"Then they will spread out. They are the ones who will be the first to endure our arrows."

Sir John asked, "Not the knights?"

"You said the banners were those of Fitzalan?" He nodded. "Thus far, he has avoided fighting us. He has let his own men do so. He will let those who came from the west, the ones who are angry at losing their lands to attack us first. They will be joined by those we dispossessed as we headed north. Dick, have you enough arrows?"

He smiled, "Perhaps we can make them think that we have used them all. If we send three flights at the fyrd that will thin them. The men at arms can slaughter them and it might tempt the mailed warriors to venture closer. They fear our arrows. That way we could give them a rude surprise."

I was satisfied and, as darkness descended, we headed back to the camp. "We will be in position before dawn. There is enough undergrowth and cover to hide us. Surprise might win the day for us."

Our men had arrived from the southern camp and were sharpening weapons. Food could wait. War was coming. Dick took his archers to the shore. They would follow the retreating tide and when they had the chance would shower the keep with fire arrows. We could not possibly hope for the good fortune we had had the previous night but any damage would keep the defenders occupied and make it easier for us to take the castle.

I gathered my knights. We had thirty-seven of them. Although outnumbered by the Scottish knights I was not worried. My men were superior. Our men at arms were also better than anything the Scots had but our secret weapon was the bow. Our archers would win the day. "I want the men at arms to dismount and they will make a shield wall. The knights and the squires will be at the southernmost end of the line. I want us hidden in the woods close to the Spindelstone Mill. When their men cross the burn downstream from the mill, then we fall upon them and cross the burn to roll up their flank." My men nodded. "Wulfric, I want you with the men at arms. You will be the rock upon which they break. With you and Dick, I know I have warriors on whom I can rely. You young knights will have the pleasure of the charge. Fitzalan will hold his knights until he has weakened our centre. Wulfric, you will have the men forty paces from Dick. When you deem it appropriate, you will fall back."

He grinned, "Fitzalan will think his men are winning and will prepare to follow up."

Irish War

"He will concentrate on you. The last thing he will expect will be an attack on his flank. We will ride boot to boot and drive them from the field. Do not chase them home. Turn and destroy the men on foot."

One of the knights sent by Henry, Henry de Beaune asked, "What about ransom?"

Sir Harold answered for me, "Better we win the battle than worry about taking prisoners and losing it. Fear not, Sir Henry, there will be prisoners. We have yet to fight the Scots and not come away as rich men. However, do not expect riches such as we had when we fought King Stephen. The Scots are as poor as church mice. That is why they fight for this land. To them it is rich!"

"We will be in position before dawn. Brief your men at arms and archers. Tomorrow they are commanded by my captains. Tell them that!"

We had no tents. Alf and I shared a hut with Sir John and Sir Harold. We left to watch the fire arrows fall on Bamburgh. The wind was not as favourable but Dick and the archers still managed to set the keep alight again. The lack of wind also meant that there was a frost and we needed fires to keep warm. That suited for it would appear to the defenders that we had been reinforced. This time they must have had seawater ready for the flames were doused but it took time and it kept their attention on the north. Sir Roger was not attacked.

I had our squires take spare spears. We would be attacking men on foot and spears were the best weapon to use. The men at arms marched first. They were followed by our archers and I led the knights and squires last. Thanks to our scouting expedition we knew the lie of the land. The ground we were to occupy was slightly more open but we would be shielded from the advancing Scots by the trees in the valley sides. When they emerged from the stream then they would see us.

As we waited Sir Gilles asked, "Will this be a total surprise to them, lord?"

I shook my head. "The Scots know that my father and I are no fools. They will expect us to be aware of their advance but they know not where we will meet them. That is why I expect scouts and the fyrd first. They will not risk their mounted men until they know where our archers await them."

Alf had grown up in Constantinople. He did not yet fully understand the English way of war. "Lord, why do not the Scots use archers? If this was Byzantium then our enemies would have similar weapons and arms to us. Are they fools that they do not use the war bow?"

Sir Harold, who had been an archer, laughed, "It takes years to make an archer. You begin when you can barely stand. I was given a bow to pull every day. I pulled it until my arms burned and when I could fully stretch I was given a stronger one. I used an axe every day to cut down trees and make logs."

"You did not release an arrow?"

"Not from the war bow. I had a hunting bow and I used that to practise on the squirrels, rats and rabbits. Then I moved on to birds. When I had seen nine summers I was allowed to use the war bow with arrows and we practised at the butts." He shook his head, "Like you, I cannot understand why others do not use archers. The Welsh do and they are an enemy to be feared."

Sir John said, "Only if you fight them in the mountains. On the lowland we always win. Their knights ride short horses and are no match for any of us."

I felt the sun begin to rise behind us and watched as the first rays lit up the west. I could not see the Scots yet. Sir John guessed that they would have marched south and camped. Most were on foot and it would have taken longer for them to reach the Waren Burn. Alf's sharp eyes spotted them. "Lord, I see banners!"

As I glanced up I saw the sun glinting off metal. They were coming. I did not have orders to issue. My men were being led by my father's warriors. Dick and Wulfric needed no guidance from me. The crucial decision would be mine. I reached behind me and Alf gave me a spear. It had a gonfanon with my gryphon upon it. I was using my new helmet, made by Alf. I rested it on the saddle. I liked it but it did restrict my view. That would be the last thing I donned. I could have charged with just my coif. I would only need my helmet when we fought the knights.

The column headed down the Roman Road. They would aim to cross by the bridge over the Waren Burn. The bridge, however, was within range of my archers. As soon as men approached it they would be showered with arrows. There was a possibility that they might stop and reconsider their actions. I did not think it likely but it was a possibility. If Bamburgh fell then Fitzalan's dreams of a fiefdom in the east would be shattered.

I saw, through the trees, scouts approaching the bridge. They would be cautious. Dick would allow them to cross unopposed. The sun was now shining brightly from behind us. It was low sun, as often happened at this time of year. It would make it harder for the Scots to see us. It was not

Irish War

the fyrd who crossed first. It was Highland warriors. They wore no helmets but they were fierce fighters. With sharp swords, helmets and good shields, they were a force to be reckoned with. When they filled the bridge then Dick ordered his archers to release. He had eighty with him. It was a tightly packed target and the arrows simply could not miss. I had a poor view of the bridge but I saw bodies tumbling into the water. Then I heard a Scottish horn and men fell back. Fitzalan or whoever was leading these men now knew where we were. His horsemen would avoid the archers.

When they began to form ranks on the other side of the valley then I had a better view. They were not doing as I had expected. They were interspersing the blocks of fyrd with better-armed men. They were supporting the weaker elements. The horse, however, was doing what I had predicted. They were behind the men on foot. A horn sounded and the blocks moved towards the burn. Dick's orders had been to attack the fyrd. He ignored those orders. Instead, he and his archers targeted the ones directly in front of them. His arrows swept through the front rank of three of the blocks as a farmer might reap barley.

Almost unconsciously, the Scots began to edge to their right and towards us. We were still hidden from view. Dick's archers sent another three flights and then stopped. This was partly because the Scots had reached the river and partly because it would make the Scots think we had run out of arrows. The lack of arrows seemed to encourage the Scots and I saw them begin to flood across the burn. My men at arms were forty paces up the slope in a three-deep line. They had a wall of shields and there was a solid line of spears behind them. The danger my men faced was the enemy hacking at their ankles but as they all had the long Norman shield I did not think that would be a problem.

I turned to my line of knights. "Be ready when I give the command. I will not shout. I will lower my spear and then we ride. That is why I use a gonfanon. Squires, stay close to your lords!"

I knew that Alf was eager to prove himself. When he had first come to me he had been a raw piece of clay. In the years he had served me, he had learned many things but he had not fought, yet, in a charge of knights.

I heard the clash of wood and metal as the two sides met. Fitzalan, if he was on the battlefield, would be wondering about our archers. Why were no arrows falling? I could see his horsemen, through the trees. They stood in a solid block. It was hard for me. I could not see the battle. I could only hear it. We awaited the moment when they tried to out flank us. When they did that they would not be in a solid block. They would be racing to get around the wall of steel and attack my men in the flank.

It was Sir Tristan who spied them. He was on the extreme right of our line and was the closest to the battle.

"Lord, they come!"

I dug my spurs into the flanks of Alciades and lowered my spear. The gonfanon fluttered as I did so. My line of knights moved down the slope. There was no point in galloping too soon. When we had ridden through their men on foot we would have to ascend the slope and attack horsemen who would have the momentum of a slope to aid them. We emerged from the trees and I slowed to allow my knights to form up on me. I was pleased that the knights who were next to me were Sir Harold and Sir John. I had trained with them. As soon as I felt their boots I spurred Alciades again.

Coming up the slope the Scots had been looking at the ground. As soon as they felt the ground vibrate and heard the drumming of the hooves on the grass they looked up. When they saw us, there was a wail. The men we saw were spread out. There was no order. I saw fyrd armed with bill hooks and axes as well as men with helmets, shields and spears. What I did not see was a lord commanding them. They turned and fled. It takes a brave man to stand before more than seventy horses, with mailed men, charging towards them. Our horses were bigger than the Scots' and must have appeared as monsters to them, I pulled my spear back and rammed it into the mail byrnie of the warrior before me. If I could avoid killing the fyrd then I would do so. There was neither honour nor glory in that. If we did not kill them then they would continue to run until they reached their homes.

I twisted my spear as I pulled it out. The entrails hanging from the end, like garlands, told me that the man was as good as dead. A highland warrior turned and faced me. I did not have to pull my arm back. He had no mail and my spear rammed through his middle. As he fell backwards his body was dragged from my spear. We had reached the stream. In their haste to cross some had fallen and I saw at least three who lay face down in the burn as they were trampled by their fellows. They drowned. I glanced to my left and right. I had knights with me and we crossed the burn. As I did so I noticed that the Scottish knights had begun to charge down the slope. They had not seen my attack and thought to exploit my archers' lack of arrows.

Irish War

We were fortunate that we were riding uphill. It enabled us to wheel. Some of their knights saw us and they wheeled to engage us. The rest of the knights and squires headed for the burn and, as we crashed into the first of their knights, Dick's archers began to send accurate arrows at their knights. At the same time, I heard Wulfric's voice as he roared, "Charge!"

We had broken their flank attack and now we had them between the jaws of our pincers. I pulled back my arm as the knight with the yellow and green striped shield rode towards me. I aimed my spear at the top of his cantle. He aimed at my head. My new helmet restricted my vision but the angle of the metal plates was designed to deflect spears. When my spear tore into his middle, his glanced off my helmet. As he fell he broke my spear. I held up my hand and Alf, riding Remus, rode next to me and handed me a fresh one. This one had no gonfanon. It was just in time. A Scottish knight, seeing me without spear, turned uphill to strike at me. My shield was on my left side and he came up the hill towards my right. Alciades was a war horse. I jerked the reins and used my knees. The spear seemed to flash across my chest before cracking into my shield. As I passed him I punched him in the side with my shield and he tumbled from his horse. I heard Alf's exultant cry behind as the Scottish knight yelled, "I yield! I yield!"

Dick's arrows and the wall of spears wielded by Wulfric had stopped the knights and they had turned. As we galloped towards them I saw that they had ridden their horses too hard. They were lathered as they struggled up the hill. I pulled back my arm and struck the first Scottish knight in the chest with the edge of my sword. As my other knights and squires appeared, the ten knights who had survived threw down their weapons and begged for mercy. I glanced to the left and saw that twelve knights had escaped. They followed Fitzalan's banner. He had escaped me again. I could have pursued but behind me, I heard the clash of metal. Wulfric and my men at arms were still engaged. I turned Alciades and rode down the slope. I did not gallop. We had all the time in the world and I did not wish to risk Alciades. Surrounded the remaining Scottish men at arms had no choice. They threw down their weapons. There were seventy bows facing them and seventy mounted men. Their leaders had fled. To fight on would have been suicidal.

My men began cheering. We had won.

Chapter 5

It was barely after noon when we reached Bamburgh. We had brought our own dead but left the Scottish. The bodies had been stripped of weapons, treasure and armour and the horses collected. The ten knights and eight squires who had surrendered were kept apart from the thirty men at arms and forty fyrd who had also chosen life over death. I sent Sir Harold, Sir Gilles and Sir John, along with their men to bolster the forces of Sir Roger.

We had one of the Fitzalan family. He had been the knight whom Alf had captured. "What is your name?"

He looked at me sulkily. Wulfric growled, "Listen, pup! You have surrendered and to a squire, no less. You speak with civility to the earl or you will be treated as a man at arms and sold as a slave!"

The words, combined with Wulfric's fierce face had the desired effect. "I am David Fitzalan. I am the Mormaer's nephew."

"And will he pay ransom for you?" His downcast face told me that he might not. "Then you are in a parlous position. Tell me all you know of your uncle's plans and I might consider treating you as a knight and selling you back to King Malcolm!"

He looked appalled at the thought. "That would be humiliating, lord! I beg you do not do that. My wife can raise a ransom."

"Have you a squire here?" He pointed to a gangly youth who had a wounded arm. "Did you yield?" He nodded. "Then take your horses and ride to your mistress. Tell her to send whatever ransom she has to Norham. If your lord cooperates then he might be here to be ransomed. If not, he could well be in Dorestad at the slave market!" In truth we did not deal in slaves but, as a threat, it often worked.

He jumped to his feet, "Aye lord."

"Alf, go with him and get him a horse. Make sure that he is not killed by our men before he brings you your coin!"

"So, David, where will your uncle go? Berwick?"

He shook his head, "No, for Berwick is held by Donnchad, Mormaer of Fife and they are great rivals. My uncle thought to make Northumbria his own."

"Then Norham?"

"Aye."

I gestured to John and Henry son of Will. "Take him and put him with the other knights. Feed them but make sure that they are watched."

When I was alone with Dick and Wulfric I said, "Now we have Bamburgh. Tomorrow morning, I want you two to go with Sir John and begin to besiege Norham. I will bring the rest of the army there when we have taken Bamburgh."

"We will be stretched thin."

"I know but winter draws on and we must strike quickly. We will use these prisoners to persuade Bamburgh to surrender. We have enough of Fitzalan's knights to ensure that he cannot cause too much trouble. Had he been in Berwick then I would have been worried. When we take Norham and Fitzalan I will give him his freedom and life. That way he will crawl back to King Malcolm with his tail between his legs. We have stirred up enmity between two Scottish lords. That is as good as a battle won."

It was a cold night with a hard frost. The next morning as my three knights and their men rode away, I left Sir Gilles to watch the sea gate. I marched the rest of my men and the prisoners around to the south gate and Sir Roger's camp. I saw faces on the walls watching us. I had the knights and other prisoners, each guarded by one of my men, line up forty paces from the gatehouse. As they were shuffled into position I saw the damage to it. We could use the ram. Before we tried the ram, I was determined to attempt to negotiate their surrender.

I stepped closer to the gate. Alf held my banner. "I am Earl William of Cleveland. I would speak with whoever holds this castle."

A face appeared. "I am Robert of Berwick and I hold this castle for Lord Fitzalan."

"Know you that King Malcolm has returned all the lands given away by King Stephen to King Henry of England. You are in breach of that treaty. Leave now and you and your men may return to Scotland without further harm."

"Our walls are high and thick. We will stay behind these walls."

I gestured to the men we had captured and walked to David Fitzalan. "These are all that remain of Lord Fitzalan's army. You recognise this knight?" He seemed to see the young knight for the first time. He nodded. "Know this, if you stay within your walls we will bring up a ram and we will break down your gate. We will enter the castle and I will slaughter everyone within do you understand?"

The castellan shouted, "Sir David, is it true?"

The knight nodded and shouted, "My uncle and his household knights fled to Norham. The burn by Budle is surrounded by our dead. We have lost, cousin."

I watched as Sir Robert's shoulders slumped and he nodded in resignation. "I have your word, Earl William, that we can go free?"

"You have my word."

"Open the gates! We surrender!"

I turned to my men at arms, "John of Chester, have the knights and squires taken to the camp. They will be coming with us."

"Aye lord."

I gestured for Sir Roger to come closer, "Sir Roger, you can use the men at arms we captured. Set them to work repairing our damage. If they satisfy you then you may let them go; without their arms, of course."

I looked at the fyrd, "You who foolishly fought against the rightful rulers of this land go now but if ever you fight me again you will pay with your lives."

They needed no urging and they took to their heels. With winter coming their farms needed attention. Some would not even make it home. I guessed that some had come from north of the Tweed. They would have to avoid Norham and would have to spend a night in the open.

I turned to the men at arms. "You men at arms will be set to work by Sir Roger. You will be fed and housed until the work on the gatehouse is complete. Then you may leave. If any of you give Sir Roger trouble or attempt to flee then you will be hunted down and hanged. When the work is finished you will take ship and leave England or return to Scotland... and never return." I stared at each and every man. Most could not hold my gaze. "You know that I could have all of you killed. This is my mercy. Do not abuse it."

One of them, an Englishman by the sound of his voice spoke up, "Lord, some of us here are just swords for hire. Lord Fitzalan paid us well."

"Then next time choose your master better."

"We would serve you."

Wulfric, standing next to me, shook his head and said, "They fought for the Scots, I would not trust them."

I held up my hand, "How many of you are English?" Twelve of them lifted their arms. That made thirteen, an unlucky number. I thought quickly, "Then if you will swear an oath to me and satisfy Sir Roger I will take you on as men at arms."

For some reason that seemed to please them. They took the oath and I had Brother Peter write down their names.

I left a handful of men to disassemble the ram and the onagers. They, with the servants, would bring them north when they had finished. It would not be for at least one day.

We left fifty men with Sir Roger and Brother Peter. The presence of my priest would help to cow the men at arms. I led my remaining knights and the prisoners, north to Norham. It was early afternoon when we neared the last stronghold on English soil. My knights had surrounded the castle. Dick and Wulfric had fought here with my father and knew both the land and the castle. The river crossing was in our hands and the castle was under siege. The Bishop of Durham, who had built the castle, had begun to use stone. When it had been taken by the Scots all work had stopped. This was not Bamburgh.

My men had made their camp to the south and west. The eastern side had a ravine and the river lay to the north. If refugees had reached Berwick and reinforcements were on their way they would have to march upstream. The prisoners had told us that the wooden bridge at Berwick had been damaged in an autumn storm. It explained why Fitzalan had headed west.

I rode to Dick and Wulfric. "Have they been given the chance to surrender?"

"Aye lord. They said they had been ordered to hold by Lord Fitzalan."

"We will await our siege engines. We now hold Bamburgh and I am loath to lose men taking this last castle in England."

"The nights are getting colder, lord."

"There are trees aplenty. Cut them and we will keep fires going."

We dug ditches and used stakes to fortify our camp. We were close to the enemy and I did not wish us to be surprised. Dick and our archers were running out of arrows. We could have sent back to Stockton for more but that would be a five or six-day journey. Our men and horses were showing the effects of a long campaign. This was the time for negotiation rather than fighting. I suspected that the will to fight had evaporated from the Scots. Those in Norham would feel increasingly isolated. I would have more men arriving the next day. I had plans in my head. I hoped that they would work and allow me home for Christmas.

The next day David Fitzalan's squire rode in with three men and two horses. One of the horses had saddlebags, He threw himself from his saddle and said, "Lord, I bring the ransom. There are two hundred gold coins in the bags."

I nodded to Alf who went to examine them. He nodded. "Sir David, you may leave." I saw the disappointment on the faces of the others knights and squires. "When you reach Scotland then tell the families of these knights and squires that when the ransom is paid they may return to the bosom of their families."

He mounted the spare horse, "Thank you, lord. I will tell them."

It was late afternoon when the wagons with the war machines lumbered and creaked their way to our camp. I knew the effect that would have on the garrison. They would see reinforcements arriving to bolster our numbers.

It took two days to assemble the war machines. During that time, the first snows of the year fell. We were close enough to the coast for it to be a mere flurry but it was a warning. I sent archers out to hunt. I wanted us well fed. The night before the assault would begin I gathered my depleted number of knights. "We will use the same method as in the previous sieges. Men at arms will use their shields to protect archers."

"This will be harder, lord. The ram will have to be pushed up a slope."

"I know, Sir John. That is why I intend to use both onagers and batter their gate into kindling."

As Norham was a smaller castle I had scouts watching the crossings of the Tweed. It could be forded in many places. As we lumbered the onagers into position and the archers loosed their first arrows, Rafe rode in. "Lord, there are Scottish riders approaching."

"A relief force?"

Rafe had been with Dick for a long time. He was reliable and I could trust his judgement, "I think not, lord. There are but twenty of them and they have a wagon. I spied a couple of priests."

"Dick, continue with the assault. Sir John and Alf, come with me. John of Chester and Henry son of Will, get your horses."

We rode along the road which paralleled the river and met the men a mile from the castle. I noticed that the banners were those of Donnachada, the Mormaer of Galloway. We waited for them to draw close to us. There were two knights with the priests and two squires and the other eighteen were men at arms.

They halted close to us and one of them removed his helmet, "I am Angus, Mormaer of Kirkcaldy. I serve Lord Donnachada. You are Earl William?"

I nodded, "Do you come to fight or is this a peaceful mission?"

"We do not bring enough men to face the wrath of the son of the Warlord. We are here to ransom the knights who foolishly followed Lord Fitzalan." He waved a hand at the wagon.

"Sir John, go and inspect the wagon. See if it is enough."

"What does the Mormaer of Galloway wish with the land to the east?"

"Nothing. But some of his younger brethren decided to fight you Normans. They are foolish but they are the king's kin. He is paying for them. He will need them."

I lowered my voice and nudged Alciades closer, "To fight England or King Malcolm?"

He laughed, "You are as clever a warrior as your father. You will not be offended if I keep that counsel to myself."

"If you do come then know that I am a lord who neither forgives nor forgets."

"Fear not, the King has no desire to make war on the Tees Valley nor Northumbria."

Sir John came back and nodded, "Then let us ride to our camp. Your knights have been well treated. Would you wish to stay the night?"

He shook his head, "We spent last night at the monastery of Jedburgh and we will do so this night too."

The ransomed knights were pleased to be rescued. Although we had treated them well their defeat must have rankled with them. They had not managed to hurt a single knight or squire. They had been badly led and they had discovered that we were far better warriors than they were. The sight of my knights was a reminder of their failure.

As my men unpacked the ransom I said, "Is your king a friend of Fitzalan?"

"No, Earl. They are rivals and enemies."

"I would ask for a favour then. Would you ride with me and tell the castellan what you do?"

"You mean persuade my countrymen to surrender?"

"No for that is dishonourable. I would have you speak the truth and tell them that you are here to ransom their captured knights and take them to Galloway."

I saw him wrack his brain to discover the trap in my words. There was, of course, none and he nodded, "I can see no reason why not."

We mounted our horses and I shouted, "Cease the assault!"

Every archer stopped instantly. The onager crews began to adjust their ropes ready for when I gave the command to begin again. I saw that the fighting platform above the gatehouse was destroyed. I had taken off my helmet and I took off my coif. I shouted, "Ho, Norham. I come to speak."

An older knight took off his helmet, "I am Robert of Selkirk. I am the castellan. What do you wish?"

"I wish you to hear the words of Angus Mormaer of Kirkcaldy."

"Speak for I know the Mormaer."

"I have been sent by Lord Donnachada to ransom the knights who fought for Lord Fitzalan."

The old knight nodded, "Thank you."

The Mormaer said, "Is that it?"

"Aye," I held out my hand, "may God be with you and have a safe journey home."

He shook his head, "I know you are up to something but I cannot devise what it is."

I smiled, "Good. That is how I like it!"

He turned and rode away.

When he had gone and I remained the old warrior shouted, "Was there more?"

"I am here to tell you that no help is coming to you. The knights who fought for Fitzalan are either dead or ransomed." I pointed to the gatehouse. "By the end of the day, you will have no gates. My men will assault and we will take the castle. You have no wooden walls. Bamburgh no longer has a keep for we burned it. I offer you the chance to take your people, with their arms and cross the river to Berwick. This is my last offer. If you refuse then there will be much slaughter and you will lose this castle. King Malcolm agreed to return it and all the other castles to England. You are the last to hold out."

I waited. I could see him working out how long they could defy us. He shouted, "Very well. How long do we have?"

"I wish to sleep in your keep this night. That is how long you have."

"Very well."

I turned my horse and rode back. My knights had been too far away to hear what was being said. Sir John asked, "Do we resume the assault?"

"No, Sir John, for I would not damage your castle any more. They are leaving. We have won."

The word spread and my men began cheering. What had seemed a daunting task was almost over. I knew that there would be the odd castle which was still manned by the Scots but Brother Peter's parchment and my men would ensure that, as we headed south, they would surrender. We had the border and the coast secure. It was time for me to go home. I sent Edgar with a letter to my wife. Edgar had a change of horses and he would be home in one long day. It would take us five. We would be moving at the pace of wagons carrying wounded and treasure we had taken from the Scots.

The Warlord

I now appoint Alfraed of Stockton to be Earl Marshal of the Horse of England. He will be the most senior knight of the realm. Only I will rank above him.

The Welsh Marches

Part Two

Stockton

Chapter 6

We headed for Chester when we had met with King Owain. King Henry was ebullient. Disaster had been averted. However, riders met us as we headed for Chester. King Rhys had realised that I had gone and was now making war again attacking down the valleys. Men had been killed and farms burned. The campaign was not over. It was merely postponed for winter.

When we reached Chester, Countess of Chester, Maud, Henry's cousin, greeted us warmly. Like Eleanor and Matilda, Maud was a strong woman. Her husband, who had died a few years earlier, had been a weak leader. He had vacillated between Stephen and Matilda. The Countess had never wavered. Her son Hugh would make a good leader one day. As it was she had to make decisions while the youth grew into his title. She would be a robust and dependable Countess.

She hugged me, "Your son is showing that he is like you, Alfraed! He has completed his negotiations with King Malcolm and he has secured Cumbria for my son. I sent Sir Brian of Stanley with a large force to invest Carlisle. We will not lose it so easily a second time."

"Do you know how my son fares?" I was desperate to know how he had done. He had my knights with him but I was his father and a father never stops worrying about his children.

She linked my arm and led me to the Great Hall. "I know that he has a harder task than Sir Brian. Many of Malcolm's lords objected to the treaty. He remained in Carlisle to complete the handover. I have heard reports that your son has had to subdue some castles, in the east, through a siege."

Henry frowned, "And was he aided by the Bishop of Durham?"

"I know not, lord. All that I have heard is second hand. Your son told me of the treaty and I gathered men to send north under Lord Stanley. Since then I have heard nothing. However, with Christmas approaching I do not think that he will be campaigning, do you? Northumbria is a harsh place." She gripped my arm, affectionately, "But then you know that better than any."

Henry said, "We need to find out about the Bishop of Durham. I like not this game he plays."

We had reached the hall and we warmed ourselves before the fire. It was warm and it was comfortable. I felt my age. "What are your plans, majesty?"

He looked at me and smiled, "I would go back to my wife in London. I had planned on finishing the campaign in Wales but that is not the place to be in winter. I will return to my family and then join de Clare and the others in spring. We must quash this Welsh insect!" He took the goblet of mulled wine the servant brought. "You fought him. Tell me of this, Rhys ap Gruffydd. Have we beaten him?"

"No, majesty. He is young and he is clever. He is well-read in matters military. De Clare might have had a chance of defeating him but the others would have been beaten. We can defeat him but we must do it decisively so that he does not dare to raise his head again."

"You are too modest. My men told me that it was you who defeated him."

I nodded, "But de Clare was a valuable ally. I think you should use him more."

He shook his head, "I accept that he is brave and not without skills but his family opposed my mother. He has yet to earn my trust. I will not allow him to have the revenues from his lands in England and in Normandy until I am certain that he can be trusted. You know that he is descended, as I am, from a Duke of Normandy?"

I knew. "He has no ambition to be king, your majesty." My heart sank. I knew what was coming.

"In the spring, I would have you and your men return south to Striguil. There we will take an army and make Pembroke safe once more. Then I will go to my lands in Anjou and Normandy. Louis the Younger is flexing his muscles. I need to exert my authority in Wales while I secure Anjou. Your son can continue to be Warlord of the North. I need you closer to me!"

Maud stroked my hand as Henry went to his chambers to change, "Poor Alfraed. It seems that your life is one of service. You gave half of your life to Matilda; will you now dedicate the other half to her son?"

"Probably." My heart sank. I had two sons, I was constantly torn. I smiled, "I do not mind and yet I would see my grandchildren."

"Then leave on the morrow! From what the king said he intends to go to London. You could be home in two or three days with a change of horses. You could be in Stockton for four months!"

I squeezed her hand, "You are a clever woman, Maud. Of course, I shall head home."

I brought up my plans and told the King of them when we ate. Henry was disappointed. "I had hoped that you would come to London with me. Eleanor always likes to see you."

"And I her, lord, but I have not seen much of my grandchildren." I smiled, "I am a grandfather now. There are obligations."

He wrinkled his nose, "They are babies! I could understand it if you were going to be able to show your grandson how to fight but you will just be saying goo, goo and baa, baa!"

I laughed as Maud shook her head and she too laughed. The King did not understand babies. He had not been there to enjoy them yet. "Cousin, they change so much that I wager the Earl Marshal will not even recognise them when he sees them." She put her hand on his. "Come cuz, he has earned the right."

Henry was not happy being counselled by Maud and he frowned, "I know he has earned the right but I have many enemies and I need the Earl Marshal to defeat them."

Irish War

I saw the chance to gain some time with my family, "As the Countess said, your majesty, it is almost winter. There will be little fighting. "

Defeated, he nodded, "Very well." He drank some of his wine and then, looking up, said, "And visit with de Puiset. If he is not willing to aid us then I may appoint another Bishop of Durham!" The King could get blood from a stone!

Maud shook her head, "He has the support of the Pope, cousin. I fear it would bring you into conflict with Rome."

"They say there is a new Pope. Perhaps he will like the English more. I would have someone like Becket as my bishop. He is a churchman who understands the needs of a king."

My men and I left before dawn. The ground was covered in hoar frost and the cold seemed to reach into my bones but I cared not. I spurred Skuld and soon the heat from my horse warmed me through. My men were also in good humour. The new men were keen to see my home. They had all heard about it. We had plenty of horses. We had captured them from the Welsh. Some were palfreys but most were small sumpters. I had my three horses and a couple of sumpters. We would ride hard and make it home in under three days. In the end, it took four. The weather over the high passes was atrocious. We lost one of the horses. It was a small price to pay. York was a welcome refuge. We reached Stockton at the end of November.

My son and my knights were still in Northumbria but the messages he had sent Rebekah were hopeful. He had subdued the land as far north as Bamburgh. I did not envy him that task. Samuel was glad to see me and he remembered me. He raced at me when I took off my cloak. Throwing his arms around me he laughed, "You smell of horses!"

"That is because we have ridden hard to be here." Ruth was shier and clung on to her mother's hand.

Rebekah shook her head, "I am sorry, father. He cannot control his tongue! He spends too long with Aiden and Masood! He needs to learn how to behave."

"I do not mind. I am just pleased to see their smiling faces."

She put her hand on my cheek, "You should be able to sit in your home and enjoy a quiet time. You have done more than enough for this land."

"I will be here until spring. By then you will be pleased to see the back of me!"

"This is your home! I would you were here all of the time. Samuel speaks of you often."

Shaking my head, I said, "It was my home but now it is yours and William's. So long as there is always a bed for me then I am happy."

I was touched by the fuss everyone made of me. Alice beamed when she saw me. She flushed when she curtsied. "I will tell cook you are at home. I am sure the mistress will not mind if we could cook some of your favourites."

"Of course, Alice, whatever you think the Warlord would like!"

William, my steward, was also happy to see me. "Your son has sent back the treasure from the raids. The manor and the town both profit. While other towns bemoan their fortune, we do not. Why, Ethelred and Alf have made so much money that they are having a church built for your chapel is too small for the town."

I nodded, "That is good. As I have to visit with Bishop Puiset, I will ask for a priest."

"You need not. Father Michael says that Brother Peter can be the priest in your chapel and he will be the priest at St. John's."

"St. John's?"

He nodded, "It will be built close to the well. There is a higher piece of ground there and the whole town will be able to see the tower as they go about their business. Ethelred is already acquiring the stone so that work can begin in spring."

"And does my son approve?"

Rebekah said, "It was his idea. He felt sorry that so many people had to hear the services from outside and, besides, he says that one day you will need a tomb next to your wife."

I laughed, "I hope he does not plan for me to use it soon."

She put her hand to her mouth, "I am sorry, I did not..."

"I jest. It is good that my son plans. All men die and he is right. One day I will meet an enemy who is faster, younger or simply better. I would like to spend eternity next to Adela."

My home was changing. It was all good. The site they had chosen for the church was a good one. I just worried that it might be vulnerable to raids. However, it would take some years to build. I would be long dead before it was finished. Speaking of the church made me wish to visit my chapel.

"Is there water for me to wash and clothes for me to wear, Alice?"

"Aye lord. When we saw you on the southern bank I had the servants prepare everything."

"Then I will change and visit Adela."

When I came downstairs Samuel was waiting for me. "Could I come with you, grandfather?"

"Of course. Put on your cloak for it is cold."

Taking his hand, we walked across the bailey and through the gate to the chapel. I had paid for candles to burn all day and night. There had been a time when William the Steward had objected at the expense. It was many years since he had done so. My chapel had the most wonderfully peaceful atmosphere. I would be happy to spend eternity here. I needed no tomb but I knew that William would build one.

I knelt next to the tomb and prayed silently for a moment then I reached around Samuel's shoulder and edged him forward, "Adela this is your grandson, Samuel. I know that William will have told you of him but William will not know how much Samuel is like William was as a child. If you were alive then you would see the likeness. Samuel and his sister are good children. I am just sad that you are not alive to see how wonderful they are. You would have been so proud and you would have adored looking after them. I am sorry, my love, that you were taken too soon."

Just thinking of that made tears spring into my eyes. They were silent tears but Samuel noticed them coursing down my cheeks, "Grandfather, what ails you?"

I stood and, picking him up, held him close to me. "It is nothing. I just ache for the grandmother you never knew. You would have adored her and it pains me that I can do nothing about it."

He nuzzled his head into my neck, "You are the only grandfather I have. Do not die, grandfather!"

I found that words would not come. I forced myself to breathe. When I had control I said, huskily, "I will do my best."

Taking his hand, I re-entered the bailey and I headed for the warrior hall, "Come, Samuel, we will see if my men have settled in here. A good lord always makes sure that his men are well looked after. They defend him and he has a responsibility to watch over them."

Roger of Bath had organised the men. I saw Ralph of Bowness helping to allocate beds. Some of the men I had left in Stockton when I followed Henry to Anjou and Wales were now married men. They lived outside the castle. Many lords did not allow that but I knew it made for happier men and it did no harm. They were never late for their duties and their wives ensured that they were well presented. It meant we had spare beds.

They all stopped and bowed as we entered. "Are you comfortable?" They beamed. It was partly the joy of being home but also Samuel's smile which could light up a room. He loved being around the warriors.

"Aye lord and Mistress Alice has promised us some proper food."

"Good. Ralph of Bowness, we will be here until after Michaelmas. My men at arms and archers can stand a watch."

"We have no need, lord, we have plenty of men in the garrison."

"None the less we will do as I command. I want every man at arms and archer to feel part of one company. My son and I have yet to fight alongside each other but that day will come. Let us start to make the bonds which tie us together now."

"As you wish, lord."

As we left Samuel said, "I like your men at arms, grandfather. They look so fierce and yet they are so gentle and kind."

I nodded, "I know. I am lucky. When you are the lord of Stockton, surround yourself with such men."

"How will I know them?"

"That is a good question. You look into their eyes. You will see there if they are true or not. If they look you not in the eye then do not trust them. Treat them as men and not as objects to be used. You have your father's blood, my blood and the blood of a housecarl in your veins. I know that you will choose wisely. You could not do other."

The cook had outdone herself. The food was plentiful and made up of the dishes I adored. Alice knew me well. When I campaigned, I ate what was there but here, in my home, it was my food and my wine from my vineyards in Anjou. I confess that, for the first time in a long time, I drank too much. I waited until Samuel and Ruth were in bed to indulge myself but James and Ralph of Bowness had to help me up the stairs to my bed.

I heard them speak just before oblivion took me, "He needed this Ralph. He carries too much on his shoulders."

"As does his son. I did right to follow him from the east."

"And I, to have found a father to replace the one that I lost!"

When I awoke I just had a mouth that tasted stale. I had neither headache nor a queasy stomach. The food and wine had been good. I only suffered bad heads and stomachs when the food or the wine was questionable. I was up before any other and I went to the stables. My horses were all there. Aiden was up too. He was grooming Skuld.

"What do you think of her?"

"She reminds me of Scout. She is not as big or as powerful as your other two and she is no warhorse but there is something about her. She is more like a person than an animal. Have you thought to breed from her, lord?"

"I confess that I had. I thought about Storm Bringer."

He shook his head, "Warrior will be better. They get on well and the colour of their colt would be more like Scout."

"Is she in season yet?"

He looked at her and shook his head, "You are here for three or four months. In that time she will be in season. When the time is right I will pair them. Of course, lord, it means that when you leave she will have to stay here."

"I know. I have other horses and the Welsh mountains are dangerous places. I would not lose my Skuld."

We left the stables and went into the outer ward. Aiden sniffed the air, "It will be a good day for hunting, lord."

I nodded, "Where?"

"The woods at the far side of Hartburn, lord. The woods to the south of Lonesome House. There are deer there. I have yet to cull them. We had good, strong stags born two years since. Old King lost an antler. I fear he will fall soon. They have been rutting for a month or so. He is a tough old animal and he will not go quietly. It would be a better end for him if we hunted him and would make the herd stronger."

"Good. I will fetch James. Should we take Masood?"

He laughed, "You try and keep him here, lord. He loves hunting in the forest. He cannot get over the changes in the landscape here. He thinks he has died and gone to heaven although he is a heathen and I think his heaven is different from ours."

"Spears or bows?"

"We had best take both. He is a powerful stag even with just one antler."

I returned indoors to change into hunting clothes. I had a leather jerkin and some soft, leather boots. I took my bow, arrows and my spears. I would not need my sword. James was keen to hunt too. The last time he had hunted his father, Sir Edward, had been alive. He needed to exorcise that ghost. The castle was awake as we descended.

Samuel shouted, "Are you going riding, grandfather? Can I come?" He turned to his mother. "Can I?"

Rebekah had not realised I was going hunting. "If you wrap up warm and do as your grandfather says."

Samuel cheered. I felt awful as I said, "I go hunting."

Samuel squealed even louder, "Hunting!"

Poor Rebekah's face fell but both of us knew that we could not say no to him now. She gripped his arm. "Go and wrap up warm. Put your good boots on." Rebekah and Alice led him away.

I turned to James, "You will have to watch over him, James."

"I will, lord. I will treat him as though he was my own son."

Rebekah looked fearfully into my eyes. "I swear, daughter, that no harm will come to my grandson." I smiled reassuringly, "And I am never foresworn." She gave me a wan smile. She was worried.

Masood and Aiden were less worried about the presence of my young grandson. "It is good, lord. The sooner he faces danger the stronger he will be. There are four of us to watch out for him. If we cannot do so then we are poor excuses for men."

Aiden was confident but he had no children of his own. He and Masood, however, had taken him hunting and they had taught him to ride. Perhaps they were better judges than I. I felt proud as he came out clutching his bow and quiver. Aiden had made him the bow as well as the arrows. He would not need either, nor the dagger he carried as a sword but he looked the part and he strode proudly towards his pony.

"This is your first time hunting. You will obey every instruction James gives you and you will be silent."

"Aye grandfather. Aiden and Masood have told me." He sounded so serious I could have hugged him but that would have ruined the moment.

The ground was hard and the air was cold. My greatest fear was that Samuel might fall from his pony and would have to suffer a hard landing. He would not have far to fall. James rode on one side and I rode on the other. As we headed south, towards the Ox Bridge, I watched him ride. He was confident in the small saddle. He stroked his pony's mane and spoke to him. All of that was good.

Once we had passed the Oxbridge and the pig farms there, we started to climb. Some of the land had been cleared. Tom and Agnes lived with their children at the Ox Bridge farm which looked down on the becks. Then the woods closed in again and we dropped slightly towards Lonesome House. It was empty now. It had been farmed by Peter Barley, so called because that was what he had farmed. His family had been wiped out during the raid when Sir Edward had been killed. Peter had been in Stockton selling barley. He became maddened with rage. His body had been found in the woods close to his house a year later. None knew how he had died. Some thought he had taken his own life others that the Scots had killed him. I had had him buried in the cemetery. He deserved that. No one else had been willing to farm the land and it lay overgrown. Perhaps that was why the woods close by had so much game. As nature had reclaimed the land and ivy crept over the house it became a paradise for all sorts of creatures. Brambles and elder colonised what had been the vegetable plot close to the house.

Aiden skirted the wood. There was little breeze, but what there was came from Hartburn. He was taking us to enter the woods from the higher ground where the wind would be in our faces. In places, we might have been able to ride our animals between the trees but it was always better to stick to the tracks. We began to climb again and Aiden halted at the edge of the woods. Here elder, hawthorn and blackthorn grew. Few had used the path and Aiden took out his short sword and hacked away the entanglement of wild blackberry bushes which encroached upon the entrance. I smiled. Had we not had Samuel with us he would not have bothered but he would not risk Samuel returning with torn clothes. He would not face the wrath of Alice!

We all dismounted and led our horses down the trail. Aiden and Masood led. James followed Samuel. We walked down the twisting trail which gradually descended. This wood was crisscrossed by streams. None were large enough to require a bridge and all led to the Tees. It made for fine hunting country. The animals had water, shelter and food. There were wild boars. I hoped that we would not stumble across them. Aiden would know their territory and we would avoid it. We reached a slight open spot. Below us was a steep bank leading down to one of the streams which fed the Lustrum Beck. Aiden tied his horse to one of the branches and we emulated him. He pointed down the stream. The trees closed in over the path and had we walked our horses then they might have brushed the leaves and made a noise. I left my bow slung across my back and held my spear. I saw that Samuel had an arrow held tightly against his bow. He had been taught well. He would be able to nock and release in a flash.

Masood dropped down the bank towards the stream. He barely made a sound and once close to the water he knelt. He pointed downstream. He walked next to the stream and Aiden led us down the trail. I turned to make sure that James was close to Samuel and then I followed. We had travelled four hundred paces, I had been counting, when a musky smell entered my nostrils. It was a deer. Each stag had its own territory. Old King's must be where we were. There would be does nearby but the other mature stags would be keeping their distance.

Suddenly we heard the crack of antler on antler. There were stags rutting. This was a disaster. They were huge beasts and seemed oblivious to all around them when fighting for the right to father young. They would trample even a man if he got in their way. A bairn like Samuel would stand no chance! Aiden and Masood had their bows out in a heartbeat. With an arrow knocked they sniffed and stared. There was lightness ahead and I caught the flash of deer as two stags thrashed and clattered through the undergrowth. I turned and saw that James had moved in front of Samuel. My squire obeyed his orders even at the risk of his own life. Like me, James had a spear.

Suddenly there was silence. I had watched this ritual before. The two stags would batter each other and then retire to gain strength for one last battle. Although stags rarely fought to the death often one would be so weakened and wounded that it would crawl off to die. I was contemplating abandoning the hunt and moving back to the horses when there was a crash as one of the stags left the open ground and hurtled towards us. It was moving so quickly that Masood and Aiden had to fling themselves to the side after each released a hurried arrow.

It was Old King. I saw his one antler and his side had been gored. There was a long wound. He had been badly wounded by the other stag. He was thundering towards us. James hurled his spear. It flew straight and true and hit the mighty stag in the shoulder. It made him turn and come directly to me. He lowered his head. He was going to charge. When the arrow flew from behind me I knew that Samuel had not moved. He had sent his arrow at the stag.

"James, move Samuel!"

Samuel's arrow hit the stag but it barely penetrated. I would not throw my spear. As Old King lowered his head to impale me I stepped to the side without an antler and thrust the spear into the side of his head. His shoulder threw me to the ground and I landed heavily. I briefly saw stars and I heard the stag crash into the undergrowth.

Aiden came to me and held out his hand for me, "I am sorry, lord. That was our mistake!"

"Samuel!"

I turned and saw a grinning Samuel holding James' hand. They were both safe. Ten paces away lay Old King. He was dead.

"Are you hurt, Samuel?"

He shook his head, "No grandfather. He was a mighty beast. Did you see? I hit him!"

"Aye, you did."

Aiden ruffled his hair, "You did well, young master. When you have a stronger bow and longer arrows then you will make the kill yourself!" He turned and looked at me, "Lord, I have never seen the like. I thought you were a dead man!"

I nodded, "Had he not lost an antler then I would have been. Samuel's arrow distracted it enough to give me the time to move out of the way."

We reached the dead stag. Aiden pointed to the wound on its side. "We have done Old King a service. He would have been dead before the end of the week. This was a mortal wound."

Masood pulled out the three arrows. "These were like fleas to the beast." He handed Samuel's back to my grandson, "But this one, young Samuel saved your grandfather's life. Keep it and when you look at it then remember this day. You took a step closer, this day, to becoming a man. I will fetch the horses."

James pulled his broken spear from the stag's shoulder, "Sorry, lord. I should have moved Samuel out of the way sooner."

Shaking my head, I said, "This was meant to be. Samuel faced death and did not flinch. You did well."

Aiden took his knife and gutted the stag. He reached in and pulled out the heart, "Young master Samuel, it is said that if you take a bite from the heart of your first kill then part of him lives in you. Old King has ruled this wood for as long as I know." He held it to him. I saw him look at me and I nodded. He leaned forward and took a bite. I had done this but that had been in the hills west of Constantinople. The heart was warm and that helped. Blood spurted and splashed down his front as he took a mouthful and chewed. Aiden shouted, "You will be a man! Your father would be proud!"

Samuel swallowed and asked, "Did my father do this too?"

"Aye, but he was older when Aiden and I brought him here. Your grandmother would not let him come with us until he was twelve summers old." I smiled, "He will envy you."

Aiden quickly gutted the stag and then, when Masood came, they manhandled it onto the back of Aiden's horse and we headed back to

Stockton. Going at a walking pace it took longer to reach the castle but Samuel rode proudly next to the dead deer as though it had been his arrow which had killed it. I was proud.

Alice and Rebekah had received word of our arrival and hurried, cloaked and wrapped into the bailey. When Alice saw the blood on Samuel she ran to him, "My poor bairn!" She glared at Aiden, "What happened to him, wild man?"

I dismounted, "Peace Alice. There is nothing wrong with him. It is deer blood and it shows that my grandson has courage. He was not harmed."

Mollified she said, "But lord, his clothes!"

Rebekah put her arm around her son, "Can be cleaned, Alice. My son is hale and hearty. Thank you, lord, I knew that my son would be safe with you. My father and my brothers would have enjoyed watching this. I suspect your son will be annoyed that he missed it."

I nodded, "Aye." I wondered just where my son was.

Irish War

Chapter 7

Perhaps the bright early winter sunshine should have told us that good news was here for Edgar and Edward rode through the gates to tell us of the imminent arrival of my son and his victorious warriors. Alice, William and Ralph knew their tasks and the castle became a hive of activity as rooms and food were prepared and beds in the warrior hall rearranged. Even Aiden had work to do. The stables we used for the men at arms and archers had been largely empty and now they needed cleaning and supplying with fresh hay. Water troughs had to be refilled. As much as we were all desperate to see our returning heroes everyone in the castle and the town was affected. The alewives began to brew extra quantities of beer. Each one had a slightly different taste. Warriors each preferred a particular brew. Our warriors had plenty to drink in the warrior hall and castle but the town held the added attraction of women. My son and I had been careful to keep those sorts of women from within the castle walls but we both knew men's appetites needed satisfying.

I sent riders to Yarm, Thornaby, Norton, Hartburn and Elton to tell them that their lords were returning. With the exception of Dick and Wulfric, the rest of my knights had families who would be keen to see their husband and father.

Samuel was desperate to show his father the new deer hide jerkin Aiden had made him from the skin of Old King. Ruth was gaining a personality now. Now used to me she spoke her mind, "You cannot! It smells!"

I smiled, "That is just the leather. It will age."

Rebekah said, "Besides you do not need to wear it. You can show it to him and the arrow Aiden told you to save. That will be a good story to tell him."

He raced off to fetch the precious arrow which was now housed in his room as his most treasured possession. Rebekah smiled as he ran, "He has grown so much since the hunt and yet I was petrified for him all the time you were away."

"I know. I would his father had been the first to take him. We will have to find something for my son to do that will bond them together."

"His father missed Samuel's first steps."

Ruth beamed, "He saw mine!"

The two children were close enough in age to be competitive. It would spur Samuel on and that was no bad thing. My son led the men down the road from the Ox Bridge. He looked weary. All of them did. Edgar had told us how they had captured every castle up to Norham. Even in my most successful days, I had not achieved what my son had. I was proud of him. When I died, the valley would be in safe hands.

Normally we arrived back by using the ferry. This time he came down the Durham Road and all my people came to greet the returning warriors. I stood by the gate with Rebekah and the children. Samuel was almost hoarse with his cheering. I wondered if he would have enough voice to speak.

William stepped down and picked up Ruth and Samuel at the same time, "I have missed you both."

Ruth said, "You smell funny!"

He laughed and put them back on the ground. "That is a polite way of saying I need a bath!" He turned to Rebekah and hugged and then kissed her. His men all cheered.

I saw as they separated that Rebekah was flushed, "Lord! Your men and all your people!"

"I care not! I am home and it feels good."

He released his wife and we clasped arms, warrior style. "You have done well, my son."

"From what I hear so have you. How long can you stay?"

I smiled, "You know I will be leaving?"

"I know King Henry. You are more than a lucky talisman. You are the reason he wins. Look what happened in Gwynedd when he fought without you alongside him."

"Each of us can lose."

"Not you."

I nodded, "We will be here until Michaelmas and then I will have to journey south to fight in Wales again. Let us not talk of that now. I believe your son has something he wishes to show you!"

Irish War

While we had been talking the rest of the men at arms, archers and servants had entered the town and the castle with the wagons. I followed them. Samuel would want to tell his father how he had saved his grandfather's life himself. I was anxious to speak with Dick.

He had just unsaddled his horse when I caught up with him, "Good campaign?"

He smiled, "It was like being with you, Warlord, when you were a young man! There must be something in the blood. I think Samuel will also be a great warrior. We took great quantities of treasure and ransom from the Scots. Our men are happy for they are all richer."

"And that means Stockton will be richer. They will spend their coin in the town and that will please the merchants." I put my arm around his back and led him to where we could talk quietly. I could have asked Wulfric but he had gone directly to Thornaby. "Will we hold Northumbria?"

He nodded. "Your son is clever. He has placed Sir John at Norham. With that held as a locked gate into England then the others can be rebuilt. King Henry has sent stone to Bamburgh and Warkworth. Your son will need to ride north regularly but I believe we can hold it this time. There is no King Stephen to give away all of our hard-won gains."

"Then my son will need you."

Dick was astute. He knew me well and understood that there was something behind my questions. "You have need of me?"

"Your archers. I would like half and Aelric to lead them. If you think that …."

He waved a hand, "You made us what we are, lord. Take us all if you wish."

I shook my head. "That would leave my son without the finest archers in the land. Half will do. I found some when I travelled. We will be fighting the Welsh and you know what their archers are like. I wanted to speak with you before I spoke with my son."

"I am honoured." He hung his saddle from the hook on the wall. "You do not wish me to come with you?"

"I would rather you watched over my son and his family. With you and Wulfric in the valley then I am content."

My son was a thoughtful lord. He rode himself to tell Sir John's wife, Edith, that her husband would be away until the new castle at Norham was ready for them to make it their new home. Many lords would have sent a servant but William knew the worry that the soon to be mother would be enduring.

We had much to talk about, that night, as we ate. Apart from Dick, it was family and squires. Samuel was rapt as he listened to all that his father had done. I recognised the gaps and words which were unsaid. He was sparing his family the unpleasant parts of the campaign. I had done the same. When Ruth began to doze and was carried to bed, Samuel still listened. After Dick had taken his leave Alice said, "Come, Master Samuel, let us follow your sister to bed. You are up later than you should be."

Samuel grabbed his father's hand, "Please father, let me come with you and grandfather to the solar. I promise that I am not tired."

I knew the dilemma my son had and, in the end, his son won. "I will fetch him to bed Alice, thank you."

She wagged a finger at Samuel, "Wilful boy. I tell you, lord, you are making a rod for your own back here!"

"I know, Alice, I know."

Alice had already put the heavy red wine my son and I enjoyed in the solar along with ripe goat's cheese and bread. She had banked up the fire and it was cosy. With just two chairs Samuel had to sit on his father's knee. He was comfortable and as good as his promise. He did not make a sound.

"The King would have me visit de Puiset before I join him. From what you said, or rather didn't say, when we ate, he is playing a dangerous game."

"Aye, he is."

"The Bishop will not be happy that you have given Sir John the castle at Norham."

"It needs defending."

"You do not need to tell me that." I looked down. "Your son is asleep."

"I shall take him down to bed."

After he had gone I cut some cheese and put it on the bread. Alice managed to procure the best goat's cheeses. There were many farmer's wives who made it but she knew my taste. It was tangy and it was robust. The heavy red wine from Chinon went perfectly with it.

My son returned, "Thank you for taking him hunting. He is still excited about that day."

"He did well." William ate some of the cheese and the bread. "You know the King has plans for me."

He nodded, "You mean after Wales?"

"Aye. I think that he wishes to show France that he is not a king to be trifled with. He has a large Empire now and the rats are nibbling at the edges."

"And having the Warlord at his side will ensure that all King Henry's enemies will fear an attack."

"For that reason, I am taking some of the archers and men at arms from the castle. I have spoken with Dick. I have some I hired in Anjou but, as I discovered in Wales, I need men I know and can rely on. I am taking Aelric and six others. I am taking the ones who are not married."

"I can get more. Sir Leofric has promised to continue sending men to us. All of us here would have you protected."

"I have done all that I can for the valley. You are the future, William. I want you to know that I am proud of you. To do what you have done in Northumbria in such a short time is more than remarkable."

"I did it with the men you trained!"

I sipped my wine. "We will enjoy Christmas before we go to Durham and speak with Bishop Puiset."

"This will be the first real Christmas the children will have enjoyed. You will be here and now there is peace throughout the land. That is rare."

The bright sunshine of the day gave way to a hard frost at night. Alice and the Steward had fires burning all night to heat the castle. When I went down early for breakfast I saw Rebekah. She had a fur around her shoulders, "I do not know how you English can bear this cold! Your summers are as cold as the winters in my land. This cold it …"

"Seeps into your bones?"

She laughed, "It does. You were born in the east, how did you become used to it?"

"I had no choice. When we came back we were fighting Scots in all weathers. You think it is cold here, you should try sleeping out in it with nothing but a cloak and a blanket for warmth. But you are right. The castle should be warmer. I will have William the Steward put the tapestries and wall hangings back up. It makes the rooms feel warmer."

Alice came in with some ale. She went to the fire and, after dropping in a large piece of butter and some spices, she plunged a poker directly from the fire into the foaming brew. It hissed and spluttered. She brought it over and poured us both a beaker, "This will warm you through, my lady. Your bairns are still wrapped in their furs. They are snug as dormice. I will go and fetch some hot food. We have porridge and fried meats."

Rebekah sipped the ale and smiled, "She is right. It is good and she is the kindest woman I have ever met. You are lucky to have her, lord."

"I know. Do you know her story?" Rebekah shook her head and continued to drink, "She was the wife of one of my archers who died while serving me. She was forced to herd swine. Her circumstances were little better than that of a slave. I found her and gave her this job. My family is hers. I know that I am lucky. I have been lucky with all of my people."

Ruth and Samuel burst into the Great Hall. As I discovered neither of them just entered a room, they hurtled in like an autumn gale. One of Rebekah's women raced in after them, "Sorry my lord, my lady, they would not listen to me."

I patted my knees, "Come the two of you and sit here. You should obey the ladies. They know what is best for you."

"We could not wait. Are we going to have an adventure today?"

I laughed, "Every day is an adventure. You just need to look upon it that way. When you have eaten your breakfast get dressed in something warm and we will visit Alf the Smith."

Ruth asked, "Is that an adventure?"

"When you see him at work then you will think so! He takes raw metal and makes it into the most wonderful things. He is like a magician!"

The eight nights leading up to Christmas were wonderful. They were filled with the children and my family. I did not spare one thought for Henry or King Malcolm. The Bishop of Durham was as far from my mind as it was possible to get. I knew that we would have to deal with him but that was for the future. The now was pure pleasure. I took the time to walk the streets of the once humble town we had built. It was now almost unrecognisable. What had been simple huts were now solid and substantial houses. The most substantial belonged to Alf and Ethelred, the richest men in the town but there were others which showed the commerce which flowed through the town. There was even a pair of brothers who made and sold crosses and other religious goods. That showed the greatest difference. When my father and I had first come people had no coin and barely eked out a living. Now they had enough to spare so that they could buy crosses to adorn their necks. The two brothers, older men, Abelard and Geoffrey, tried to sell me a silver cross. It looked to be the most expensive item they had to sell. I had bought presents for the family in York when we had passed through. I did not buy.

Christmas, too, proved to be joyous beyond words. Since Adela's death, the castle had been empty. We had had brief highlights such as when the families of my knights stayed but this was as it had been in the old days. My knights spent Christmas day with their families but they all came to spend some time with us during the ten days of feasting in the shortest of days. As a bachelor knight, Wulfric was there the whole ten days. Samuel was delighted. The grizzled old warrior played all sorts of silly games with my grandchildren. He went on all fours to pretend to be a bear. He played hide and seek. He even sat them on his knee and told them the stories his mother had told him when he had been a child.

Ten days after the feast of St. Stephen, William and I left, with an escort of ten men at arms and ten archers. I had sent Sir Gilles to warn the Bishop of our visit. I told him that we intended to stay the night. As we headed up the Durham Road William and I began to plan our strategy. One of us would speak while the other would watch. The Bishop surrounded himself with political creatures. They would bear close scrutiny. We agreed that it would be William who would speak. He would be around more than I would. It made sense. I also had more experience of watching for deceit. We had chosen the best archers and men at arms. That was not because we feared attack. Since my son's foray north there had been peace. It was more as a statement to the Bishop that we had warriors who were the best. The twenty of them were also clever and they would pick up any news and gossip which might tell us what the Bishop was up to.

The castle looked magical. We had had no snow in the valley but Durham had a blanket all around. It was further north and closer to the hills. It was a daunting castle. Set on a high rock and with a river curving around it would cost many men to reduce it. I could see why the Scots had never attempted to take it. We were admitted and due deference was shown. Our men were taken to the warrior hall and our squires took our horses to the stables. While we waited for them I scanned the walls. The Bishop did not employ as many men on his walls as we did. I had heard that he liked to hoard money. In my view that was short-sighted. However, it was useful information. If I had to take the castle then I might be able to take it by stealth rather than force.

Our squires soon arrived. The Bishop had ensured that there were grooms to care for our horses. I was riding Storm Bringer for Warrior had been covering Skuld and Aiden was hopeful that she was with foal. The black horse with the white blaze had made a grand entrance in the sea of white.

A knight greeted us, "I am Sir Ralph D'Aubigny. I will take you to the Bishop."

William said, "Did I not meet one of your relatives in the Holy Land?"

He nodded and smiled, "My cousin. It is good of you to remember, earl."

"And what of you? Did you go on Crusade?"

"I did but I was laid low in Acre by some vile disease. I have only recently returned. I spent some time with Raymond de Puy Provence, the master of the Hospitallers. He spoke often of you."

William smiled, "How is the old knight?"

"The same. He still strives to do good in a world where men are driven by greed."

I nodded, "And now what is your position?"

"The Master gave me a letter of introduction to the Bishop of Durham. I hoped for a manor. I believe there is one vacant at Fissebourne. I would like to be given the manor." He shook his head. "I am not hopeful. The Bishop cannot ignore the letter of introduction but without connections, it appears that I am of no use to him." He smiled, "It is why I am used as a doorman!"

"And if you are not given Fissebourne?"

"Then I would present myself to King Henry."

"What of your family's lands?"

"I am afraid my family chose the side of Stephen. We lost all. I am the last of the line and a penniless knight. I suppose I could be a sword for hire. My squire and I are quite handy with our weapons. As you know, lord, if you are not then the Holy Land will take your life." He gave us a wan smile, "We must go. The Bishop does not like to be kept waiting."

I shook my head, "He can wait for an Earl Marshal!"

The Bishop had decided to impress us. He had his chair, one might call it a throne, on a raised dais. As we entered my son said, quietly, "It seems he has been lessoned by King Malcolm's advisers. He wishes to look down on us."

I gave a slight nod, "Your Grace."

He frowned. I had not shown obeisance. William had told me, on the way north, that he had annoyed the Bishop by a similar action. "I pray you to take a seat. Sir Ralph, we are done with you. You can wait without." The young knight had been dismissed like a servant. The Bishop smiled and it was a false smile, "We will eat and drink but first I have some questions, Earl William, about your campaign in the north."

This suited us for William would be able to talk and I could watch. The priests who flanked him looked not like the priests I knew. These were well fed. They had jewelled fingers. They looked like men who knew how to accumulate coin. There were also two knights there. These were not like Sir Ralph. These were grizzled warriors. Their surcoats and mail were unfamiliar. The pommels on their swords told me that they were neither English nor Norman. I did not recognise either and that caused me concern for I had fought alongside most knights. The others I had fought against. Where had they come from?

The Bishop asked, "Your campaign was successful?"

"Yes, your grace, we have recovered that which King Stephen gave away and the Countess of Chester has also recovered Cumbria. The King will soon have his taxes eh?"

The priests looked at each other and there was worry on their faces. The Bishop spread his hands, "We have much reconstruction, Earl William. Castles must be strengthened." He looked at me and I nodded. "And that brings me to Norham. I realise it is an oversight but it has come to my attention that you gave the castle to one of your knights, Sir John of Elton."

William smiled, "I did. We need the castle as a bastion against the Scots. The Tweed is the natural boundary between our kingdoms."

"But it belongs to the Palatinate."

"Then, perhaps, you should have recovered it, your grace. It was my men who took it."

"You had my knights with you."

"And..."

"And..." he waved his hands before his face. "I am not happy with this situation. I shall speak with the King!"

I had been watching the two knights and their eyes had never left William. I spoke, "I am Earl Marshal and King Henry has given me certain messages to pass on to you. I will do so in private but for the purpose of this meeting regard me as the King's voice." I smiled.

The Bishop flustered and fussed about the castle for some time. William answered all of his questions well. Eventually, the Bishop realised he had been outwitted and he slumped in his seat. A young servant came in and whispered in the Bishop's ear. He stood, "The food is ready. Let us eat. I am weary of this debate."

I noticed as we sat to eat that they had placed the two knights well out of earshot of William and myself. I wondered at that. Sir Ralph was seated next to William. The food was, as I had expected, excellent. The priests were too well fed for it to be other. We had had three courses when the Bishop, who had been just picking at his food while drinking heavily, turned and said, "Earl Marshal, I cannot eat while I wonder what King Henry wishes to say to me. Come to my chambers and tell me so that I may enjoy the rest of the meal."

"Of course."

Everyone watched us as we left. There was a guard at his door. We entered and sat down. He looked at me expectantly. "I will be blunt with you, Bishop Puiset, the King is not happy with your lack of vigour against the Scots."

"What can I do?"

"I said that I will be blunt and I shall. He is keen to have another Bishop here in your stead. He would have a man who can fight the Scots."

His face fell, "But the Pope himself...."

"The Pope is in Rome and you are here." I smiled, "It is why my son put Sir John in the castle at Norham. We need a strong leader."

"What if I had a strong leader to put there?"

"Have you?"

He gave me a sly look. "I may have. Allow me to have the night to think about this. You can reassure King Henry that, from now on, he has a Prince Bishop who will be a rock against the Scots."

"Good and when the taxes follow he will, indeed, be a very happy king!"

We rejoined the others and the wine had been flowing. I was pleased that my son and our squires had not emulated the others and he had refrained from drinking too heavily. As we passed the two knights I noticed their accents. They were speaking Norman but they were French. I felt the hairs on the back of my neck prickle. What was going on?

The Bishop had given me, my son and our squires a chamber to use. It may have been an insult, I was the representative of the King, but it suited us. The four of us sat and spoke of what we had learned.

"The Bishop is taxing his people heavily. His knights are unhappy."

I looked at William, "How did you learn that?"

"The priest who was on the other side of Sir Ralph told me. Sir Ralph was asking about Fissebourne. The priest told him that the knight who had been there had tired of the taxes and gone to the Holy Land. He laughed when Sir Ralph said that he hoped for it. I saw Sir Ralph's spirits sink."

"Fissebourne is almost a neighbour. I would rather it was Sir Ralph there than a knight appointed by the Bishop." I told them about the two French knights.

James nodded, "I was going to tell you that, lord. They have been in the castle for two months. They have men at arms with them. That had not travelled from France but Rome. One of the priests who was seated close to Alf and I said that they were hoping for a manor. There was Fissebourne. I think the other hoped for Norham."

I stood and smacked one hand against the other. "Now it all makes sense. I wondered at the sly look on the Bishop's face. I see the Pope's fingers in this. Thank you, James, forewarned is forearmed. I can now wrestle for a solution to this dilemma." I began to undress. The Church and the other rulers were resentful of the power which Henry wielded. Thanks to his wife and our conquests he now ruled the largest Empire save the Byzantine. Henry did not listen to Rome. His grandfather had been the same. It was why he appointed free-thinking priests like Thomas Becket to positions of power. This was the Church's chance to infiltrate the Palatinate with knights who would advance Rome's cause. The fact that they were French was even more sinister. The King of France was a great supporter of the Pope. However, he also wished to make England less stable. Thanks to our conquests in Wales and the peace with Scotland King Henry could not turn his attention to Anjou, Normandy and, perhaps, France. By the time I had fallen asleep an idea had formed in my head and sleep strengthened it. I awoke refreshed and eager to meet with the Bishop.

We were the first ones up. Sir Ralph joined us. He looked depressed, "What is amiss, Sir Ralph?"

"When I was speaking with your son and Canon Michael last night I discovered that I could wait until the end of time and not be granted a manor. My squire and I will have to seek our fortune elsewhere." He forced a wan smile. "At least I have my letter from the Master of the Hospitallers."

I shook my head, "I fear they have less influence here than the Templars. It is why the Templars are such a rich order."

We ate in silence. Eventually, the Bishop appeared. He was followed by the two French knights. "Ah Earl, I am pleased that, like me, you are an early riser." I nodded although we had been up a good hour already. "As I said I have slept on the problem and come up with a solution." He pointed to the two knights. "These knights seek a manor. Both are doughty warriors. I would give one Fissebourne and one Norham. Your Sir John can return to his wife at Elton. He will be pleased, will he not? It will mean he will be home when his child is born."

I flicked a glance at William. The Bishop had a spy in our land.

"And who are these men? Remember, Bishop, I have to approve them."

"You? But…"

"Remember our conversation in your chambers?" He nodded. "Who are they?"

"One is Jean of Auxerre and the other is Guillaume de Nissa."

"Frenchmen."

He adopted an innocent look, "Does that matter?"

"This is England, your Grace. The King would have either Normans or Angevin if he cannot have English. That is not an acceptable solution."

He sat back in his seat and the two Frenchmen glared at me. One said, "I am insulted, my lord."

"Why, because I told you that you are French or that you are not English? Either way, it matters not. You are foreigners in my land. Watch your words or it may end badly."

The Bishop spluttered, "My lord, this is my castle!"

"And I am Earl Marshal. Now listen to me, Hugh de Puiset, I have a solution. You have one knight who is acceptable to me. And I will allow you to have Norham."

He brightened, "I can have Norham?"

"In exchange for Fissebourne. You and your knights have proved inept at stopping the Scots from entering my land through Fissebourne. I would have that and Sir Ralph here can have Norham."

"Sir Ralph but…"

"But he is one of your knights. He has the backing of the Master of the Hospitallers and I believe he would hold Norham against the privations of the Scots. Is that not right, Sir Ralph?"

I could see that I had taken him by surprise, "Of course lord, I…"

"And we know that he has the right qualities for a church manor as the Master of the Hospitallers has recommended him. Is there a problem?

You get Norham and I get Fissebourne. We both know that Norham is more valuable and your new lord of the manor will ensure that you receive all that is due to you." My voice and tone told him that I would brook no argument. His shoulders slumped. I had won the argument. He would come up with some other plot and device but, for the present, all was well.

We spent some time debating the logistics of the handover. The Bishop and his two angry Frenchmen left us. William and I spent time with Sir Ralph. "I do not know how to thank you, lord but how do you know that I will do a better job than either of those Frenchmen?"

"Because they are French and the Master recommended you. My son trusts the Master and that is good enough for me."

William said, "But there is a problem. You have but your squire. You will need men to garrison the castle." He shouted, "Alf, fetch quill and parchment!"

"Aye lord." His squire hurried off.

"There are thirteen men at Bamburgh. They swore an oath to me. They were Englishmen who fought for the Scots. I believe you can trust them. You can have those as the heart of your defence. You will need more but the Bishop will have to pay for the other men. You should choose your own men. If they come from the Bishop then I would not trust them. If he has any sense then he will have the castle improved and made of stone. It is a good castle to defend. You have a river and a gully to protect two of the sides of the castle. Bamburgh is King Henry's castle and it is close enough to you to be of assistance."

"Thank you both. The Master was right, Earl William. You are a man of honour and integrity."

Later that morning, as we rode south I was even prouder of my son. The land would be in good hands when he took control.

Chapter 8

William was aware that Sir Ralph had no archers and so he began to spread the word, further south, that he was seeking archers. It took less than a month for us to see the results. His reputation and, I must confess, mine meant that ten archers arrived at the castle. My son equipped them and sent them north to Norham. When they arrived Sir John could return to his new estate.

"And what of Elton? It is not as rich as Fissebourne but it is a good manor and guards the road from the west."

"Father, this is still your land."

I shook my head, "King Henry made you the Earl. You will be living in Stockton, not I. You make the choice."

He nodded, "Then I would appoint your old squire, Sir Richard. His wife comes from Long Newton. She still has family there. Sir Hugh's other knights are all men from Gainford and Headlam."

"Good, then you had better write to him."

I knew that my time in Stockton was coming to an end. I had had a letter from King Henry reminding me of my obligations. His missive gave a date for the meeting. It was twenty-one days hence. He confirmed the meeting in Striguil with de Clare. I wondered if he was softening towards de Clare. Would he give him back his title and his English and Norman lands? With my impending departure in mind, I took to spending more time in Stockton. I had old friends and none of us was getting any younger. How many more times would I speak with them? I had lost friends when serving the Empress and I regretted the opportunities I had missed to speak with them.

When I spoke with Alf he gave me a present. "It is a helmet such as I made your son. It will protect you in battle."

"I thank you for the gift but I do not think that I will be in battle as often in the time to come. Now I sit on a horse and order others to fight."

Alf laughed, "I have never seen you in battle on a horse but I have spoken with those that know you. I cannot see that you would sit idly by while others fight. I am certain this will see good service and keep you safe." It was a fine helmet and almost the twin of the one he had given to my son.

"I thank you, old friend."

It was good to sit and talk. We spoke of the old days when we had had to defend Stockton's walls against Scots and brigands. We talked of warriors now dead. He told me how his children and grandchildren were doing.

When I saw Ethelred, it was a different conversation entirely. Ethelred was rich. He had become rich through me. As a result, he never charged me or my men for using his ferry. He and I were partners in *'Adela'* and he had another five ships which plied the east coast and beyond. When I needed ships, I knew that I would not be robbed if I used Ethelred's. He too spoke of his children but it was not as with Alf. He did not talk of grandchildren nor their health but he spoke of their success and how much money they were making. He meant nothing by it. It was just his way.

"Warlord, I have something to ask you."

"Ask away, old friend. I can always say no."

He had laughed, "You have rarely done that. You know that my son Ethelbert is my shipwright?"

"Aye and a good one too."

"He needs specific trees to make good ships. He spends a long time finding the perfect y-shaped trunk. We buy them and it makes a sound ship."

"I know, in the past, he has paid me, and now my son for the wood."

"We thought to save time for the future. We seek permission to be able to go in the woods and to make young trees become the perfect shape. He will have to spend less time seeking the trees for we will know where they are."

"That will take years!"

He smiled, "I have grandchildren and they will thank me. My family will become rich long after I am dead."

I had been wrong about Ethelred. He did think about his children and grandchildren; it was just differently from Alf. "I will speak with William but I cannot see anything that he would object to."

He clasped my arm. "Thank you, lord!" he then went to explain how they would find the young trees and make them the perfect shape for a sound ship's keel. I left knowing more about shipbuilding and also about Ethelred. I had done him a disservice by my thoughts.

As I passed the house of the Smithson brothers, who made religious goods, I saw that they had opened an inn. I was not aware that one was needed. I called into their workshop.

"Good morrow, Earl Marshal, can we interest you in a cross? I will give you a good price." Abelard was keen to sell to me. I had no doubt that if I had bought one then he would have let all his customers know. It would increase his sales.

"No, thank you." I pointed at the building next door. "I am just intrigued that there is a need for an inn in Stockton."

The elder brother, Geoffrey, smiled broadly, "There are many travellers now, lord. Since your son scoured the north of the Scots then there is more trade going through the town to Durham. This is the shortest route, save the sea, and we all know how parlous that can be."

The younger, Abelard, added, "And people come to Stockton. The iron and the metal goods produced by Alf are in great demand. Do not worry, lord. We have been open but a month and have been more than half full for at least twenty of those days."

"Good." That seemed good for my town. Would we become as big as York, I wondered?

As I left I saw some of the guests as they headed down to Brigid the Ale Wife who served ale at the tavern she had named The Hope. Perhaps the brothers were right. I had been so busy with war that I had not noticed the real growth of my town. Thanks to the vigilance of my men it was now a place which could grow and prosper. I saw that the men who walked to the Hope were all foreign-looking. That was not a surprise. Being a port, we invited those from foreign climes. Their clothes and accents marked them as different. I heard Flemish being spoken.

I returned to the castle. I had much to do and yet I begrudged the time I would spend in planning. I decided to delegate. When I reached the castle I found James, he was practising with Alf son of Morgan. I hated having to stop them but my needs were greater, "James, I would have you ensure that all the men at arms and archers who will be travelling to Wales with us have a spare horse and all the equipment we need."

"Aye lord."

"The same goes for Lame Tom and the servants. I suspect we will be sleeping in the open more than we will be sheltered and housed."

"Aye lord. Do you mind if Alf helps me? He is keen to learn what duties he might have to perform for Earl William."

"Of course." I handed him the new helmet, "And we will need to pack that too. I will ride with my old helmet but this one will be for when we go to war!" That done I sought William and his family. They were in the Great Hall. I heard squeals and giggles. They were playing some sort of game. I stood in the doorway, unseen and watched them. I had missed this with my son's first family. I relished every moment of it now.

Eventually, Ruth spied me and she squealed, "Granddad!"

They all turned and my moment was gone. The two children rushed up to me. "Where have you been? We were looking for you."

"Well young Samuel, I too have friends and I was speaking to them before I go."

His face fell, "You are leaving now?"

I laughed, "No, we still have much time but I needed to say my goodbyes early. I have a great many things left to do."

Rebekah said, "We are planning a feast in fourteen nights time. We have invited all of your knights, including Sir Hugh."

William nodded, "We know not how long you will be away and, by then, Sir John should have returned."

I knew what was going through his mind. I was getting old and he was afraid that something would happen while I was away. It had happened to me with Adela. "Good, it will be a good opportunity for us all to catch up with one another. I have not seen Wulfric since Christmas and then I had little opportunity to speak with him. He was too busy playing the fool with the children."

"You know Wulfric, he never changes but I think he sees in Ruth and Samuel the grandchildren he might have had if he had ever married."

Samuel nodded, "I like Wulfric. He is like a huge bear that can talk! He has promised me his sword when I grow up."

"Then you are lucky for that is a mighty sword. Come let us go into the bailey and you can show me your skills. Fetch the wooden swords."

When he ran off Ruth said, "I cannot use a sword. What about me?"

"Then what say that tonight I tell you a bedtime story from the east. I can tell you of the Princess Scheherazade."

"Who was she?"

"She was a storyteller from Persia. My nurse was an Arab and she told them to me."

She clapped her hands in delight, "I want to go to bed now and hear a story!"

Rebekah laughed, "Let us tire you out first." She gave me a grateful smile. Ruth often felt left out of things.

Our meals had become simple affairs. Alf and James had realised that we needed the time as a family and they actually preferred to eat in the warrior hall. Dick presided over that table. The drink flowed more freely and the language was a little more relaxed. It was not that my men were crude or boorish but they were men. Instead of the large table we used for feasts William used the table I had used for so many years when he lived in Normandy and I lived alone. In those days, I had eaten with my squire and then retired to my solar. It was cosier now, eating before the fire and waited on solely by Alice. She loved to have the family to herself.

That night I was aware that I would be telling Ruth a bedtime story and so I donned my silk tunic. I had brought it from the east on my last visit. William had brought me a curved Turkish dagger and I strapped that to my waist too. I would play the part. Putting a cloak about me I decided to watch the sunset before we ate. I walked around the walls to the western gate. It overlooked St. John's well.

The watch was set for the night. Walther of Thorpe was the sergeant at arms and with him were Aethelward of Thirsk, James son of Abelard and Wilson of Aycliffe. It was still light and so they were gathered above the gate. Once it was dark they would patrol the walls. They were taking the opportunity of watching the herons come down to the river for one last feed before dark. My castle was compact and the riverside was almost inaccessible to men. It made it more secure. It was really the gate to the west which presented the danger. The north gate came out in the town. That was busier these days. Sentry duty was not what it was.

They smiled when they saw, beneath my cloak, the fine surcoat. "That looks expensive, Warlord."

"It is Walther, and that is why you rarely see it but it is for my granddaughter. I wish to tell her a story."

"They are fine children both of them. It is good to hear children's laughter in the castle."

James laughed, "It is better than Ralph of Bowness' snores."

Just then the sun began to dip and the sky began to turn orangey-pink. I had seen sunsets in many parts of the land but this one was always special. The five of us stood and watched the sun slowly slip down and the rainbow of colours filled the sky. When the last light twinkled out I turned, "I shall go now. I always feel fulfilled when I see a sunset."

"Aye lord, it is one of the benefits of this watch. When we do the early shift, we are too tired to appreciate the sunrise and that always feels colder. Enjoy your meal and we will watch the walls for you this night."

I could see that Samuel was tired for his eyes drooped. We had practised for a good hour. However, he was forcing himself to stay awake. He would not admit defeat and go to bed before his sister. Alice had prepared a leg of mutton. She had slow cooked it with spring greens, last year's beans, some early vegetables and barley. With herbs from the kitchen garden, she had outdone herself by using half a bottle of old wine. It was delicious. There was far too much for the five of us. The children had good appetites but it was William and me who made inroads into the mutton.

When Samuel almost collapsed into the remains of the steamed pudding Alice had made, we took the children to bed. Samuel was laid in his and almost asleep when Rebekah laid him down but Ruth said, "Remember grandfather you promised me a story of Sherhez, er, Shraz…

"Scheherazade. And I shall. The Warlord never breaks his word." I sat on the bed and began to tell her one. I got through one story and had begun the second when I saw that she was asleep. I pulled the covers up and said, "Good night princess." I kissed her on the top of the head. I went to Samuel but he had disappeared down beneath the covers.

When I reached the hall Rebekah and Alice were just beginning to move the mutton. "What will you do with that, Alice?"

"The bone to the dogs and the rest for soup. Why lord?"

"It will be a cold night for it was a fine sunset. I will take it to the night watch."

"I can do that!"

I took it from her, "I am neither too grand nor too lazy. They are my men I will take it." I saw Rebekah yawning. "William, take some wine to the solar. It is a night for talking."

"Aye, father, it is. I would hear what you discovered in the town today."

"What makes you say that?"

"John of Craven drinks in The Hope and he said there were many strangers there and that they were staying with the new merchants."

"Aye, I met them. They seem to have a good eye for business."

"They may do but their guests were Flemish and French."

I frowned, "I knew there were Flemish but not French. I will speak with them again. They did not say that. I like not being deceived however innocent it may seem."

I went up the back stairs. One of the sentries would be in the gatehouse. The dish was still warm and the smell filled my nose. The men would enjoy this feast. When I emerged into the night I felt the chill. I had, foolishly, forgotten my cloak. It was too late to go back for it. I looked for one of the sentries. There should have been one on the river wall but there was no one there. I wondered if they were having their mid-watch meal. If so then I would be in perfect time.

As soon as I stepped into the gatehouse I saw that they would be eating no more. Walther and James lay dead. There were three armed and mailed men dead near them. I recognised one of them as one of the guests from the inn of the two brothers in the town. I dropped the dish and, picking up Walther's sword shouted, "Alarm! Enemies afoot!"

My family! The warrior hall was in the outer bailey. There would just be William left to defend himself against however many other killers had managed to get inside. Even as I was racing back to the Great Hall I was wondering how they had got in and surprised my sentries. I heard the clash of steel as I entered the door to the interior of the castle. As I leapt down the stairs and landed heavily I saw three men. Their backs were to me and William had his sword and dagger in his hand, facing them.

I roared, "Die!" It was not bravado. I wanted to distract them. They were good. Only one of them turned around and he had fast hands. I had had fast hands but I had been younger then. He lunged at me with the tip of his sword. That was unusual. Most men used the side of the sword. I barely had time to flick it away but I still had the Turkish dagger. I slashed it at his throat. He jerked his head back and, as he did so I punched at his face with the hilt of my sword. It smashed into his nose making it erupt. Briefly blinded, I managed to tear my dagger across his throat.

Pushing his body to the side I leapt at the two men who were fighting William. I had seen how good they were by the man I had fought. There was nothing elegant about my move. I clattered into their backs. They both wore mail and my blades did not hurt them. What did, however, was my weight for it drove them forward. William's blade was driven through the body of one. It came right through and scored a wound down my left side. The other was lithe and he was quick. He threw me off and brought up his dagger. I used my own dagger to counter and then William sliced into his neck.

"The children!" I had no idea how many men were loose in the castle. William nodded and ran from the hall.

Alice had come in and she and Rebekah lifted me to my feet. They saw the blood, "Warlord, you are wounded."

I shook my head, "It is nothing." I went to the three bodies to make certain that they were dead. I would have liked to question one of them but with just two of us left to fight them we could take no chances. I heard no noise from the children's room. "You two follow me." I knelt and picked up two of the assassins' daggers. I gave one to each of the women. "If there are others then defend yourselves."

I saw William, as we neared the room. He was backing out of the room. He put a finger to his lips and mimed sleeping. I said, "You two go in the room and lock it. Do not open it for any save William or me."

Rebekah put her hand on my arm, "Be careful, lord."

William must have joined me when I heard footsteps. I looked around and saw Ralph of Bowness leading ten of my men at arms. "There were killers. Six are dead. Walther and James are dead too. I know not about the others."

Ralph nodded grimly, "Stay here, lord. We will seek them out."

William noticed my wound, "I will get Brother Peter."

I looked at my most precious garment. "It is ruined! Whoever was behind this will pay."

"Have you any idea who they are?"

I nodded, "I recognise one of them, perhaps another two. They were staying at the house of those two brothers. As soon as Ralph returns we will go and see these two men. They have questions to answer."

Brother Peter, Alf and James appeared. "Brother Peter, see to my father. James, go and fetch his cloak and his sword."

"Aye lord."

As Brother Peter took out his medicine and began to clean the wound William knelt by the bodies. "Alf search the one in the passageway."

In the time it took for my wound to be bandaged the two of them had searched the bodies and James had returned with my cloak and sword. William held open his hand, "French coins and freshly minted."

I nodded. "Those two knights at Durham were French. That was no coincidence."

Ralph appeared and dropped to his knee. "I am sorry, my lord, I have failed you. We found the other sentries, they are dead. There is another dead man close by."

"Rise, this could not have been avoided. Did they come over the town wall?"

He nodded, "Aye, lord, how did you know?"

"I saw these in the town today. It is I who have been lax. There was a time I would have questioned every newcomer to my town. Four of our men have paid the price for my carelessness. Leave enough men to secure the castle and bring the rest with us."

We hurried out of the keep and left by the town gate. I saw that Dick and his archers were there. He looked at me and saw my wound, "Lord?"

"Guard the walls, Dick."

William was as angry as I was. I could tell it by his gait. We reached the house of the two brothers and I sent Ralph of Bowness around the back. There were two front doors. One led to the workshop and one to the accommodation. Others had come into the street. I said, "Back in your homes until I say!" They obeyed my commands.

"Alf, James, take four men and search the workshop."

I nodded to William and he tried the handle. The door was not locked. We entered with swords at the ready. Ralph of Nottingham had brought a lighted brand and he held it aloft. The place was empty but we saw signs of a hurried departure. "Wilfred, take some men and get to the stables. See if their horses are there."

By the time we had confirmed that both the workshop and the rooms were empty Wilfred was back. "Three horses are gone, lord, but there are six other horses there. They must belong to the dead men in the castle."

I nodded, "We can do nothing this night. I will have Aiden, Edgar and Edward find their trail."

We fetched Alice and Rebekah from the children's room. Poor Rebekah was visibly shaken. Alice said, "I will make a posset. That will help people to sleep." That was Alice's way. There was always some food or a drink to remedy any situation.

Rebekah asked, "What did they want?"

William said, bluntly, "They wanted my father and me, dead."

"But why?"

I sat down. My wound had begun to ache. "Many reasons. As they were French and Flemish then I can see that the French King had a hand in this. However, we have upset the Bishop of Durham and he had two French knights at his court."

"We will ride thither tomorrow and confront him. Pope or no Pope we will not be attacked in our own castle."

After they had drunk the posset Rebekah and William retired to the room they shared with their children. The rest left Dick and me alone. "When I go to Wales, Dick then you and Wulfric will be even more important than before. We will speak with Alf and Ethelred. I need those two to interrogate every newcomer. We did it once before. I thought that with the Scots subdued and Stephen dead we had no reason. I was wrong."

"We have enough guards now. We can strengthen the defences. It has cost us, four dead men, at arms and that is sad but it could have been worse. It might have been you and your son."

Alf and Ethelred were summoned first thing. Aiden and his two men had ridden out directly we had returned. Aiden said that he could track in the dark. The two senior burghers were distraught that such a thing could have happened. We had once had a town watch. The two men promised to reintroduce it and to use the gates again. Peace had been an illusion.

When Aiden returned it was with the news that the two men had taken ship to France from Hartness. It had been waiting for them. Hartness was the Bishop's port. The questions we had for him mounted. We left just before noon. I took six knights with men and a large conroi. I wanted the Bishop to be worried. If he had fled too then I would know who had caused this problem.

I suspect he knew something for he was there to greet us as we entered the castle. He was coming from his cathedral, "Earl Marshal, Earl, what can I say? That you came so close to death..."

How did you know?"

"My official at Hartness was questioned by your men. He sent directly to me for he knew that the enemies you sought left by my port. If there is anything I can do to make it up..."

"Where are those two Frenchmen; the ones who came from the Pope?"

"They left a month since. They were disappointed not to be granted manors."

I nodded, "Brother Peter, go to the Cathedral and fetch the Bible which therein resides."

"That is a valuable book!" The Bishop was outraged at my audacity more than the fact that the Bible would be brought from his church.

Brother Peter said, mildly, "I will be careful. I know how to carry a Bible, even a valuable one!"

I led the Bishop inside his hall. Many of his priests and knights were gathered. That suited me. When Brother Peter returned I said, "Place it on the table." He did so. "Bishop Puiset, I want you to put your hand on that Bible and swear that you had nothing to do with the attempt on our lives."

"I told you I knew nothing."

"Then you can swear with a clear conscience."

"Earl Marshal, this is unseemly. I should not have to swear."

"If you do not swear then I will put you on trial for attempted murder." My voice was calm but inside I was seething. He had to have known something. My fingers itched. I wanted to draw my sword and lay it at his throat.

His eyes narrowed and I saw the hatred he bore me and my son in them. He placed his right hand on the Bible and said, loudly, "I swear that I knew nothing of the attack on the castle at Stockton, the attempt on the Warlord and his son's life nor of the men who committed this. I knew nothing about their ship which was in Hartness." He lifted his hand as though it burned. "There!"

It was at that moment that I knew he was lying and yet he had sworn on the Bible. I saw the outrage on the faces of his people. They were outraged that I had made him swear and yet some of them had to have known too. I could do nothing.

"One more thing then, Bishop, unless you wish Hartness to be taken from you have your people there scrutinise and examine every ship which enters the harbour. The French are not our friends."

He nodded, "I have learned much from this, Warlord and there will be changes!"

Part Three -Wales

Chapter 9

My wound was just itchy when we set off for Chester. That was a good sign that it was healing. My son had been embarrassed that his sword had wounded me. I found it amusing.

This would be the first time I had travelled the road since Cumbria had been returned to the Countess. It meant an easier journey. My title also afforded me accommodation in churches, castles and monasteries. Gone were the days when we slept in woods with stakes and armed guards. We would return to that in Wales but, for the present, I enjoyed the seven-day ride. Enjoyed was not the right word. My mind was filled with the treachery of my enemies. Even in my most precious of sanctuaries, I was in danger.

As we rode I did what I had done when I had served the Empress. I went through every enemy and worked out if they were part of the plot. I was just pleased that she was safe, within her priory. Since her son had become king and she had retired then she could enjoy a life of contemplation. I was sad that we could not be together but I was sadder that she was denied the joy of being close to sons and grandchildren. I doubted that I would ever see her again and I often wondered if she thought of me.

As we descended the road across the hills towards our next halt I dismissed the Scots as the ones who had sent the killers. Galloway, Fife and Argyll were all leaders who were capable of murder but they would not hire French or Flemish men to do the deed. I still had enemies in Normandy and Anjou. Any of those could have hired the men. The problem with those as killers is that they would have found it easier to do so in battle. When I had fought alongside Henry in the last rebellion there had been no attempt on my life. Nor would it have been the Welsh. I might be a thorn in their side but they would have waited for me to come into their lands again.

It was then that I realised that the attempt had to have been on both William and myself and that left just one person who stood to gain, Hugh de Puiset. Louis VII would have backed the attempt. It suited him to have discord and dissension in the north. The Bishop of Durham was the one who had pulled the strings. I could not believe that he had been foresworn. William and I had spoken, along with my senior knights, before I left. A closer watch would be kept on Hartness. The Bishop would be visited once a month by one of William's knights. We had decided to put the valley on a war footing. Knights would patrol their manors and beyond. Strangers would be questioned and those who came from France specifically scrutinised. If that discouraged foreigners from our land then it would not hurt us. Our ships would still trade with other ports and their ships would be welcomed. Armed men with strange accents would not. Not one of my knights had dissented.

Countess Maud made us welcome. She always greeted me warmly with hugs and smiles. Whenever we walked she linked my arm and walked close to me. She was still an attractive woman. Some widows seemed to diminish when their husbands died. Not so Maud. I had known her for a long time. We were able to have comfortable silences and we understood each other well.

"I have to thank your son for what he did for the King and my family. The handover of the castles went easier for us. Already the revenue is flooding in once more and Chester can become what it was before Stephen gave away that which was not his."

"And what of your Welsh border? The King and I campaign in the south. Is the north safe?"

"King Owain Gwynedd ap Gruffydd has kept the peace since your battle in the Clwyd. We had begun to strengthen the castles there. What we need is a castle which is closer to the mountain of Snowdon where the land between the sea and its slopes is narrow."

"We would need to make war on him first and take that land. I do not think that King Henry has the appetite for that. The mountains yield little that he wants. The Welsh Marches are rich."

"Then why does he have you going to war? We hold the marches do we not? Surely de Clare and the lords who are there can hold on to them. Striguil and the other castles are mighty fortresses are they not?"

Irish War

We were walking by the Dee and I pointed to its water, "They are but they guard the coast. The waters of the seas guard them. King Rhys ap Gruffydd is young but he is clever. He uses his mountain strongholds to launch raids. They take slaves and cattle. The lords lose income and the King loses revenue. This will not be a long campaign. If we are still there at harvest time then I will be surprised. We will use our mobility to strike quickly. The young Welsh king needs to be discouraged. He can raid his neighbours but the Marches must be peaceful."

We headed back to the castle for darkness was approaching and I was still wary of a knife in the dark. "But he knows you are coming. It is common knowledge that King Henry and Count Striguil are gathering an army to punish King Rhys ap Gruffydd."

"Knowing that an enemy is coming and defeating him are two entirely different things. Remember Lincoln? Stephen knew we wanted the castle but he did not know that we would take it with a handful of knights and a pair of very brave women!"

She squeezed my arm, "You always know the right thing to say. Have you never thought of remarrying?"

I smiled at her, "Is that a proposal?"

She laughed, "That is not the worst idea in the world, I would not be averse. I am a woman and I have needs but I do not think that King Henry would like our union. The daughter of the Earl of Gloucester and the Warlord of the North might be a combination which would threaten his throne." She continued to squeeze my arm and said, huskily, "But you are always welcome in my home. You know that."

I nodded, "I know that and I too am a man who has needs but I would not risk damaging a lady's reputation." I put my hand on her hand and squeezed her fingers. "You are a fine lady and deserve to be happy."

She laughed, "Sadly I am the daughter of the bastard son of the old King and as such, I am a prize heifer! Come, let us make merry this night. I would have each day joyous!" I enjoyed a wonderful evening in Chester Castle.

When we reached Striguil King Henry had not arrived. We had travelled quickly and all of my men were mounted. I guessed that Henry had more baggage than we did. We had used sumpters for our equipment. King Henry preferred wagons.

I liked Richard de Clare. I knew the reasons for Henry's suspicions but I thought them unfounded. All that Richard de Clare wanted was his title and his lands returned. It would not have cost Henry anything to give it to him for the title lay vacant. Richard de Clare's Welsh lands were Pembroke. To give the title to another he would have to give the land to another. Henry was no fool. Count Striguil was a powerful knight. His family was also descended from a Duke of Normandy. He could trace his lineage back to Richard Duke of Normandy. The de Clare family also had other estates in England, in Surrey, as well as Normandy and Anjou. As a warrior, he reminded me of William. He was a fierce fighter and a superb rider. He led men well and, more importantly, they followed his banner.

He greeted me warmly and appeared excited. "Earl Marshal, I am to be married!"

I smiled, "Congratulations. Who is the bride to be?"

"Eva, Aoife MacMurrough, the daughter of King Diarmait Mac Murchada of Leinster."

I showed my surprise. "Does King Henry know of this?"

"Not yet." He looked worried. He looked around and, taking my arm said, "Let us walk by the Severn. I need your advice. I know that you are an honourable man. What I say will remain in confidence."

I nodded, "Unless it threatens my king."

He shook his head, "That it will not." We walked close to the river. There was no one near us but had there been then the sound of the waters would have masked our words. "Last year the king was deprived of his kingdom by Ruaidrí Ua Conchobair, High King of Ireland. He visited King Henry and asked for his help. The king said he was too busy. The King told him to seek help from the marcher lords." He looked at me and watched my reaction. That meant that King Henry had begun this course of action. "He came here on his way back and asked me and my brother lords for help. I met Eva and I was smitten. King Diarmait noticed this and offered his daughter's hand in exchange for my help."

I felt my heart sinking. This was the sort of action which could cost a lord his head. "And what do you say?"

He shook his head, "I am no fool, Earl Marshal! I told him that I could supply men but King Henry would have to give permission in order for me to lead them. I thought to ask him when he comes but I need your help. He listens to you. Everyone knows that since his father died you have become a father figure. Help me to keep my word."

"Then you have promised."

He sighed, "I have land here but no title. I will serve King Henry but…"

"If you took your men then what of this land?"

"That is why I am pleased that you come on this campaign. I believe we can subjugate the men whom King Rhys ap Gruffydd leads and when the land is secure, with your help, I can persuade the King to allow me to regain Leinster for King Diarmait Mac Murchada. It would gain another ally for King Henry."

I nodded, "Then I will help you so long as you heed my advice and obey me. I know the King. I have been with him since his birth. Do not speak of this until I say it is the right time."

"I swear."

I nodded, "Now tell me of King Rhys ap Gruffydd. Where is his stronghold?"

"It is in the heart of Cantref Mawr. The Carreg Cennen Castle is almost impregnable for it sits on a high cliff. There is but one way to assault it."

"What is nearby?"

"The King has built a monastery called Talley Abbey and there is Dinefwr Castle which overlooks the River Tywi."

"How far away is it?"

"From here ninety miles. It is longer to go by the coastal route and safer for we have castles there. We would be crossing Bannau Brycheiniog. That is a high wilderness filled with bandits and outlaws not to mention bands of warriors who serve King Rhys. The land we call Brecon is a dangerous place."

"Those are often the best routes to take for they can be travelled unseen. If we go by the coast then this king will know exactly where we are. He will place his men to stop us."

We had reached the castle and the Great Hall. "Will not King Henry make the decision?"

"King Henry will be guided by us. The journey is not what concerns King Henry. It is the destination. He wants secure borders so that he can concentrate on Normandy, Anjou and Aquitaine."

The King did not arrive for another four days. The other Welsh Marcher lords gathered with their retinue. I had not brought my scouts and so I asked for two of de Clare's. Rhodri and Thomas were both typical Welshmen. They knew their job. I went with them to scout out the approaches to Brecon. I took James, Aelric and Tomas ap Tomas. The two local scouts knew the land well.

"If I wanted to get to Carreg Cennen unseen which way would I go?"

They looked at me and saw the grey on my beard. "Riding a horse lord, or in a carriage?"

I saw the anger on Aelric's face at the insult. I smiled. "Do not let these grey hairs fool you. I have travelled over worse than Bannau Brycheiniog before now. Answer me this then, if you were to get to the castle unseen which way would you go?"

They smiled and Rhodri said, "Now that question I can answer, lord. I would travel north, along the Usk Valley. That way you could approach the castle from the north and their eyes would be on the south."

"And the Welsh Abbey?"

"That is not far north. You would have to pass Dinefwr Castle to reach it."

"Good then let us see how far we can get in half a day."

As we rode I saw the mountains rise to our left. They were a natural ridge. Once you chose your approach then there would be no chance of crossing. A plan began to emerge in my mind. We passed isolated farms and one castle before we stopped at noon at the castle of Abergavenny. It was part of the land ruled by William de Braose. The knight who was in residence was Hamelin de Balun. He was an old knight. I had met him in the last campaign. He had the look of a man who was waiting to die. He greeted us warmly but he would not be fighting alongside us. He did, however, provide valuable information about the land over which we would travel. He confirmed my scouts' opinion that it would be the best route to take. We returned to Striguil.

It was dark when we returned and, after eating I pored over maps with de Clare. I missed William for I could use him to test my ideas. Dick and Wulfric were also useful for that. I found Richard de Clare equally receptive. He knew how to listen and to be able to question. Those skills were what I needed. James meant well but he would agree with everything I said. I needed someone to see problems and Richard did that. By the time we had finished, I was confident that I had a plan which would yield results.

King Henry brought knights with him. They were young and they sought land. This was how the King managed to gain favours. He took the younger children of rich lords so that they could win manors. It cost the King nothing and ensured that he had the support of the most powerful of his barons, counts and earls. His grandfather and great grandfather had also been astute, politically. He also brought with him Thomas Becket as an adviser. He was a very organised man. He knew little of war but he understood lists and numbers. Henry needed someone like him.

Henry greeted me warmly. "You and your son have, once again, served me well, Earl Marshall."

"If you speak of Scotland then that was all my son."

"It was your son leading the men you trained. I take your point. William has done well. And Bishop Puiset?"

I lowered my voice and told him of the attempt on our lives and my conclusions.

"But you have no proof." I shook my head, "And he swore an oath?"

"Your majesty, he lied. I know when a man lies."

"I think you are wrong, Earl Marshal. It is his eternal soul he is wagering."

I did not argue. There was no point. Pressure had been applied. I dare say it was from the Pope.

"And I have devised a plan to defeat King Rhys ap Gruffyd."

He beamed, "Good, for I wish to be away before the harvest is collected in. You are wrong about the Bishop but what you said about the Flemish and French confirms what I have heard. King Louis is building an alliance. He knows that you and your son are my bastions against the Scots. King Malcolm is under pressure from his own people. I think King Louis would hope to use him to divert us in the north while he eats into Normandy and Anjou. What is your plan?"

"You and the main army will head down the coast and follow the main road through Novo Burgus, which the Welsh call Casnewydd-ar-Wysg. That way you would draw the Welsh towards you. The farmers will be in the fields sowing crops. Their sheep will be lambing. King Rhys will not be able to allow us to roam at will in his land. He will have to bring us to battle. They have two castles close by and it would be tempting for them to try to trap us between them."

He nodded. He had a good mind for strategy. "And you would have us make that a trap?"

I nodded, "You would take three-fifths of the army. That would tempt him to try to take us. Then we could use our horses. The last thing we need is for him to sit behind his walls. That would not suit your majesty's plans."

"No indeed." He looked thoughtful as he digested my words. "And you, with two-fifths of the army?"

"I would be approaching from the north and the side they least expect."

"You would fall on their rear." I nodded. "It would be a hard plan to time."

"Richard de Clare has good scouts. I have ridden with them. We would send them to tell you when we were in position and then you could appear to fall into their trap. They will use archers but we have enough archers to counter them. It is you and your knights who will hold them."

"You expect me to do much."

"If you wish, majesty, we could reverse roles. I am more than happy to hold them and you fall on their rear. However, …"

He stared into my eyes. I think he sought to see if I was mocking him, "However, they know that I have made reckless mistakes like that in the recent past and you have not. If they see your banner then the king will be suspicious. You have defeated him before."

I shrugged, "We can fool him. We must hurt him so badly that he cannot begin to expand again. The reparations you make King Owain pay means that the men of Gwynedd will be weak for a while. You do not want Deheubarth to become more powerful. We need weak Welsh kingdoms."

He studied the maps I had shown him and he nodded, "Who would you take with you?"

"De Clare and Fitzgerald. They have sound men. It would be slightly less than two fifths but I am content for all are mounted and we need to move quickly."

"I approve. I know not why you like this de Clare so much. His father fought against us."

"If we chose only those who had fought for us we would have a small army. All the rest are dead!"

"A little blunt."

"And he has something he wishes to ask you later. I beg you to listen to him."

"If he asks for Pembroke again…"

"He will not!"

He took me to one side, "What you have said about the Pope may no longer be true, Earl Marshal."

Intrigued, I asked, "Why not?"

"We now have a new Pope and he is English! Nicholas Breakspear is now Pope Adrian IV. He has written to me. He has something he wishes me to do. When you return home, I think you may find the Bishop of Durham a little more compliant."

Before we ate that night at a feast for the senior leaders, I told Richard that he should approach the King after the meal. "So soon?"

"If you do not then he may hear of it from another and I know that would annoy him and aggravate the situation."

"Very well. Who goes with you on the sneak attack?"

"You and Raymond Fitzgerald."

"Good. He is a fine leader. A little rash but brave as a lion. I will have him seated close to us so that we can get to know one another. When do we leave for the attack?"

"We wish to rest the horses which recently travelled from London. Three days at the most."

He shook his head, "Then this visit will cost me a fortune."

"See Thomas Becket. He handles the King's coin. He will reimburse you." It happened that Thomas was heading for the King's quarters as we spoke. He had sheaves of papers with him. "Lord Chancellor, a word."

"Of course, Earl Marshal. You and your son have saved the kingdom a fortune and brought it great wealth. I always have time to speak with you."

"Good. Count Striguil here is concerned that his finances will be stretched if the army stays here three days. You can see his point."

"Of course. The army outside fends for itself but here...send me your bills Count Striguil and I will scrutinise them. We are more than happy to pay for that which the King and his guest use but none other!"

"Of course." When he had gone from earshot Richard said, "An old man in a young man's body. Is he always so serious?"

"I believe he does enjoy hunting and hawking but he is a serious cleric that is for certain. He appears to have principles."

The King had surrounded himself with the sons of the important lords. He was making friends for the future. We had had to fight for the throne and he was not going to relinquish it easily. His major commanders were also seated with him. Others might have felt slighted but not I. I knew that I was held in the highest regard and I did not need to listen to the boasting of young knights who had yet to do anything and older lords whom I had beaten during the civil war. I needed to get to know the two men whose knights I would be leading.

There could not have been a bigger contrast between the two lords. Where Richard was sophisticated and witty Raymond was more like Wulfric. He was a bear of a man. His nickname was Le Gros and I could see why. He was enormous. He seemed a little in awe of me.

"Earl Marshal I grew up listening to stories of how you saved the kingdom for the Empress and her son. I am honoured to serve with you."

"You flatter me." I disliked people talking of my exploits and I changed the subject. "I knew your grandmother, Nest ferch Rhys. I met her when she lived in the tower back in Old King Henry's time."

He nodded, "She mentioned you. She said you were the one true knight. My father, William, was lord of Carew and he admired you although he sat out the civil war holding on to the village of Carew for the crown."

It was a diplomatic answer. "When we leave I want us to ride and ride quickly. The aim is to appear as ghosts who move unseen through the land. When we are in position then we must appear as twice the number of men we actually have. This will be a test of your skills and those of your men but if you are successful then your reputations will be made."

Raymond banged the table, making others turn, "By God, Earl Marshal! I should like to leave right now!"

I laughed, "There would be little point as the King does not leave for three days. Do either of you have archers?"

"Raymond said, "I have ten Welsh archers. They are deadly!"

"I have ten also."

"Then I will put them under the command of my captain, Aelric. He knows how I like my archers to be used." They both nodded their agreement. "And how many knights?"

Nest's grandson said, "Four."

"I have fifteen." Count Striguil noticed my raised eyebrows and he shrugged, "After our success against the Welsh, men begged to serve me. I have manors I can promise them. I could have more but that would mean leaving border castles unguarded." He lowered his voice. If I go to the aid of King Diarmait Mac Murchada then I will need those knights."

I shook my head. He had spoken too loudly and Raymond had heard. "What is this? The chance of land in Ireland?"

He was a loudly spoken man. Richard said, "Keep your voice down! I will tell you more in the morning but keep this to yourself!"

He smiled, "Of course."

I leaned over, "I am telling you to keep it to yourself. If you speak of this to another…."

He recoiled, "I am sorry Earl! I swear…!"

I held up my hand, "Let us enjoy the feast. Count Striguil, I think that before the King retires you should speak with him."

"Aye lord. I think I should."

As usual, I drank little and I was pleased that my two companions emulated me. I had trained Henry well and he also drank sparingly. I had taught him that men had loose lips when in their cups. As knights staggered from the table I nodded to Richard. He rose and approached the King who had Geoffrey Mortimer with him. That knight could barely raise his head from the table.

Sir Raymond said as Count Striguil left us, "I know I am loud and vulgar, Earl Marshal, but you shall not find a truer knight in the whole of Wales. I swear."

I smiled and put my arm around his shoulder, "Take some advice from an old knight. Swear less and let your actions speak for you eh? I can see that you mean well. Go to bed and we will speak with you in the morning. I would talk with all the men we take. You will learn that when I lead I do so in a manner different from other men. It is why I have the luxury of grey hairs and my limbs intact!"

He clasped my arm, "Thank you, Earl Marshal. I shall not let you down."

I waited for Count Striguil to speak with the King. I saw their heads together as Count Striguil put his case forward. The King listened. Sir Geoffrey was lying face down in the remains of his venison stew. He would hear nothing. King Henry waved me over. I took my wine and joined them.

"Did you know of this?"

"Count Striguil apprised me of the situation and I advised him to speak with you. But I believe you had an idea, your majesty, as the Irish king approached you first."

He nodded, "Why should we help the Irish? What can we gain?" There was a strange look in Henry's eyes. He was not drunk and yet I thought he was testing de Clare.

Count Striguil looked nonplussed, "He might become an ally!"

Henry laughed, "If he cannot regain his own kingdom then he is of little use to me. I would rather you stayed here and guarded the borders, Count Striguil."

I put my hand on the King's arm. I was one of the few who were permitted to do so. "Do not be so hasty, your majesty."

"I will listen to your words, Earl Marshal, for you have rarely led me astray but I will need convincing."

I spread a hand at the young knights who were staggering from the hall. "You have many young knights who require a manor. Do you think that we will take enough from the Welsh to make the prospect attractive?"

"No, the best land has gone. All that is left is rocky hillsides filled with sheep."

"Ireland is a primitive land. There are hills rather than mountains. They do not have castles and they have no knights. They fight half-naked and their horses are overgrown ponies."

"So?"

"Count Striguil could take the lords you brought for land to Ireland. In exchange for service, he could demand manors. Your knights would have land, villeins and an income. Who knows what that might lead to?" I appealed to Henry's love of power. His grandfather and great grandfather had had it too.

Henry's eyes showed that he was excited. "You are talking about extending our land to Ireland."

Count Striguil frowned, "I thought that we were going to help King Diarmait Mac Murchada?"

"We are but when we have recovered Leinster the knights who are there can take the other kingdoms. The Earl Marshal is right this is an opportunity." He smiled, "I will tell you now what the Pope asked of me in his letter." He lowered his head and his voice. "The Irish have a corrupt church. They are also the last bastion of slavery. It is almost a trade there. They are savages! The Pope has issued a papal bull and he has asked me to intervene. Matters in Anjou and Normandy prevent me from doing so but I see that we now have an opportunity to gain favour with the Pope and to extend the land which we control."

"Then you are agreeing, your majesty, that Count Striguil can help the King of Leinster."

Henry looked first at de Clare and then at me. "I agree, Earl Marshal, but on one condition." I nodded. "You will go as my representative! I need an old head who can negotiate and knows how to take advantage of the circumstances. I want no Norman king of Ireland save me and that is unlikely to happen in my lifetime. Is that clear, Count Striguil?"

De Clare nodded. There would be no going back to Stockton in the near future. My honour and the need to do right by de Clare had been my undoing. "Very well, majesty, just so long as Count Striguil has his titles returned to him."

I saw Henry's eyes narrow and then he laughed and clapped Count Striguil on the back, "God, Earl Marshal, you are the last of a dying breed. You are like my grandfather and Uncle Gloucester! You know how to win. Very well, Earl Richard!"

Chapter 10

We left three days later before dawn had broken. I was anxious to disappear into the woods and hills of the Brecon before any spies around the castle were about. We would be seen but the longer we could delay discovery the better. King Henry would take the longer, albeit quicker route, along the Roman Road which went along the coast. He would do so with much noise and fanfare. Our purpose was to alert the Welsh to King Henry whilst keeping my men hidden.

The two scouts rode ahead of us followed by Aelric and the archers. We had thirty-eight and I was pleased with that number. In five flights, they would send more than a hundred and fifty messengers of death towards the Welsh. With twenty-two knights and twenty-two squires we had heavy cavalry that could more than hold their own. Finally, we had thirty-six men at arms. My men were the equal of any Welsh knight and I was satisfied. We made Abergavenny by the end of the first day and we entered the castle of Sir Hamelin. He could not fight. He was too old and we needed youth but he gave us food and accommodation. Better than that he gave us six of his own men as scouts. They were like gold for they knew Brecon well.

When we left, before dawn to avoid notice, we knew that was our last night in a castle. Our next night would be in the open or within the eaves of the forest at least. We were close to the hamlet of Finni-Fach when the Welsh brigands attempted to ambush us. They had obviously not scouted us out but saw the archers on horses and mistook them for, well I know not what, but whatever the reason they launched an attack. It was worrying that our scouts had not spotted the ambush.

When we heard the clash of metal I spurred Warrior and pointed my spear ahead. The men at arms, led by Roger of Bath spread out and rode to flank the attackers. It was only later we realised that they were brigands. For all we knew King Rhys had ambushed us. Aelric had dismounted the archers and they were using the horses for shelter. They were releasing arrows into the forest. I rode to the left with James in close attendance. A surprised Welsh archer turned and pulled back his bow. I leaned down and lunged as his arrow flew over my head and my spear impaled him. I withdrew it and galloped after another brigand who was trying to evade me. My spear took him in the back. We had to be ruthless. The last thing we needed was for King Rhys to know that Normans were to the north of him. When I saw John son of John ahead, then I knew we had destroyed them and I rode back to the road. My men reported that we had slain over thirty brigands. They would no longer prey on travellers.

Rhodri dropped to his knee, "I am sorry, lord, I have let you down. You commanded me to lead these scouts and I have failed."

"No, Rhodri, you have not. It is a lesson and we shall learn. From now on two scouts ride the road and the rest ride in the forest. We will be forewarned!" We had escaped without too much damage. We had been lucky and we could not rely on such luck all the time.

We found a campsite before dark. As I walked around the perimeter checking the sentries I saw Rhodri alone. I could see that the scout was still angry with himself. "Aelric, go and speak with him."

"I know why he berates himself so. We lost a scout and three archers today. That is his fault."

"Aelric, remember when we were learning. You forget the years we have between us. The grey hair on our heads and in our beards is testimony to the dead."

He bowed, "You are right, Warlord. In the valley, we are used to the best. Here they are still learning."

Count Striguil asked, "How did your men at arms know what to do? Mine and Sir Raymond's just followed yours."

"We have worked together for many years. Our men at arms are paid well and learn how to think for themselves."

Sir Raymond said, "You pay them well? Why?" He was not trying to be argumentative. I could see, from his face, that he was genuinely confused.

"It is simple. It is cheaper to equip a man at arms than a knight. Often, they are better. I can have three men at arms for the same price as a knight. If you add a squire then it is five men at arms. A knight will seek glory. A man at arms seeks to win. I would rather have a good man at arms than a poor knight."

Irish War

They were both silent for a long time. I liked both of them and that night they showed their true character. They listened and they learned. I do not believe that the Irish War would have been so successful if they had not listened.

The next day was the most dangerous. We had to move within striking distance of the two castles without being seen. I had also come up with this plan as we would be able to threaten the monastery at Tally Abbey. It had only recently been built by King Rhys. He would not wish to see it damaged. We moved down the Cennen valley. It was not a large river. We could have forded it anywhere but it did provide cover. When Thomas returned to say that the castle was two miles away we left the river and headed through the woods until we were halfway between the Cennen and Towy rivers. We were deep in the heart of King Rhys' land and, so far, we were hidden.

I summoned Rhodri, "You know what you must do?"

"Aye, lord and I will make up for my mistake. I will find the King and tell him that we are in position."

While my men made camp I rode with Thomas, James and Aelric. I wished to scout out the castle for myself. As soon as we neared it I saw that it was an impregnable sanctuary. Perched high on a cliff and surrounded by trees, defenders could laugh away a siege. The trees gave us a good vantage point for we were to the west. The trees to the south had been cleared so that the defenders could more easily see an approaching attacker. Welsh archers would make that a killing ground.

As we watched I saw a pair of riders gallop up to the castle. Inside I heard trumpets. We were almost a mile away and even at that distance, I could hear the sounds of horses and men shouting. After a short time, a small column of ten riders emerged and, after riding south for a short time headed down the road which led west. It was but three hundred paces from our vantage point. We moved further back into the shelter of the trees. The ten riders were obscured from view but I heard their hooves. As the hooves drew closer I put my hand on my sword. I did not think that they were coming for us but it paid to be prepared. I saw that it was a knight with a squire and eight men at arms. They were typical Welsh men at arms. Their hauberks were short ones. The knight had a yellow dragon on a red background. I had seen it before when we had fought King Rhys.

Moving back to our original position we heard trumpets sound as the main body of men left the castle. I saw many banners. King Rhys had fifty knights with him. I saw at least sixty men at men arms and the rest were archers and fyrd. They did not head west, they continued on the road south. They were going to fight King Henry. We waited until the gates of the castle slammed shut and the sound of the army receded before we headed north and west back to our camp.

I dismounted and waved over my two lieutenants. "I think that King Rhys has taken the bait. His scouts must have seen King Henry and his army approaching. He has sent riders to Dinefwr for help. If Rhodri reaches the King then we can close the trap."

Count Striguil looked thoughtful, "The timing of this worries me, lord."

I nodded, "That is why I want you to send Thomas and the other scouts to shadow the Welsh. If we can arrive as the Welsh begin to array their forces then we can achieve victory before we have even drawn a sword."

As we had passed down the Cennen valley we had seen in the distance the dots of sheep. Although it was still early some had lambed. Farmers would be busy making certain that as many animals survived as possible. Our appearance would strike fear into their hearts. We could end the threat of the Welsh in one battle. As I helped James groom Warrior I reflected that if we failed then all that we had won in our last campaign could be lost. The King was gambling that my plan would succeed. It was a great responsibility.

Lame Tom and the other servants would remain in the forest with the spare horses the next day. I had only brought one war horse, Warrior, and James would not be required to bring another if Warrior fell. I would fight on foot. I was praying now that Warrior would not fall in battle. If he did then I would have to fight on foot and that would likely result in my death. We rose in the middle of the night and ate cold fare. Although all Welsh eyes would be on the south, the smell of wood smoke wafting from the north might alert them. One of the scouts had returned before dark to say that Thomas and the other scouts had found the Welsh army. They were camped in the hamlet of Llandybie by the small river, Marlas. King Rhys was cleverly using his land as an ally. The river would prevent him from being outflanked on his left and he had men coming from the west.

Rhodri rode in just as we were about to leave. "Lord, King Henry has received your message. He and the rest of the army are at Tyr-y-Dail by the Afon Loughor. King Rhys is less than two miles from him. I had to sweep west to avoid them. I almost fell foul of another force. There are three hundred men coming from Dinefwr. Half are mounted. There are many on foot."

"Where are they?"

He pointed to the west, "They are travelling south on the main valley road. They are less than two miles away."

Sometimes the Fates give you an opportunity which you must seize or risk losing all. King Rhys was clever. He was using the night to move his men, just as I was. Although we would be outnumbered, if we could strike at this column then we would deny the king his reinforcements and still be in a position to attack and support King Henry.

"Rhodri, if we rode to this column how far from Llandybie are they?"

"Less than three miles."

I turned, "Count Striguil, Sir Raymond, we will attack this column. Aelric, take the archers and go with Rhodri. Get ahead of this column and ambush them. When they engage you, fall back to the woods. We will attack them in the rear. When I sound the fall back then head for the woods to the east of the road."

All three shouted their affirmation.

I would be leading eighty mounted and mailed men against three hundred. I hoped that my archers would draw their horses so that we could plough through the men on foot and then fall upon their horsemen when they were disordered. Most men would not risk a night battle. I had rarely fought one but this time I had weighed up all of the factors. They would be on a road. We would know where they were. We knew where they were heading. My archers would be able to attack their front at the same time as we attacked the rear. There would be little likelihood of us being hit by our own arrows. Most importantly, if things went awry, I could have James sound the fall back and we would have lost nothing. We would have damaged half of the enemy's forces and unnerved their king.

As we rode I said, "James, your most important task is to have the horn ready. You will have the chance for honour and glory when the real battle is joined. I cannot waste this opportunity."

"I know, lord."

The sound of our hooves thundered on the cobbled road. The Welsh would know riders were coming. I hoped they would be confused or at least uncertain. We might be reinforcements. I wanted hesitation.

We were travelling at twice the speed of the column and, as I heard screams shouts, and clamour from the head of the column, we struck the rear. My men had spread out on both sides of the road. Count Striguil was to my left and Sir Raymond to my right. Their knights were eager to claim first blood. The horses and donkeys fled as the men leading them were slain. My spear was unbloodied but I saw dead Welshmen in the ground as we ploughed through the baggage train. The Welsh would now be short of arrows!

A handful of men at arms had turned to face us. I saw their shields but I did not slow down. I pulled back my spear and thrust down. One of the Welsh spears grazed Warrior's flank and slid across my chausse. My spear cracked into the face of the one in the centre. Warrior's hooves trampled a second and James' horse a third. Harry Lightfoot speared the fourth. The scene was repeated along the line. The Welsh foot could have stood if they had prepared defences. If they had been protected by archers then they could have held us off but we hit the rear of their line. They were surprised and they were leaderless.

The eager knights of de Clare and Fitzgerald hurtled ahead of us. I pulled back my spear and skewered a sergeant at arms who was trying to rally men. Then I heard a Welsh horn. Someone at the fore had realised that he was chasing shadows. We would soon have horsemen to contend with.

I yelled, "Ware horsemen! Slow down and prepare to meet horse!"

I knew that my voice would only be heard by those men around me but I could see both of my lieutenants and saw them nod their acknowledgement and shout orders to their men. I reined in Warrior. There was little point in lathering him. Most of the Welsh foot had left the road and either fled across the fields to the west or taken shelter in the woods to the east. I heard hooves and, as the first grey appeared in the eastern sky, I discerned horsemen riding towards us. They were in for a shock. The shadows they had been chasing, my archers would be remounting and moving to attack them in the rear.

Neither line was solid and neither line was boot to boot. When we clashed it was not the almighty crack of thunder it usually was, it was a series of small encounters. A knight and his squire came directly for me. Arne Arneson, aware that James was my signaller, nudged his horse next to me. I couched my spear and rode at the knight knowing that the squire was as good as dead. Arne Arneson was a frighteningly powerful warrior. The Welsh spear clattered off my shield as the knight leaned forward to lunge at me. Using my cantle for support I drove the spear towards his shield. He was unbalanced and my spear drove under his shield and into his side. He was thrown from his horse. Even as I withdrew my spear a man at arms with a sword came at my spear side. The spear was unwieldy. I just swung it in an arc as I wheeled Warrior. My spear caught the man at arms a glancing blow to the head and, while he was distracted, James rammed the standard at his middle. He too was thrown from his horse and trampled by James'.

I shouted, "James, sound fall back! Head for the woods."

We had done all that I intended. We had damaged their morale, dispersed their baggage train and slain great numbers. We could afford to lose no more men. The sun was beginning to break in the east and I reined in once I was safely in the woods. I turned to face any Welsh who might have followed us. I was relieved to see all of my men at arms ride in. Count Striguil followed.

"I lost a couple of men at arms and Sir James has a wounded horse. He is heading back to the camp to remount."

Sir Raymond's men had suffered more than any. He shook his head, "Sir Jocelyn was too reckless. He was pulled from his horse and butchered along with his squire and three men at arms who went to their aid. We slew the Welsh but we were too late to save them."

"It could have been worse and it was as I said, Sir Raymond, you need to train your men to think and act as one!"

Aelric joined us. He was in ebullient mood. "We discovered six sumpters. They were loaded with arrows!"

I smiled, "Then God has been kind to us. We chased them when we attacked the column. The Welsh will not have them and we shall. Did you lose any men?"

He gave me an offended look, "Lord! We were fighting Welsh horsemen. They could not catch my grandmother and she has been dead these twenty years!"

"Back to the road. We advance on King Rhys. I think his men from Castle Dinefwr should have reached him by now."

Sir Raymond said, "You wanted him reinforced?"

"I want all of them in one place so that when we defeat them none escape. That was the problem the last time. He has his two finest castles and they are empty of men. The King will have to sue for peace if we defeat him." He nodded his understanding. "Aelric, you and your archers act as our vanguard. If there is trouble ahead sound your horn."

As Aelric and his men rode away, James said, "Can I put my horn away now, lord?"

"Aye, we can use the standard to signal."

Sir James returned. Despite having lost a horse he looked pleased with himself. "I came upon three Welshmen on my way back here. Two are dead!"

"Did you see any others?"

"There was just twenty or thirty of the fyrd. They were in the distance and they were heading away from the road. I saw some heading up to Bannau Brycheiniog."

I waved my spear and we moved forward. The road descended as we went. Soon I saw the smoke from the hearths of Llandybie. We passed a Welshman. He was lying on the side of the road. He had succumbed to his wounds. His companions had not helped him. That told me much about the morale of the army we fought. My men would have brought our wounded with us. They would not have left a man to die alone.

Aelric sent Rafe back. "We have found the Welsh, lord. They are fortifying Llandybie."

"Is there any sign of King Henry?"

"He and the army are forming up on the south side of the settlement."

"Good." We had the Welsh surrounded. The river which had been the Welsh king's defence would not trap him.

We stopped five hundred paces from the defences. I had great respect for the Welsh archers. We would move closer but only when the men at arms and archers had thinned out their ranks. A rider appeared from the east. Aelric's archers had him covered with their bows as he galloped up. He held up a hand, "Earl Marshal, I am sent from King Henry. He is going to begin his attack."

I nodded, "Tell him we have routed more than a third of his men and we will attack too."

He turned his horse and retraced his steps. Like us, he kept well away from the Welsh archers.

"Aelric, dismount and have your horses taken away. Roger of Bath, dismount the men at arms. You will advance behind your shields and protect the archers."

"Aye lord." I smiled as I saw that half a dozen of them had picked up discarded shields. They had anticipated my orders and now had a second shield.

I saw Sir Raymond frowning as he tried to work out the reason. When he finally did so, he smiled. "And what of us, Earl Marshal?"

"Let us dismount. The archers will do their work first." We dismounted. And I handed my reins to James. "We soften them up. We form a long line behind the archers and men at arms. I hope to make them think that there are more of us than there are. They may risk charging us. If they do then they will learn that our paucity of numbers does not mean that we are weak!"

Aelric nodded to Roger when they were ready. The secret would be a slow and steady march. The archers pressed themselves into the backs of the men at arms. They were no fools and knew the skill of the men they faced. The Welsh waited until my men at arms were three hundred paces away before they sent arrows towards them. They did not send them in large numbers. They were testing the range and the efficacy of the shields. One or two arrows reached the shields. I heard Aelric shout something and forty paces later the men at arms stopped. It was a confident move by Aelric. He was gambling that his men were better archers than the Welsh. Many men would dispute that but Aelric's archers had one advantage over the Welsh. They were, generally, a hand span taller. That meant they could use a longer bow. Both sets of archers would have the same rate of arrows but Aelric would have the longer range.

I heard arrows crack into the wood of the shields. I even heard a couple ping off helmets and mail. Unlike the Welsh, all of our men were mailed. They had quantity but we had quality. Aelric shouted, "Draw!" It was a perfect line of men and bows. When he shouted, "Release!" the thirty-eight arrows soared. Even while the flight of arrows was in the air, a second and then a third flight sailed into the enemy ranks. Aelric had been correct. Every arrow reached the Welsh lines.

I heard a trumpet as King Henry launched his attack. He was sending in his horsemen. He was still too impetuous. Having destroyed the reinforcements King Rhys was not going to get any help. We had plenty of arrows and he had a diminishing supply. After ten flights of arrows, Aelric rested his men.

"Mount, let us see if we can worry them." As I mounted I was able to see the fighting at the far end of the settlement. Banners of both sides vied with each other. It was hard to see who was winning. However, King Henry, by closing with the Welsh had negated the effect of their arrows.

Pulling my shield up I nudged my horse closer to my archers and men at arms. Arrows were sent towards me. Warrior's caparison was made of heavy material. He would be unlucky to be hurt by an arrow intended for me. The Warlord was still a prime target. I held my shield high. They had to use a plunging trajectory. Had they been able to use a flat one then I would have been in trouble.

Aelric looked around, "Lord?"

"Ten more flights of arrows and then I want your archers to go to the flanks. Roger, make a wedge and you attack their eastern defences. I will lead the knights and squires to attack the western defences. Aelric your archers can pick off their leaders."

They both nodded. I deftly slipped my shield around my back as I galloped away. When I reached our lines, I swung my shield around again and saw that there were eight arrows stuck in it. That was at least eight arrows less to send at us when we attacked.

"I want two lines. The squires behind the knights. We are going to attack the western side of their defences."

I held my shield tightly and rested my spear across my saddle. "Forward!"

We did not need to ride boot to boot. We were not charging knights. We were charging men who had improvised defences. Aelric and his archers kept the attention of the defenders on the arrows. As soon as Aelric stopped then we would be the target. By then I hoped to be within charging distance. This was not like charging a solid wall. The men would see our huge horses coming towards them and it took a brave man to stand up to one. As the last arrows sailed over to the Welsh defences, Roger and his men began to move. At the same time, the Welsh saw us and they had a dilemma; which force was the most dangerous? In the heartbeat it took for someone to make the decision, we were a little closer.

Roger of Bath's wedge was impregnable. The Romans, the Saxons, even the Vikings had used just such a formation and when the men in it were fully armoured then it was hard to break. The Welsh arrows flew. I saw one of Count Striguil's knights struck in the upper shoulder with an arrow and one of Sir Raymond's knights had his horse hit too but the line was unbroken. Men were shouting. I was not a shouter but I knew others, like Wulfric, who were. They seemed to fight better if they were cursing their enemies.

I lifted my spear. There was no point in having a couched one. I would thrust over their defences. As I closed I saw that they had just used barrels and blocks of wood to make a barrier. They had not embedded stakes in the ground. I suspected they had to the south but they were not expecting an attack from the north. I rammed my spear into the shoulder and neck of a man at arms. He had mail but my spear was sharp. I saw a mounted knight fall backwards as one of Aelric's men's arrows pitched him from his saddle. I pulled out my spear and then urged Warrior on. He clambered, somewhat ungainly, over the barrel which barred our way. I thrust the spear into the chest of the archer who had his bow fully drawn. As he fell he knocked away the chest which also barred my route. I was in the clear.

"James! On! Follow me!" I spurred Warrior. His front hooves came up as he leapt. They smashed into the skull of an archer. There was a sickening crunch as his rear hooves smashed the man's chest when we landed. Before me, Welsh warriors were fleeing and I could see the rear of their line which was busily fighting against King Henry and his men. I thrust again with my spear and it hit a man at arms in the shoulder. He was a tough man and, using two hands, he wrenched the spear from my hand. I drew my sword and hacked across his throat as I passed him. I saw that James had drawn alongside me and he was using his sword to hack at any Welshman he passed.

I saw ahead King Rhys and his household knights. They spied my banner and he charged at me. I know not if he sought to fight me or he had seen an opportunity to escape. It mattered not. "Count Striguil! To me!"

James and I could not take on King Rhys and his six knights alone. I heard the Count's voice, "Striguil! To me!"

I reined in Warrior. He was tiring and had been wounded early on. He was a brave horse and I would not waste his life needlessly. One of King Rhys' knights came directly towards me. He had no spear but he swung a war axe. He came at my right-hand side. I watched as he stood in the saddle to reach forward and take my head. I jerked Warrior to the right. We were not moving quickly and he slid silkily to the right. The knight hit the air and I lunged with my sword. It was not a clean strike but his speed made the blade tear through his mail and into his stomach. I barely had time to move Warrior to my left as King Rhys himself launched his horse at me. I guessed there was hatred in his move. I had thwarted him twice. His sword swung at the place I had been.

I continued my turn. His horse slid by. I saw James bravely take on a much more experienced knight and Harry Lightfoot galloped to help my squire. I knew that I could end the battle with one blow and I concentrated on the king. I swung my sword, more in hope than expectation at the King's back as his horse galloped by. I connected with his mail. As I would have expected the King had good mail but I knew that I had broken some of the links. Another of his knights galloped at me and swung his sword at me. I barely managed to block the blow with my shield and the end of the sword rang against my helmet. Alf had made a good helmet and I barely felt it. I lunged with my sword and felt its tip pierce the mail and touch something soft. He wheeled away.

King Rhys ap Gruffyd was desperate to end my life. He could have ridden away but he had stopped and wheeled his horse to face me. More knights had joined the mêlée. It was a confusing picture. My men at arms, led by Roger of Bath were trying to protect my back. I forced myself to be calm. I was older than the King. He had more strength than I had. I needed to use my head. I used my knees to switch Warrior. The move threw off the aim of the King who hacked down towards my head. The blow caught my shield and slid down it. I swung a wide sweeping blow. His sword was pointing to the ground as my sword hit his back again. This time it was higher than the first blow but I saw that it had hurt him. His back arced.

I whipped Warrior's head around and stood in my stirrups as I pulled back on the reins. He reared and brought his mighty hooves down on the shoulder of the King's horse. Warrior was powerful and the King's horse struggled to keep upright. He failed and I saw the King pitched from his horse. I knew I had to act quickly. When Warrior landed I slipped from the saddle and had my sword point at the King's throat before he could move.

"Your majesty, yield. You are too young to die but if I must end your life I will." The tip touched bare flesh.

Time seemed to have stood still. A knight slid from his horse to the ground. He had a second mouth. His throat had been opened by a mighty blow by John son of John. Another fell from his horse with his leg hanging by tendons. The King himself was still winded. His last household knights moved towards me. If he did not yield I would have to kill him. Even then I might die. I was surrounded.

He nodded and gasped, "I yield, I yield! Warlord, you are the devil incarnate. May you rot in hell."

I raised my sword, "The King has yielded! Lay down your weapons!" I dropped my shield and held out my left hand. I said, quietly, "That may well be my fate, your majesty but I have done my duty for my king."

My men began to cheer. We had won. I was not surprised. The King was young. He had shown great skill and his plan had been a good one but he had been outwitted. King Henry galloped up to us. He was grinning. I saw that his sword and surcoat were bloody. He had not been an idle bystander.

"Earl Marshal, once again I am indebted to you. King Rhys ap Gruffyd you have yielded to my Earl. You are now my prisoner."

He glared at King Henry, "You are a greedy man, Henry Plantagenet. I curse you. One day your sins will come to haunt you."

Henry sheathed his sword. "Perhaps. We will retire to your castle now and decide on reparations."

"Reparations?"

"Aye, it has cost us coin to take back the land you stole."

"It was our land first!"

"As my Earl Marshal told you the last time, and now it is ours. Make war on me or my people and you will suffer the same. You are a minor king of a tiny kingdom. Do you think that you can defeat me?" He turned, "Mortimer, take the King. De Clare, you and Fitzgerald ride to Carreg Cennen Castle. Demand their surrender. We will follow."

I know that this was a test for de Clare. Could he do what the King demanded? I believed he could. I turned, sheathed my sword and looked for my men. If any had been lost then I would blame myself. I saw that James had a new scar on his cheek but he was smiling. He would need a new ventail. That was a small price to pay. John son of John was being tended to by James of Tewkesbury. He had a gashed leg.

We had lost men. I saw their bodies being taken by their comrades. We would bury them when time allowed. I raised my hand, "King Henry!"

Every warrior raised his sword and chanted the King's name. I saw that he was pleased. I knew that he would have lost too many knights but the glory he had gained compensated for that. He had lost in Gwynedd but here he had won. We would have peace in the Marches and he could go to Anjou knowing that his kingdom in the north and the west was secure. My son and I had won that for him.

Part Four- Ireland

Chapter 11

It took six months to prepare for what would, in effect, be an invasion of Ireland. King Henry managed to send many of the young knights who sought his patronage and they joined Count Striguil. I left the organisation to him. I was there to help the King of Leinster to win back his kingdom. I wanted to return to my son in Stockton but I had been promised by the King. He had returned to Anjou. I think he wanted to prove that he could win without me at his side. James thought that the King secretly hoped I would fail. The King was young and wanted the world to see him as a successful general. I spoiled that image. I did not mind. Henry was my son.

We had travelled to Bristol. It had been King Stephen's prison and I remembered it well. As Earl Marshal, I was afforded fine accommodation in the castle. It was the King of Leinster and Richard de Clare who had to worry about finding hay for horses and accommodation for men. They were the ones who had to pay for ships to take us to Ireland.

De Clare had three hundred knights and as many archers and men at arms. We had but one hundred archers in total but I knew that they would be the difference between success and failure. Raymond Le Gros was second in command and he threw himself into the task. The two knights worked well together.

King Diarmait Mac Murchada was a different proposition. I did not like him. He was older than me and he seemed like a fussy old man who was just concerned with his position. His daughter I liked and she and Richard were well suited. They were married before we left Bristol. I think the King was keen to tie Count Striguil to his family. It seemed to me that he had lost his kingdom because he was not a very good king. I spent most of the time ensuring that my men were well equipped. The reparations from King Rhys had brought me a fortune. I sent half of the treasure home to William along with half a dozen men at arms. The rest I used to buy another ship just for my men and to buy the horses, armour, swords and tents. De Clare was trying to win a kingdom. I was looking after my men. The ship would be useful and I could use the *'Maid of Portishead'* back on the Tees.

We set sail for Ireland. King Diarmait Mac Murchada had chosen the landing site. That decision I allowed him to make. The rest would be mine! Having my own ship was a luxury. It felt like an indulgence but I now had the freedom to sail back to Stockton. Carlisle was a short journey away and I could be in the Tees Valley in a day with a change of horses. It gave me reassurance and I was happier about this campaign.

The Irish we would be fighting had no knights. They had no archers and they did not wear mail. At the time we landed, there were no stone castles in the whole of the land. They had wooden palisades and earth bothies. I intended to use the mobility of our horsemen and the skill of our archers to make a lightning quick campaign which would retake Leinster before the High King even knew we were in Ireland.

We landed south of Wexford. It had been full of Vikings a hundred years ago. It still remained a largely Viking town without much Irish influence. The two ports we might have used, Wexford and Waterford were both in Viking hands yet. We had to land by using cranes to lower the horses into the water. It took some time. Had there been opposition we would have struggled but none came near and after three days all were landed and the ships moored offshore and awaited our capture of a port.

When we landed, King Diarmait Mac Murchada sent a summons for his people to join him. As soon as he did so it alerted the High King to our presence. I knew we needed Irishmen to fight for the king. If it was just Normans then we would be seen as invaders. The Irishmen who would join us would not help us to retake his kingdom. That would be done by knights on horses but it would make an army which might intimidate our enemy. I made certain that the site for our camp was defensible. The sea protected two sides while a lake protected a third. We just had a narrow neck of land to defend.

We were forced to use Irish scouts. I was unhappy about that. I did not know them but we had little choice. Aelric and his archers did not know the land well enough to perform that function. King Diarmait Mac

Murchada had recognised my importance and had assigned me a translator so that I could speak with the scouts. The King, himself, spoke our language well. The translator was a slave called Padraig. I liked him as soon as I met him. He was thirteen summers old. He had been taken as a slave when he was but four summers old. He was of Norse origin. Given the name of the Irish saint he had shown great skill with languages and it had been his salvation. He not only interpreted, he told me of the people who spoke the words. That too was important.

We waited by the sea for the men of Leinster to flock to his banner. It was not so much of a flock as a trickle. I saw the disappointment on Count Striguil's face. This was not proving to be a glorious homecoming. The King had just two hundred men by the end of the week. Eight had helmets and wore metal torcs and carried wickedly long swords. They were chiefs. The rest were half-naked with small shields and either short swords or fire-hardened spears.

The High King forced our hand. A week after our arrival Aelric had led my archers north towards Wexford to hunt. He and his men came back so quickly that I knew something was amiss. De Clare was in command but old habits die hard and Aelric reported to me. "Lord, there is a large host of men heading here from the north-west."

"Horses?"

He shook his head. "Their leaders have horses but the men they lead do not." He shook his head, "I saw little armour lord. They are half-naked."

Turning to Count Striguil I said, "There is little point in moving far from here."

He nodded and pointed to the north. "We can line up there. The knights on one flank and the mounted men at arms on the other. The men at arms on foot and the archers can be between. King Diarmait Mac Murchada can wait there with his men too.

I smiled, "You have been watching me."

He returned my smile, "Aye lord."

We moved quickly for the banners of the horde which were approaching could now be clearly seen. It looked like a sea of men. Without any discernible order, numbers were difficult to estimate but they would outnumber us many times over. As I mounted Storm Bringer I noticed that Aelric was using the stakes at the edge of our camp for defence. With the men at arms in three ranks before him, he and the archers would be safe from the enemy.

Irish War

I saw Padraig standing by my horse. I pointed to the camp, "I will not need you until after the battle. Go back to the camp and stay with lame Tom and the others."

"Yes lord. I am not afraid to fight alongside you."

I leaned down, "You are like the people we fight today. You have never seen us fight. After the battle tell me again if you would fight with us." He nodded and headed back to the camp.

I spurred my horse to join the other knights. I saw King Diarmait Mac Murchada exhorting his two hundred men to fight well. Simon of Striguil who led the dismounted men at arms had wisely ignored the king and placed his men some ten paces behind them. If the Irish did not stand they would have to flee to the sea or the lake. They had a wall of spears and shields behind them.

The High King, Ruaidrí Ua Conchobair, was leading his army. I knew him just by the number of horses he had around him. There were eight horses. That was more than half the total number we could see. The horde was a mile away and they were moving rapidly. Padraig had told me that was how they liked to fight. They closed rapidly with an enemy. Battles were over quickly for they fought savagely until their enemies fled.

Count Striguil said, "I do not think we will stand here and let them attack us."

Raymond Le Gros nodded, "Let us charge them."

They both looked at me for confirmation of the plan. "We need the Irish to hold where they are. James, ride to Roger of Bath. Tell him that the mounted men at arms will charge when we do. Count Striguil, you had better give your instructions to the King."

By the time both James and de Clare had returned the Irish were less than half a mile away. I had never seen such a primitive army. Even the Scots had more armour. They did, however, have numbers. I estimated it to be at least three thousand men we faced.

Count Striguil looked at me and I nodded. He lifted his lance and said, "Forward!"

We began to move towards the Irish. We were trotting rather than galloping. Had they met mounted men before they would have halted and prepared a hedgehog of spears but, as Padraig had told me, they had never seen knights before. They continued to charge towards us. They had such numbers that they were able to charge on three fronts. I think they thought to overwhelm us by sheer weight of numbers. It might have worked with barbarians. We were not barbarians. I rested my spear on my horse. I did not use a lance as the others did. I had fought too long with a spear and I found it easier to use a spear rather than the longer lance. Behind me, James carried a spare spear for me.

   Some of the younger, wilder warriors had outstripped their peers and they reached our line first. Already our horses were stretching their legs a little more but we still had a continuous line. I saw Sir Raymond spear one who had a surprised look as the lance emerged from his back. His body dragged the weapon from Sir Raymond's grasp and he had to draw his sword. I pulled back my arm and punched my spear towards the half-naked warrior who swung his sword wildly above his head as he tried to get at me. The punch meant that the spear tore into his stomach. I twisted and allowed his body to fall from my spear. As soon as I raised it I found another victim. Their headlong charge had spread them out. Soon we would be amongst thicker ranks but, for the present, we had the luxury of time. We could choose where to strike.

   The next Irishman tried to fend off the spear. He merely directed it towards his shoulder but there it caught on a bone and was torn from my grasp. As we were approaching larger numbers I did not have time to take the spear which James carried. I drew my sword. The first three men I next slew were isolated and the edge of my blade tore into their skulls as I hacked left and right around my horse's head. Then we were slowed by the mass of men before us. Storm Bringer was a mighty horse and he powered his way into their ranks. His snapping jaws and huge hooves intimidated those before him. As I continued to wield my sword in wide sweeps I felt the blows on my shield and my chausses. The swords they had were not made of the best metal. After the battle, we found many which had bent. They did not keep their edge and, although the blows on my legs were painful, they did little damage.

   There were almost three hundred of us in that charge and we had cut a swathe through the heart of them. They were all brave and reckless but the bravest had been killed first. Some of the ones we now saw merely had wooden clubs or spears which had a sharpened, fire-hardened tip. Count Striguil was leading us towards the High King himself. If we could capture him then King Diarmait Mac Murchada would have his kingdom back in one fell swoop. It was not to be. He turned and, along with his chiefs and kings, he galloped from the field. Those around him fled with him.

There was a wail and the whole of the Irish army turned to join the flight. We were still outnumbered but they had fled. We pursued them until our horses were weary. It was not only our horses. My blade had been blunted by bone and my arm ached from the repetitive action of slicing, chopping and hacking. Count Striguil's horn sounded the recall and the pursuit ended. We stopped just half a mile from Wexford. The Irish had not gone there. They had fled north and west. I reined in Storm Bringer and Count Striguil led his weary horse towards me.

"I cannot believe it was so easy."

I pointed my bloody sword at the town. "We should take that tomorrow, Count Striguil. There is no wall. We could take it now but our men are spread across the battlefield. Better we rest and take it fresh."

"Aye, I will let King Diarmait Mac Murchada have that honour."

"You are becoming quite the thinker, Count Striguil."

"I am thinking that we could take this whole island. Why do I need to be an earl when I could be a king?"

"Do not get ahead of yourself, Count Striguil. I agree that this land is ripe for the plucking but King Henry will not be happy if you rival him."

"And you are his Earl Marshal, lord, I know that. I am just speculating. There is no harm in thoughts are there?"

As we rode back I wondered at his ambitions. He reminded me of other lords who had had some success and it had gone to their heads. I would have to watch him. Had we ridden straight away to Wexford then we might have taken it without a battle. We delayed. That was my fault but King Diarmait Mac Murchada had not been entirely open with us. He had not told us of the men who would defend Waterford, Wexford and Dublin. Our dead had been collected. Horses had been slain. I saw two knights angrily beating the dead body of an Irishman who had slain one of their horses. It was futile but I understood the value of their horses. A warhorse could cost forty marks. The knights would have no treasure from this battlefield.

When we reached our camp, James took Storm Bringer for feed and to groom him. He had suffered no wounds. I would ride Warrior the next day. Padraig and Lame Tom appeared with water to wash and a beaker of ale. Tom was an old soldier. He pointed to the dead, "That was not war, lord, that was slaughter. They are brave but by St Michael, I have never seen such foolish men to attack with so little armour."

Padraig said, "What I do not understand is why they did not use the warriors of Wexford and Waterford."

"Are they different?"

He nodded, "Yes, lord. They are Vikings! They also live in Dyflin. They call Waterford, Veðrafjǫrðr. It is their town. They still raid from there."

"And they are in Wexford too?"

"Aye lord, even more of them. They call it Veisafjǫrðr. They wear mail too and have good weapons." He picked up one of the discarded Irish weapons which lay in the camp, having been collected by the servants. He showed me that it was bent.

"Thank you, Padraig." I did not like the fact that he was a slave. "So tell me, Padraig, what do you say to fighting with us now that you have seen us?"

He shook his head, "I am Norse, lord and I know war but I have never seen beast and man combine as I did today. It was as though you were one beast."

He was an intelligent boy. I saw that there was more to him than just being an interpreter. "Who owns you, Padraig?"

"The Bishop of Ferns."

I now saw why the Pope had issued his papal bull. If the church-owned slaves then it explained why he wanted the churches cleaning of corruption. "Come with me and we will speak with the King and the Earl." I waved over de Clare who, like me, had washed the blood from his mail and drunk some beer.

"My lord we had best see the King."

"Why?"

"He has been less than honest with us. We have an enemy who will give us a much harder battle than that which we fought this day." I took Padraig not as a translator, King Diarmait Mac Murchada could speak our language well, but to ask for his freedom. The King could be heard long before we reached him. Bodyguards were using sticks to play a game with the skull of one of the enemies who had been killed in battle.

He roared when he saw us approach, "By the heavens above you and your beasties are a terrifying sight! The very ground trembled when they passed over it."

I nodded, "King Diarmait Mac Murchada I understand that there will be greater tests for us in Wexford and Waterford."

He frowned and glared at Padraig who quailed. The battered skull had ended up by the King's feet and it had upset the youth. Perhaps he saw his skull being used in the same way.

"You mean the Vikings?"

"You know of them?"

"Of course, I do. That is why we did not attack either Wexford or Waterford. They do not bother us. They raid Munster, Wales, and Connaught. They did not join with the High King, did they? Leave well alone I say."

I shook my head. "We need a port. We have to take one or both of them."

He laughed, "Good luck then. We have made a fine start to retaking my kingdom. When that is mine I will see about evicting the Vikings."

I looked at de Clare who shrugged. I would speak with him later. "There is another matter. Padraig here, I would have him freed."

"He is not mine. He belongs to the Bishop of Ferns. Take it up with him."

I smiled, "I will." Turning to Padraig I said, "As of this moment you are a free man. Will you stay on as my servant and translate for me? I will pay you a stipend."

"I will lord and gladly."

"You cannot do that!"

I turned to the King, "The Pope says I can and besides you said he belongs to the Bishop. He can always argue his case with me. Come Count Striguil, we need to speak with Sir Raymond."

Padraig said, "Thank you, lord."

"I was not lying, Padraig, the new Pope wishes slavery abolished."

Count Striguil said, "The King of Leinster is not going to be happy about the way you spoke to him."

"Remember Richard, I represent King Henry. Would he have done it any different?"

"No. What do we do about Wexford and Waterford?"

"We take one of them. We may have to take both. We need a port and we cannot have a large band of armed men loose in the land."

Sir Raymond was keen to take on the Vikings. "There will be more treasure and plunder in the town than we can take on the battlefield. My knights are already complaining about the lack of gold."

I cautioned them both, "These are Vikings. I have fought them before and I have Arne Arneson who is descended from Norse stock. If your men become angry when they lose their horses then do not fight Vikings. They use two handed axes and are quite happy to use them on horses. They are fond of horsemeat."

Irish War

Sir Raymond looked appalled, "Savages! Have they no honour?"

"It is a different honour to ours. However, first, we will speak with them. If they agree to pay homage to the King of Leinster and allow us to use their port we may not have to fight. Padraig, can you speak their language?"

He nodded, "It is why the Bishop kept me, lord. I learn languages easily. My father was Norse and he took one of your people as a slave when he raided the west coast. I spoke with him until he was whipped too hard and died."

"And how were you taken?"

"We lived on Man. There are still Norse there. The Irish raided us for slaves. My father was slain."

"The rest of your family?"

He shrugged, "We were separated at the slave market. I know not. I have almost forgotten what my mother and two sisters looked like."

This was a sad story. And there had been a Norman child who had been enslaved and whipped to death. I thought about Samuel. Aiden had been a slave but we had soon freed him. I could not remember the last slave we had had. I liked to think that the serfs who worked our land were treated better than others. Certainly, they all seemed happy enough. I felt better about what we were doing. It seemed to me that we were bringing civilisation to the Irish. Perhaps we were doing it harshly but they would be better off for our protection.

The next morning, I assembled all the knights and we rode to Wexford. There was a wooden palisade which ran around the walls and a ditch. It would not stop us if we chose to attack. Their houses were unlike ours and were more like an upturned ship. They lived in larger groups than we did. We were seen from a distance and a large number of armoured warriors greeted us. I counted at least eighty and, unlike the Irish we had fought, all had a helmet, a shield and a substantial-looking weapon. Many had a hauberk. They called them byrnies.

"Hold! What business do you have in Veisafjǫrðr?"

I noticed that he spoke our language. It sounded a little awkward but he knew who we were. Padraig's services might not be needed. "I am the Earl Marshal of England. We are come to reclaim the throne of Leinster."

He grinned and said something to the men behind. They laughed. Turning back to me he said, "I am Jarl Sigtrygg Haakenson. I rule here. This is not Leinster! This is Veisafjǫrðr. The Irish learned long ago not to annoy. I will be generous and not kill you at first sight. Begone horseman and do not bother us."

"I am speaking pleasantly to you, Viking, but do not think to abuse us. We wish to use your town and your port."

He laughed, "Hell will freeze over first."

"Think carefully before you answer me again. We have three times your number here and more than that in our camp. Reconsider your words!"

In answer, he turned around and bared his backside at me. His men began laughing and banging their shields. I heard Sir Raymond draw his sword, "Sheathe it. They are words only and the actions of a child. We will return to our camp." As we turned I said, "What did the jarl say to his men?"

"He said if the High King couldn't enforce his rule then…" he hesitated.

"What is it?"

"He used a word that I cannot translate for I do not know the meaning. He used the word that means a man who lies with horses."

I laughed, "The Viking knows how to insult. We will return in the morning and end their rule here."

James said, "Lord, I see one of their dragon ships. It is heading down the coast."

I looked at Padraig for enlightenment. "I think they may be going for more men. Vikings are independent, lord, but they are all tied by blood. You will have to fight more than those we saw today."

"I realised that. Those longhouses we saw would house more men than came to taunt us."

When we reached the camp, we discovered that King Diarmait Mac Murchada and his men had departed. Aelric said, "The King said as he had his kingdom back he would return to his capital, Ferns." He looked at Count Striguil, "Your wife is with him, lord."

De Clare smiled, "Then she will be safe at the very least."

As we dismounted I said, "I think the lack of men flocking to his banner has made him realise that he is only going to win by letting us fight."

Sir Raymond was not happy, "You mean we do the fighting and the dying and he gets the rewards?"

De Clare was older and wiser, "The trick, Raymond, is to do the fighting and not die. Then we can be rewarded when we win. Tomorrow will be a sterner test for us."

Chapter 12

Sir Raymond was all for a charge of heavy horse to break the Vikings. I waved over Arne Arneson. "Arne, tell his lordship how the Vikings will fight us tomorrow."

He nodded, "They will make a shield wall which is three men deep. The shields will be before and above them. There will be no gaps. Our arrows will not penetrate it. They will have spears sticking out. Before them, they may have stakes and they will wait for us. They are patient. They will stand. When we close their spears will seek weaknesses. After we are exhausted they will push forward and become an armoured killing beast. They will thrust and stab. They will use their shields as a weapon. They use their helmets, heads, hands and teeth as weapons. If you take a Viking's sword he will use anything to kill you. If you think you have killed a Viking then kill him a second time, just to make certain."

Sir Raymond said, "Their only tactic is to wait for us to hit them? They will not move?"

Arne laughed, "They can move my lord but they will choose not to. They know you cannot break their shield wall and they know that our horses will not be able to jump over them."

Poor Sir Raymond looked deflated, "Then how do we beat them?"

I waved Arne away. He would go back to the men at arms and tell them of the look on Sir Raymond's face. "We have superior numbers and we use them. We probe for weaknesses. This will not be a quick battle. We will fight on foot. I want relays of knights and men at arms to attack the shield wall. We will be able to rest between fighting. They will not. Their shields are twice as heavy as ours. They may be strong men but holding a shield above your head tires a man. When their spears are broken and blunted they will use swords and axes. They will be equally deadly. We can replenish our spears and sharpen our swords. They cannot."

"That takes time."

"My father was a housecarl who fought for Harold Godwinson. He was not at Hastings but I know others who were. Duke William charged the Saxon lines many times. It took hours for them to tire the housecarls. When they did then they used their archers. We conserve our archers until they are tired."

"That does not sound glorious."

I laughed, "If you expect the war to be glorious then you are in for a disappointment."

My personal disappointment was that the Vikings had been reinforced. As we returned the next day we saw the masts of three dragon ships. I had forgotten that the Vikings did not need to use horses to move for they had the fastest ships in the world. There were three more crews to fight and that could mean almost a hundred and fifty warriors. As we approached the Viking warriors marched from the town and arrayed themselves before it. There were more than three shiploads of them. Behind them, I saw archers too. I knew, from Arne, that although a Viking bow was not as good as a Norman war bow their archery was good. I reined in half a mile from them. They were singing and banging their shields. I turned to Padraig, "What are they singing?"

"It is an old song of a warrior whom the old gods honoured by touching his sword with lightning and making it magical." I raised an eyebrow. "I have heard the song before. When I lived with my father he did not sing it but he told me the story. It was said to have happened not far from my home."

"Do you believe it?" Count Striguil sounded incredulous.

I looked at de Clare, "What matters, Richard, is that they believe it. The fact that they are supposed to be Christian and yet they sing of an old god should tell you how much they believe it." I turned and saw the men at arms dismounting. "We will have to change our plans. Aelric!"

He galloped up, "Aye lord?"

"They have archers. Can you outrange them?"

"Of course."

"Then either destroy them or make them take shelter in the town."

He nodded and rode off to collect his men. I watched him speak to Roger of Bath and six men at arms rode with them. Sir Raymond said, "Why only six men at arms?"

"They need horse holders, lord." James' voice answered the question for me. Sir Raymond was getting a lesson on tactics from a squire.

"We cannot fight along the whole line. It is too long. We will attack at the two ends where they are the weakest. I will attack the left flank and Count Striguil the right. When I withdraw, Sir Raymond will take over my attack and then we will relieve Count Striguil. That way we always have one-third resting and sharpening weapons. Their best warriors will be in the centre. We will make them wait. Come we will get a little closer." We rode towards the archers.

I saw that Aelric's archers had dismounted and he had one of his archers send an arrow towards the rear of the Viking line. He would be using his weakest archer and testing the range. When he was satisfied I heard him shout, "Draw!" We stopped just a hundred paces from them. "Release!" The Vikings had heard the command and they sent their own arrows at the same time. Three of their arrows found flesh. More than half of Aelric's struck Vikings. The three wounded were able to move back to the horses. I waved the priest forward to see to their wounds.

I dismounted, "Have our horses taken to the servants and the reserve men at arms."

The second Viking flight only resulted in one arrow hitting one of our archers in the foot. It would not stop him releasing! Five flights later and the Viking archers withdrew. We had won that battle by superior numbers, weapons and the skills of my archers. Aelric and his men remounted and moved back to allow us to make our attack. The shield wall began singing their song again and banging their shields. More men came from the town. I saw that some were the archers who had fallen back. These had no mail but they all had a shield and they formed another two lines. They would be a reserve to fill in the gaps made by the fallen and to help push when we attacked. If we had had an onager it would have been a wonderful target but we had none. We would have to do it the hard way.

I took my spear and raised it. "First wall, with me!" I had the unattached knights with me. They were eager to fight alongside the Earl Marshal. Some hoped that I would bring their heroism to the notice of the King. They wanted advancement. We marched obliquely across their front, as Sir Raymond's men were waiting in the middle. The Vikings would expect us all to attack at once. The waiting would unnerve them. When we were forty paces from them I raised my spear again and we formed a block of metal which was fifteen men wide and five men deep. I had knights in the front rank and my men at arms in the second. I began banging my shield with my spear. It was not for bravado. It was to get a rhythm for marching. When every man was banging I shouted, "Spear leg!" We began marching. After three paces, I stopped banging and lowered my spear.

The place I had chosen to attack was the right-hand side of the Viking line. Those in the second rank and third ranks had had to use their shields to protect the right side of the shield wall. They had to hold their spear in their left hand. Few men could use a spear as effectively with their weaker hand. I pulled back my spear. Roger of Bath and John son of John allowed my spear to slide back between them. I saw the Viking I would be fighting. He had a red beard and he had painted his face red to match. He had an open helmet with a nasal. My head was enclosed. He was shouting something at me but as I could not speak his language the words were wasted. I had my shield held tightly to my side. His spear came not for my shield but for my helmet. He was trying to hit me through one of the eye holes. He had never seen a helmet like mine before. His spear slid off the side. The warrior in the second rank rammed his spear at my head too and it had the same effect.

I punched with my spear upwards. My helmet protected me but it restricted my view. I was guessing where to strike. I hit something soft and someone grunted. I did not know if it was the man I was facing or the one behind. I twisted the head and pulled before ramming it again. Roger of Bath slid his spear over my shoulder and it struck a shield. I pulled back and punched again.

"Everyone, push!" We had five men behind me. We were facing three men in the shield wall and the rear two ranks had no mail. I felt the weight of my warriors behind me and I was face to face with my foe. Neither of us could move our arms. My spear was still stuck in one of them. I could move my head and so I pulled it back and head-butted the Viking. My helmet was well made and heavy. There was a metal strip, like a cross down the middle. That hit him and I heard his nose break. Blood, bone and cartilage covered his face and I saw his eyes watering. He would not be able to see very well. More importantly, he began to slip. Whoever I had wounded had been bleeding and the man was slipping on his blood.

Spears began to punch at our shields and helmets from the Viking second and third ranks. I was able to pull back my spear. This time, when I punched forward, I struck something hard. It was metal. I continued to push and twist at the same time. I guessed I had hit a byrnic and my spear was caught in the mail links. I kept pushing and twisting until the pressure stopped and it hit something soft. A spear found a gap and hit my shield. It slid off my shield and into Sir Simon next to me. He grunted.

I shouted, "James, sound fall back. It is time for a change!"

The horn sounded and a voice from the rear, Arne Arneson, shouted, "Shield leg, back!"

I trusted the judgement of my men and stepped back. The Vikings thought us defeated and cheered. A Viking voice shouted something. I guessed it was to stand. The last thing they needed was to chase after us. That had been the undoing of Harold Godwinson. As we stepped back I saw that we had moved their right wing back six paces. There were two knights lying on the ground. I could not see if we had had success other than a bloody patch of grass. Even if wounded they would stand and try to fight. That was the Viking way. Any dead or badly wounded would have been dragged away and replaced by other men. What I did see was that there were not as many spears. Sir Raymond and his men were already marching into position.

I shouted, "Halt!" When we were stopped I pointed to the place Sir Raymond had vacated and we marched there. Our servants had new spears for us. They would be sharper. As I took mine I saw that Count Striguil had also pushed back his wing. When my men had rearmed we watched as Sir Raymond's men marched into the Viking right flank. It had been weakened and I saw the huge Marcher Lord push the Vikings back a pace.

While we watched we switched positions. A new line of knights formed the front rank. We became the third rank. When we took over from Count Striguil the men who fought would be fresher.

I heard de Clare order his men backwards and we began to move towards the Viking left flank. There were dead knights and men at arms but I also saw that the Vikings had suffered losses. Once we were close enough I shouted, "Spear foot!" We began to march towards the Vikings. All of our men had fresh spears. I saw that the Vikings had fewer spears. The men at arms in the second rank were led by Günter of Swabia. His shield covered the heads of the two knights in front of him: Sir William and Sir Stephen. He was as solid and reliable as my old friend Rolf had been. Even if the knights in front of him were novices he was a veteran.

As I was in the middle I had my shield in the middle of Günter's back, I rested my spear on his shoulder. If I held it at the bottom of the haft I could punch with it. It might not have much power but the effect of a spear coming at eye height could be alarming. The young knights were keen and they all swung their spears at the same time. Günter and I thrust our spears forward too. Mine struck metal but Günter's found flesh. It tore into the cheek of a Viking. The man did not move. When the spear was retracted there was a hole large enough to see inside his bloody mouth. The Vikings were tiring. Had this been earlier in the battle then the Viking might have moved his head out of the way.

Suddenly an axe swung overhead towards Sir Stephen. Had it been any other than Günter the blow might have caused damage but Günter's shield held. At the same time, two Vikings in the front rank fell to the ground. As the warrior behind stepped forward John of Norton thrust his spear into him. The Viking's shield had caught on the sword of the warrior next to him.

I shouted, "James! Archers!"

The horn sounded twice. We now had a gap in the Viking flank. Men were filling the gap but, as they did so, they were exposed. Our archers could now do what they could not before. They could find flesh.

It was time for us to send in our reserves. Count Striguil would lead his knights and the remainder of the men at arms. They would be our largest force and they would be attacking the centre of the line. Although they were the best warriors the arrows and our flanking attack might just turn the day in our favour. I saw the arrows begin to fall and heard shouts as they found their way through shields held by weary men. I heard the crash as our reserves struck the Viking line. I watched as two more Vikings fell close to us. There are decisive moments in a battle. We had, with us, twenty warriors who had yet to be engaged. Roger of Bath and a line of knights were behind me.

I shouted, "Roger of Bath, lead your men at arms and the knights. Attack the line to our left."

"Aye, lord! On my command turn left and move. Move!"

The pressure went from behind me. Once again, the axe came over and Günter stopped it but this time he thrust forward with his spear as he did so. The spear went under the arm of the man swinging the axe and into his body. The axe slid to the ground. I saw Günter release his spear and reach down for the axe. He shouted, "Ware behind!" I moved out of the way and Günter swung the axe. It struck a shield already battered by spears and arrows. It split asunder and the man's arm was severed in two.

Sir Stephen saw his chance and he leapt into the gap, ramming his spear into the side of the next warrior. The shield wall was broken. Now

Irish War

it was a mêlée. My men at arms excelled in that form of combat. With our longer, lighter and narrower shields we could outmanoeuvre the Vikings with their large and extremely heavy shields. They had been holding them for hours and now they paid the price.

I hurled my spear at the chest of a warrior without mail. He fell backwards clutching at it. My sword was in my hand and I leapt at the stunned Viking who had just been knocked aside as Günter smashed his axe into the face of the man next to him and bundled him out of the way. I brought my sword down on his helmet. Even if I did not break the helmet I would smash his skull. The battle was now shrunk to within the sweep of my sword. I could not see the rest of the battle. I was aware that James was behind me and I was following an almost berserk Günter. He was swinging the axe with deadly accuracy. The Vikings were tired and their shields were dropping.

I knew that the Vikings would fight to the end. The young knights would expect them to surrender. They would expect ransom. That was not going to happen with Vikings. "No mercy! Kill them all!" It was harsh but I was thinking of my young knights. The men they were fighting were the toughest warriors they would ever face. Athelstan had told that the only way you could be sure you had defeated a Viking was to take his head.

I saw a Viking lurch towards Günter's right side. Günter was busy with a Viking who was also armed with an axe. I hurled my shield, with my body behind it at the man and he fell to the ground. I barely kept my feet. He lay below me and I skewered his neck. The mailed Vikings were still fighting. They were still dying but the ones at the rear, the ones who had no armour, now ran. My father had told me the same had happened at Hastings. The housecarls had stood and the rest had fled. As we butchered and slaughtered the Viking warband, the others ran.

It was not quick. The Vikings died hard. The men at arms were more methodical and logical than the knights. The knights fought furiously and tried to end it quickly. The men at arms, knowing that we had superiority of numbers, were looking for weakness in tired men. I found myself with no enemies to the fore. I looked to my left and saw isolated bands of Vikings being cut down.

"James, bring our men. Let us destroy their ships else they will flee and we will have to fight them again."

"Aye lord, to me! To me!" I looked down and saw that many of the Vikings, despite being Christian still wore amulets around their necks. I saw a Thor's hammer, a wolf and a dragon. The Vikings were not natural Christians.

"Ready my lord."

I turned and saw that James had gathered forty knights and men at arms. I led the column towards the harbour. We did not run but went at a fast walk. Tired men could fall. I saw, as we neared the quay, that one of the dragon ships was almost loaded. When they saw us, the sail was unfurled and mooring lines cut. The breeze took her away. There were still five others being loaded.

"Fetch fire! Burn the others!" Men ran into the houses. I could smell the smoke. There would be burning brands. One ship had escaped. Had they managed to push off the others then they might have escaped too. These were not mailed warriors. These were Vikings and their families. That would not matter, they would all fight as hard as the ones we had just slain. One ran up to me, as I was leading the column, and he swung his sword at me. I pulled up my shield and as his sword slid down my curved shield I swung at his head. He had no helmet and the edge of the sword bit into his skull.

Harry Lightfoot lived up to his name. He had run, with a burning brand in hand, and reached the furthest ships. Although not fully loaded, as they saw him approach they hacked through the mooring line. As the sail unfurled Harry threw the brand and it caught on the billowing sail. The wind fed the flames. The canvas was bone dry as was the mast. The fire raced up and down the mast. The ship was doomed. Before the flames could spread the people on board hurled themselves into the water. Even as I watched I saw heads disappear beneath the waves.

The quay was a maelstrom of battling bodies and whirling weapons. It was our mail which saved us. I was struck from behind by a sword. I whipped around and hacked my sword sideways. My sword bit into the side of an old man. He had a smile on his face. His sword in his hand he had died a Viking. The last four ships remained tied to the quay and they were doomed. Brands were thrown and soon all four were alight. Some on board jumped into the sea, others came back to the quay. The women and the old gathered the children around them and awaited death. The last men stood defiantly with weapons ready.

Padraig ghosted next to me. He was out of breath. He had run from the camp, "Padraig, tell them to surrender. They will not be harmed."

He shouted to them and one of the men answered. "He said they will not be slaves."

"Tell him that they will not be enslaved and they can continue to live here in, what did you call it, Veisafjǫrðr. The only difference will be that there will be a Norman who rules the town."

This time it was a longer conversation. Eventually, Padraig turned, "I told them that you had freed me. He says if you will swear on your sword that they will still be free then they will surrender."

I took my sword, kissed the blue stone and said, "I swear that the people of Veisafjǫrðr will not be enslaved."

The swords were sheathed. We had won. I wondered at the one ship which had escaped. Whither would it go? Would we have to fight at Waterford too?

This time there was a great quantity of treasure for the knights, men at arms and archers. Vikings liked to adorn themselves with copper, silver and jewels. They wore battle bands and carried their gold with them. Their swords were well made and their mail was valuable too. Once again, we had lost a few of our younger knights but my plan of attack had minimised the losses. I was acutely aware that there would be no reinforcements and the King of Leinster was a poor ally. If we retook his kingdom then it would be by our efforts. We found the body of Jarl Sigtrygg Haakenson. He had died well. All of the wounds were to his front. He had a metal dragon around his neck and his sword was in his half-severed hand. He would be in his Valhalla.

The servants brought our horses and supplies into the town. It was safer than our camp and we would have houses in which we could stay. We had slain over a hundred Vikings in the battle and as many more had died in the attempt to flee. We had room. We took over one of the longhouses. It was like a warrior hall. The Vikings made good beer and there was plenty of it. I sat at a table with my lieutenants and their senior knights.

"Did you send word to the king that we have taken Wexford?"

De Clare nodded, "I sent my squire."

"Then we must strike quickly at Waterford. I hope that there will be fewer men. We cannot afford to lose knights and men at arms." I turned to Padraig. "Is it far?"

"No lord, as the crow flies it is less than thirty miles."

"And Ferns is the same distance north?" He nodded. "Then King Diarmait Mac Murchada will be of no use to us."

De Clare wiped the beer froth from his mouth, "I am not certain, lord. The High King still has plenty of men. I cannot see him suffering the one defeat and not trying to retake Leinster. At least we have our backs protected. Ferns has a wall does it not, Padraig?"

My translator nodded, "Aye lord and it has a stone cathedral."

I was not sure how that would help them but the Irish king might be able to defend walls. The simple fact of the matter was that we had little choice. We had to secure the other major port before we moved to Ferns and retook the rest of the kingdom.

"Count Striguil, as the King of Leinster did not want Wexford, I think you ought to appoint a lord of the manor for it. Or, perhaps, take it for yourself. You could start work on a castle."

"I think I will take this as my castle." He turned to his uncle, Hervey Montmorency, "Uncle, would you be castellan for me and start work on my castle?"

He grinned, "Aye for I am getting a little old for this campaigning."

We left the next morning for Waterford. We did not take all of our men. Sir Hervey would need a garrison and men to begin building the motte and bailey castle. We had discovered spare wood for dragon ships and that would be the palisade. It would not need to be a large castle. It was more of a refuge in case of attack. From what I had seen the Irish would not be able to take even a simple castle.

We reached Waterford not long before sunset. I rode to view the town. It had a wooden wall. I was relieved to see just two dragon ships in the harbour. We would not have as many men to fight. We made an armed camp with sentries at regular intervals and I had the horses hobbled. We were as far away from help as we had ever been.

My servants had my tent erected quickly. They were old campaigners. I knew that I was lucky to have them. They had hot food started quickly too. With a couple of logs for seats, it was quite cosy. James had taken Padraig under his wing and had given him one of the captured swords. He was showing him how to defend himself. With no knights in my retinue, I sat with Aelric and my men at arms.

"If the rest of the war is as the first part then we should be home by Christmas, Warlord."

"We should Aelric but I would not count on it."

Roger of Bath picked up some of the soil and rubbed it between his fingers. "It is fertile soil but I have seen few farms."

"I was speaking with Padraig today, as we rode across this land. He said that the people are too busy raiding and fighting each other to be successful farmers. Perhaps a firm Norman hand might make it a rich country."

Roger sniffed the soil, "I am betting they could grow wheat here."

Tom and the other servants brought over the wooden bowls with the stew they had made. Salted meat mixed with water and greens they had found may not sound appetising but after a long day riding it was more than welcome. James and Padraig joined us, "I hope that Sir Hervey begins work on a bread oven. The stew is nourishing but I like my bread."

Padraig shook his head, "There are few bread ovens here, master. The Bishop has one."

"Then we shall have to change that, eh James?"

"Yes, lord! I did not think that Ireland would be so primitive. I thought Wales was bad enough but that is sophisticated compared with this land."

My men slept in the open normally but, as a drizzle descended they improvised tents with their cloaks and the eaves of the trees. The drizzle became heavier rain as the night progressed. As I had grown older so I had needed to make water more frequently in the middle of the night. I rose and donned my cloak for I could hear the rain. Sir Raymond's men had been given the night duty. It was rotated each night. The password was '*Eleanor*'.

As I neared the place we had designated as a toilet I saw a figure. "Eleanor."

The reply was supposed to be, '*of Aquitaine*'. The figure did not move. I wondered if the rain had masked my words but, as I repeated it I drew my dagger and took a step closer. The Viking turned, with a bloody sword in hand. I saw, as he turned, that he wore a cloak made of a whole wolf skin. The wolf's skull was attached to the skin and formed a helmet. Beneath it, he was bare-chested.

"Alarm! Alarm! We are under attack!" I undid my cloak and held it in my left hand.

The wolfman leapt at me with his sword swinging. I whirled the cloak and it wrapped around the blade of the sword. I pulled the man towards me. I took him by surprise and as he came at me I rammed my dagger into his throat. I saw another three figures. They all wore animal furs. Roaring, they raced at me. I dropped the cloak and picked up the sword. Even as I was switching the sword into my right hand two arrows flew from behind me and hit one of the fur-covered figures. He stumbled but still came on at me. There was a roar and Günther the Swabian leapt from the side swinging the axe he had taken. It struck one of the Vikings in the chest. The one with two arrows sticking from him swung his sword at me. I blocked it with my sword and ripped the man across the stomach. The last warrior was surrounded by my men at arms and butchered.

James had brought lighted brands from the camp and he looked at me with concern on his face, "Are you hurt lord?"

I shook my head, "Shaken. What were they?"

Padraig said, "Shapeshifters. I thought they were a legend. There were stories of warriors who could turn themselves into wolves and bears. It was said they could not be killed."

Günther pulled his axe from the chest of the Viking he had killed, "Well we disproved that theory at any rate."

Aelric pulled the two arrows from the chest of the one I had killed. "I do not know, this one almost did for the Warlord with two arrows in him."

"Find our dead sentries and bury them. Then search them for signs. Take their heads and put them in a sack. We will return them to Waterford tomorrow. I am guessing that is where they came from."

Count Striguil and Sir Raymond appeared through the trees, dripping from the rain. They looked in horror at the four dead men. In the light from the brands, we could see that the men had sharpened and blackened their teeth. Their bodies had scars which had been impregnated with natural dyes. They looked as though they were from another world.

"Are we to fight more of these tomorrow?" Richard de Clare was visibly shaken by the four dead Vikings.

I looked at Padraig. He shook his head, "I have been to Waterford before and I have never seen the like. I would doubt it, lord."

I returned to my bed but I had difficulty in sleeping and so I sat up and planned what we would do at Waterford. When I had my plans clear I examined the sword I had taken. It was shorter and broader than my sword. The hilt was smaller and it was unadorned save by a dragon carved into the blade. It had a good balance. I would have Lame Tom make me a scabbard for it and I would keep it on my horse.

As I had not slept, I rose early. The rain had stopped. It had cleaned away the blood. The four headless bodies lay in the woods where they had fallen. My men were also up and about. The attempt on my life had shaken them. They were all old-fashioned warriors. I was their lord and they were my oathsworn. If anything happened to me then they would blame themselves.

Waterford was a wonderful harbour. I could see why the Vikings had made it their own. They had built a wall around the burgh and they had two towers over the gate. This time they did not form up before the wall, they lined them. We reined in beyond bow range. Here their archers would have the same range as my bowmen for they had the advantage of a fighting platform from which to send their arrows. When I had made my plans, I had two choices. If they had formed up then we would have attacked as we had at Wexford. I had a plan for the defence of their walls too. We would build an onager and reduce the walls. I would not risk my men in an attempt to storm their walls. We had too few for that.

"Padraig, do they understand the concept of a bare head?"

"You mean as a sign that you wish to talk, lord?" I nodded. "They do. The jarl here speaks your language too."

"Count Striguil take off your helmet and you too James. Sir Richard be so good as to fetch the sack with the heads." I took off my helmet and handed it to Roger of Bath. I lowered my coif and I slipped my mail mittens from my hands. Spurring Warrior, I led James, Padraig and Count Striguil towards the gate. When we were two hundred paces I saw bows drawn. A voice shouted something indistinct and they were lowered. The first test had been passed. They would speak.

We stopped by the bridge over their ditch. "I am Earl Marshal of England. I am here to ask for your surrender."

A grizzled warrior nodded, "I am Jarl Finni Siggison why should we surrender? We have stout men and strong walls."

I nodded and held my hand out for the sack. Count Striguil gave it to me. I emptied the sack and the four skulls fell from it. "You mean stout men like these who came to our camp to murder me?"

I saw the warrior glare at a younger warrior who was nearby. "That was a mistake. They are not the same as my warband. We are warriors and we have never been defeated."

"Good. For we would not make war on such men. We would have you as allies."

"Allies?"

I saw the question in his eyes. Could he trust a Norman? I guessed this was the first time he had dealt with one. I chose to be as honest as I could be. "I offered the same to Jarl Sigtrygg Haakenson. He declined and he and his oathsworn are dead. I suspect many of your warriors fought with him too." The look on the jarl's face told me I had hit the mark. "You can carry on here as lord of Veðrafjorðr. You will acknowledge Count Striguil here as your lord."

"And what does that mean? I have to bow and kiss his arse?"

I smiled, "No, jarl. It means that if there are common enemies then you fight under his banner but you lead your own men." I sensed hesitation. "I do not ask for an immediate decision. I will return in the morning and you can give me your decision then."

"Thank you."

"But know this, Jarl, I will not leave belligerents behind us. You will either be our friends or I will reduce your walls to kindling and slaughter every one within your walls. I would prefer to be allies but…"

"I understand and I thank you for your honesty. You are a man. That Irish lord, Mac Murchada, is not to be trusted but I believe that I can trust you. You spoke well to our kin at Veisafjorðr."

As we rode back I knew that some had left Wexford to warn the men of Waterford.

"Will they accede to our demands?"

I turned to Count Striguil, "I hope so for if not we will have to spend time building war machines and I am concerned that the High King may be gathering another army."

"What if he does not?"

"Then we can secure the borders of Leinster and you can begin to build castles!"

We made our camp even more secure by planting stakes around it and digging a ditch. The ditch also helped to make the camp drier. Tomas ap Tomas and his Welsh archers hunted and we ate venison! It was a better meal than the one we had eaten the night before.

When we approached the town the next day I knew we had won for the gates were open. We had Waterford and it had only cost us two sentries. That was a small price to pay.

Irish War

Chapter 13

With Waterford as an ally and Wexford under the command of Sir Hervey, we sent a ship back to England for more men. I hoped there would be young knights who were eager for land. Already de Clare was looking for sites which could be defended and made into manors. It was not the Irish way but I knew that Richard de Clare was going to rule the Norman way.

When we reached Ferns, I saw that more men had arrived to serve the King of Leinster. Perhaps our victories had made their backbones stronger. The King had a hall but it was hardly palatial. They had a wall but only the gates were made of stone and the wooden walls were just two paces high. I could have cleared them with Skuld. I saw the disappointment on de Clare's face. As we rode up he said quietly, "And he expects me to lie here with my wife?"

I shrugged, "When the borders are secure find yourself a good place to build a castle and use stone."

The King came from his hall to greet us. He had the Bishop of Ferns with him and his chiefs behind him, "Welcome, husband of my daughter. I hear you have quashed the Vikings! Now we can begin to take more land from our enemies. If you have taken Wexford and Waterford then Dyflin should be easy."

I looked at the Count. I was willing him to speak but he did not. He was looking at his wife who had come to join him. She looked radiant and I think Count Striguil was somewhat distracted. I spoke, "Your majesty, we will need your men in order to take Dyflin. We lost men in our attacks."

He scowled, "I know not why you are even here, Earl Marshal. I invited Count Striguil, who is the husband of my daughter."

It was my turn to smile, "I am the representative of King Henry. As I recall you asked him for help and he allowed his knights to aid you. If I return to England then you will lose half of the Count's army."

He turned and nodded to the Bishop. The Bishop stepped forward, "I believe that you have freed my slave, Padraig. Who gave you the right to do so?"

"The Pope, Bishop. He is not happy with your practices. Slavery is no longer acceptable. He is also unhappy at what he sees as corruption. I have yet to do as my king asked and write a report on the activities of the Church for we have been too busy fighting the enemies of the King of Leinster. When time allows then I will do so." The threat was enough and he backed off. I turned my attention to the king, "Well?"

"We have men ready to fight but I would have them fight under the banner of Count Striguil."

"And that is perfectly acceptable. We will make a camp yonder." I pointed to a slightly higher piece of ground about half a mile from the cathedral. "Are you coming, Count Striguil?"

"I think I will stay in the hall with my wife this night."

I think the king saw it as a victory for he beamed. When we reached the open ground I said, "Sir Raymond, I would have you make a camp but I would have you use this higher ground. I think we will make this a castle for Count Striguil."

As it seemed likely that we would be at Ferns for some time I intended for us to be comfortable. I went with four of my men at arms and we laid out the lines for a simple square keep. I had spotted the only ground higher than the cathedral. It would have to do. I did not plan on using my own men to build it. I would use the men of Leinster. I sent James, with Padraig, to find a quarry which was close by for the stone. At the end of two days, we had a strong, defensible camp and James had found stone. Count Striguil remained in Ferns. That suited me for it meant I could act without being watched. When all was ready I went with Sir Raymond and Hugh de Lacy to visit with him and the king.

When we were announced I saw that Count Striguil was a little embarrassed. "I am sorry that I have been absent, Earl Marshal. The King has been telling me of his plans. They are grand and achievable. I believe that we can take County Meath. It is weakly held."

I saw the King preening himself at the praise. I nodded, "Excellent, then perhaps the King will provide us with labour to build you a castle here."

Silence fell, "A castle?"

"Your majesty, surely you must see that you can only hold this land if you have a strong castle. I have laid out the lines of a castle just half a mile away. I know where we can source the stone. Is there a problem?"

"What of the High King?"

"I had planned on taking a body of knights and men at arms to find his whereabouts. When we know where he is then we can plan to defeat him." I had prepared my answer before I met with the king. I could now see how he had lost his kingdom. He was indolent. The only way the Count of Striguil could regain Leinster was with Norman knights and men at arms backed up by English and Welsh archers.

"Very well. I can see no problem with a strong castle."

That night I walked around the projected castle. I had decided on four towers around a central keep. From what I had seen so far that would be more than an obstacle for the Irish. I needed a mason. I did not believe that there would be one in Ireland. It would take time to collect the stone and have the foundations dug. I had time to send to England for one. The payment would come from the Irish. King Diarmait Mac Murchada was regaining his kingdom and the price, so far, just his pretty daughter.

I took just my men at arms and archers along with Hugh de Lacey and his men. I liked Hugh. He had had problems in Wales and this was his chance to regain his fortune. He did not complain nor bemoan his situation. He worked hard and his men were as loyal and hard-working as he. We headed north-west. The High King had his centre of power in Connacht. That lay to the west. I intended to head there and see if I could find him and his army. If he was not preparing to march against Leinster then we might be able to take some of his land.

The land over which we travelled was largely flat. I knew that there were mountains in Ireland but, thus far, I had only seen them in the distance. It was land made for horses. The only horses we had seen had been large ponies. It was no wonder that our charge had come as a total surprise to them.

We were about to turn and ride back to Ferns when Tom the Fletcher's sharp eyes picked out something. "Lord, up ahead, there are huts and beyond them, I see armed men."

"You have good eyes." Confident that we would be able to outrun the enemy if they were in large numbers we continued up the narrow road. I had learned that the Romans had never built any roads here. They were, at best, cobbled but normally, they were a greenway. The recent rain had made them somewhat slick and slippery. Men would find it as hard to move quickly as we did.

If we could see them then it was certain that they could see us. The thin sun sparkled off metal. They were moving. We kept heading towards the houses. It was not a large place. I counted no more than twenty huts and buildings. Given that I guessed that it was a gathering place. The High King had summoned men. We must have arrived shortly after the summons for there did not appear to be a great host. What was most interesting was the river. From the direction it took I guessed it was the river which flowed through Wexford. Had this been England then I would have expected a castle to guard the bridge. There was none.

As we headed closer the Irish formed up with one flank on the bank of the river. I turned to Hugh de Lacy. "How many would you say?"

He stood in his stirrups. "I would say more than two hundred."

I nodded my agreement. "Let us get a little closer. Aelric, if we get the chance, see if you can make them charge us."

"Aye lord."

My eighteen archers were all mounted. No matter how close to the Irish they went they would be safe. We closed to within two hundred paces. The warriors banged their shields. The ones without shields banged their chests. There were the usual warriors who bared their backsides at us. Four of them dropped their breeks and began to make water in our direction.

"Aelric!"

While my archers dismounted and nocked an arrow I studied the banners. There were six different ones and I had not seen any at the first battle. What I needed was an Irish warrior who knew the lords. Aelric and his archers did not just send the eighteen arrows randomly. They targeted those who had bared themselves. As soon as the fourteen who had done so fell the rest fell back or sheltered behind shields.

"Now the leaders on horses."

Switching targets my archers sent their arrows at the six men who were mounted. Three of the men fell. Two horses were struck. One died quickly. The other ran around for a while, throwing its rider and careering into men on foot before a warrior with an axe ended its suffering. Another three flights later and the Irish withdrew into the relative safety of the huts.

"Come, we can return to Ferns. The High King is coming but not yet. We have time to prepare." We had not inflicted a large number of casualties but we had damaged their morale. We had struck and killed with no loss to ourselves. When we met them then those who had been at the river would remember.

The King had provided people to dig the foundations. I suspect that many were slaves. The stone had yet to arrive and my request for a mason would not have even reached England yet. I waved over Padraig. "There is a small settlement by a river north of here."

"Athy."

"Thank you. Next time I will take you with us for your knowledge will be invaluable." I rode directly to the King's hall. Count Striguil and Sir Raymond were both there. "The High King is gathering an army but they will not be ready for some time." I looked at the King. "If you could have scouts out, your majesty we might have a warning. We found them gathering at the place you call Athy."

The Bishop frowned, "That is close, your majesty. If they have left already then they could be here within half day. Perhaps instead of having our people build the castle for these Normans, we should have them preparing defences."

I laughed, "Stick to the church and your books, your Grace. Leave the strategy to warriors. We will meet them long before they get here so long as the scouts give us warning when the High King arrives. I did not see his banner yet."

"What if he brings an even larger army, Earl Marshal?"

"It matters not. If we meet them in the open then they will be slaughtered."

"Pride and arrogance are both sins."

"I have pride but it is pride in the men I lead. As for arrogance then I can tell you that I am not but I know my trade." I left and Count Striguil and Sir Raymond followed me. Once we were outside I said, "How many men does the King bring?"

"We now have a thousand, Earl Marshal."

"Good, then I want to find a place to bring them to battle. We will end it with one battle. This time I want none to escape." It was not in my nature to be so ruthless but I knew that it would be the only way to make the High King realise that this was a war he could not win.

Over the next few days, the scouts went out to find the dispositions of our foes. Twenty knights and squires arrived three days after I had returned from Athy. They were young but they were more than welcome. Forty more riders, the majority of whom were mailed, would make all the difference. My plan was simple. We had scouted out the land. If they gathered at Athy then they could not make it to Ferns in one day. The Bishop was no warrior. He assumed an army could travel at the speed of a horseman! They were on foot and it was over thirty miles. I gambled that they would stop at the tiny hamlet of Bunclody. It was on a river and would allow them to reach Ferns in a few hours. I intended to wait for them five miles from Bunclody and use the King of Leinster as bait. There was a bridge over the River Clody at Ballycarney. Once I knew that they had left Athy I intended to cross the river there and ride to Bunclody. We would cross and attack their rear once they were engaged with the King of Leinster. We would stiffen their ranks with the knights of the Count of Striguil. I would lead the rest. The archers would also be behind the men of Leinster but they would be hidden.

The scouts reported, two days later, that the standard of the King was at Athy. The King of Leinster gathered his army. They prepared to march out. I did not rely entirely upon the Irish scouts. I used Ralph of Wales and John to watch Athy. They would not be seen and they would be able to tell me when the army left.

James had found a helmet for Padraig to wear and a cut-down hauberk. A full one was too heavy but, as he would be riding with me, I wanted him protecting. James made sure that he had a good horse too. We were able to leave our spare supplies and horses at the castle site with the servants. The foundations were almost finished and we just awaited the masons.

Early one afternoon John rode in, "Lord, the Irish have left Athy. Ralph of Wales is shadowing them. They are coming down the road to Bunclody. He has four thousand men. We were able to count them as they left the settlement. They are spread across the land as they march. There is no order to them." The professional soldier in John was outraged.

"Good, rejoin Aelric." I found the Count. "We will leave this afternoon and cross the Clody. We will camp tonight south of Bunclody. You know that all of this fails if the King does not do exactly what I said."

"Do not fear. He wants it over. His eldest son is held hostage by the High King. He sees this as his chance to get him back."

"Good then leave now. It will take the king some time to reach Clohamon. He needs to tie one flank to the river. You must be on the other flank."

Irish War

I hated leaving the Count alone with the King. The Count was reliable but not so the King. I led my two hundred knights and squires along with two hundred men at arms south-west towards the river crossing. This was another place which needed a castle. We clattered across the wooden bridge and turned to follow the track which ran alongside it. There were farmers but they fled when they saw us coming. If we had frightened the army of the High King then we absolutely terrified the farmers. They saw mail-clad giants on unbelievably large horses. It grew dark and we stopped to make a cold camp. I walked with Roger of Bath and James. We headed along the river until we heard the noise of the Irish camp. We travelled more than two miles before we found them. I saw the spirals of smoke from their fires. We were close enough. They would not see us and we could head away from the river before dawn. I wanted the High King to take the bait. I needed him to see a strong army of Leinster with Norman horses. He had to believe that he had enough men to defeat them.

We ate cold rations and slept close to our horses. James and Padraig were still talking as I fell asleep. I was pleased that James had someone to take under his wing. Since I had knighted my other squire, Richard, he had led a solitary life. My time was always taken up with matters of what others deemed to be of greater importance. James was left to do much on his own. My men at arms and archers had their comrades for companionship. When we fought, the next day, it would James who would be responsible for keeping Padraig safe in case we needed him to translate.

Roger of Bath shook me awake before dawn. James and Padraig were still curled up asleep. I rose and walked away from my sleeping squire, "What is it?"

"One of the sentries woke me, lord. He heard noises across the river." I waited. Roger would not have woken me just because a noise was heard. "The Irish camp is awake, lord."

"Then they may move early." He nodded. "I want everyone awake and mounted but no trumpets or horns. Do it man by man."

"Aye lord."

I went to James and Padraig. I woke them and told them what to do. I hurried over to Sir Raymond and woke him. Most of the knights were young and they soon roused the camp. There was noise but the strident blast of a horn or a shout would have been much louder. James returned having woken sufficient squires for the ripple of rising to continue. He began to dress me. Padraig arrived back and he helped James to dress. We had no servants with us. I found a jug with some ale left in and I drank some of that before giving it to James and Padraig. They offered me some of the dried meat they carried. I shook my head.

We saddled our horses and we three mounted. As soon as we did so it was a silent signal for the rest of the conroi to do the same. Making the sign for silence we headed away from the river so that we would not be heard from across the river. Roger and I led. We had scouted the path the previous night when we had returned from our trip up the river. I could hear, in the distance, the sound of the Irish as their camp came to light. The Count and the King might not have their own camp roused but they were in position and they would hear the Irish as they approached.

We turned and headed towards Bunclody. The first grey could be seen in the east. The noise of the enemy receded. As we neared the bridge I waved forward Roger of Bath and Harry Lightfoot. They galloped off towards the bridge. If the Irish had left any men there then we would still be able to attack but we would have lost the element of surprise. When there was no noise from the dark and they did not return then I knew that the bridge was unguarded.

By the time we crossed the bridge and entered the hamlet the sky was much lighter. Roger and Harry had still to return. We found them at the Irish camp. The High King had left servants and women there. I saw that Roger and Harry had slain the three men left to guard it. Roger came from one of the huts and held aloft a torc. "Lord, the King's treasure is here. They left three men to guard it."

"Sir Raymond, leave a knight and six men at arms to secure this camp and the treasure." I lowered my voice, "A trustworthy one!"

There might have been a time when Sir Raymond would have been offended at my suggestion but he had changed since first we met. He nodded and said, "Aye lord. Old Sir Geoffrey will be perfect! "

We were now riding on what passed for a road in these parts. We were able to move faster. All of my men at arms now rode before us. They were there to warn us of the enemy. As the sun rose in the east over the Wicklow Hills, I heard the clash and clamour of battle. The High King had clashed with our men. The river and Count Striguil would mean that the High King was pressing towards the centre and I had no doubt that the Leinster line would be bowing. I could picture Aelric and his archers as they slowed the inexorable press. As we rose from the slight hollow I saw, a mile away, the rear of the Irish army. I spied the banners of the

High King and his lords. They were at the rear of the army and looked to be mounted. I raised my spear and pointed first to my right and then to my left. Our line began to form. My men at arms galloped back and joined James and Padraig, behind me. I was flanked by Sir Raymond and Hugh de Lacy. Spurring Warrior, I led the line at a canter towards the distant battle.

As soon as our four hundred sets of hooves struck the ground the sound travelled south. We would be heard. The sound of the battle would disguise our direction but they would feel the ground tremble and know that horsemen were coming. Each moment that delayed our discovery took us twenty paces close to them. Already the jaws of my trap were closing. I saw the river to my right and Count Striguil's banners to my left. We were less than half a mile away. I lowered my spear and rested it on the cantle of my saddle. I spurred Warrior. He began to open his legs. The rest of the line reacted and began to move faster.

I heard a horn from the Irish. We had been seen and I watched as shields and spears turned to face us. It was too late. We had a line which was a hundred men wide and four men deep. The men on the flanks of our army were closing in. I saw the black shadow of arrows as they descended into the heart of the Irish army. They were surrounded and the mailed mounted machine was about to chew them up and spit out the remains.

Their horsemen did not ride to face us. That would have been suicide. They only had twenty and they were the High King, his sub kings, chiefs and his chieftains. Instead, they placed themselves behind a wall of shields. Their bodyguards and oathsworn formed two ranks before them. That suited us. I spurred Warrior when we were just a hundred paces from them and I moved my spear so that it was pointed at the line of warriors. They had few spears. They had swords and small shields. Some had limed and spiked hair and I saw a few helmets. They were not afraid. I watched one warrior break ranks, throw away his shield and race towards us with his sword held in two hands. He ran and threw himself into the air. His sword was sweeping down to strike at Warrior's head. My spear was on the wrong side and we were boot to boot. Sir Hugh's spear took him in the head. His sword flew backwards and his body fell beneath our crashing hooves.

Then we struck their line. I punched with my spear and it rammed into the bare, tattooed chest of the red-haired giant who roared at me. I allowed my hand to trail back as Warrior's hooves clattered into the shield and chest of the man behind him. He screamed as he was crushed. The red-haired giant slid from my spear and I moved it back into position. I punched again. This time it hit an Irishman in the shoulder and he was able to wrench it from my hand before falling beneath Sir Raymond's horse's hooves. I drew my sword and swept it around at the warrior who lunged at my leg. His sword slid along my mail chausse as my sword hacked into his skull.

We were now through the oathsworn and the chiefs and kings awaited us. They were mounted. They rode at us. These were not cowards. One rode at me, for our line was now disjointed. He had a helmet with a metal bird on the top. He had plaited, lime spiked hair and beard which made his head look twice the size of a normal man. He had a sword which was longer than mine but, he had no stirrups! He swung his sword at me and it clattered into my shield. I saw that he almost fell from his horse. His mount was smaller than Warrior and I had the advantage of height. I stood in my stirrups and brought my sword down. He raised his shield to block the blow and my sword shattered it asunder. The blade bit into his arm. I whipped Warrior's head around as I lunged at his, now bare, chest. My sword sliced across his chest and, bleeding from two wounds, he could no longer keep his seat. He fell from his horse and was trampled by the terrified beast who backed away from Warrior's snapping teeth.

Another warrior, a chief I guessed, lunged at me with his sword. I took it on my shield. I saw him anticipate me standing in my stirrups. He lifted his shield. I hacked across his leg. With no mail to protect him, my sword ripped through to the bone. Had he had stirrups he might have kept his seat but he slid from the horse, his lifeblood pumping away. There was now a gap and I urged Warrior into it. King Ruaidrí Ua Conchobair had one bodyguard with him. He was on foot and he held a two-handed axe. He had a fine helmet but was bare-chested. I walked Warrior to him. I could see from his stance and the position of his axe that he intended to take Warrior's head. A two-handed axe is a terrible weapon and can inflict great damage but once it has begun its swing then it cannot be stopped. I waited for him to swing and then I whipped Warrior's head away from the blow and pirouetted around. The axe caught some of Warrior's tail; it would regrow. I was swinging my sword as I came around and it sliced across the Irish bodyguard's throat.

I reined in next to the king and pointed my sword at him, "Surrender or die!" He jabbered something at me. "James, Padraig!" My squire and my translator stopped their horses by me. I saw that they were both spattered and besmeared with blood. They had not been idle. "Padraig tell him to surrender or die!" Around us, men were still fighting furiously but here, in the heart of the Irish army, there was quiet for we were surrounded by a sea of dead. The king's standard-bearer was still on his horse but he had been wounded in his right arm and he clung to the standard with his left.

Padraig spoke to the king. He was answered and Padraig spoke again and swept his arm towards me. The King nodded and said something to the standard-bearer. The standard was lowered and he sounded four blasts on his horn. Gradually his men stopped fighting.

"What did you say to him, Padraig, to convince him?"

"I told him that you had defeated the Vikings and you had more men coming from England. I said that they all rode horses as you did."

I nodded, "You both did well. Search the bodies of the chiefs and kings I slew. Whatever treasure they have is yours."

I saw Count Striguil and King Diarmait Mac Murchada heading towards me. The Bishop of Ferns was with the King as well as the chiefs who rode with the King of Leinster. He was beaming. "Thank you, Earl. You have repaid my trust a thousand-fold." He turned to King Ruaidrí Ua Conchobair and began berating him.

I could leave the rest to the King and Count Striguil. James and Padraig had gold and silver bangles and amulets they had taken from the dead and remounted. "James, sound for my men. We will head back to Ferns. Our work here is done."

We rode south and had to pick our way through waves of Irish dead. I saw that almost half had been slain by arrows. Aelric and his archers joined my men at arms. "We do not stay, lord?"

"You like the smell of death, Ralph of Wales? I assume you have taken what you wish from the battlefield?"

Aelric nodded, "They were poor pickings."

Roger of Bath said, "Then we will share with you for we fought the chiefs and they carry their treasure with them."

My men fought as one. You could not buy loyalty like that. We reached Ferns as the sun began to set. We would have a good and safe night's sleep free from the smell of dead flesh and the sound of carrion feasting.

Irish War

Chapter 14

We were wise to ride back early. The rest of the army did not arrive for a week. There were hostages to be recovered and hostages taken. Oaths were sworn and peace was made. During that week the masons arrived. I used some of the treasure we had taken from the Irish camp to pay them and they began work on the castle which would become the home of Count Striguil.

Sir Raymond and his men reached us the day before the King and the bulk of the army. He took me to one side, "We need to speak, lord."

I found a quiet part of the camp and said, "Go ahead."

"The King is grown greedy. He wishes us to take more of Meath now."

"And the Count?"

"He is in agreement."

"But you think that I will disapprove."

"You are a man of honour, Earl Marshal. King Henry asked you to come and help the King of Leinster regain his kingdom. He has done so."

"You are right. I need to return to speak with King Henry." Sir Raymond was not telling me all. "Speak in confidence, Sir Raymond. Do not hide your thoughts from me."

"There is one part of the kingdom which is not yet recovered. Dyflin now has a Viking king, Ascall mac Ragnaill meic Torcaill. Count Striguil has promised that we will take it with our men."

"King Diarmait Mac Murchada wishes us to bleed for his town."

"It was his son's idea."

"His son?"

"Domhnall Caemanach mac Murchada was one of the hostages held by the High King. When he returned to his father it was as a conquering hero. He and his brother Conchobar fell out. That continued when he met the Count, the first night after his return. The Prince said that just because the Count had married his sister did not mean that he would inherit the kingdom when his father died."

"What did the King say?"

"He was not there. He and the Bishop were praying. It was the next day that Domhnall Caemanach mac Murchada made the suggestion to his father. He said it would prove that the Count truly cared for King Diarmait."

"Clever. It means that the Count could not refuse. If he did then it would appear as though he was disloyal. I thank you for telling me. Then we shall take Dyflin and then I will return to speak with King Henry. It means a long sea voyage for he is in Anjou but…"

He smiled, "You are the King's man. I know."

The foundations of the castle had been laid by the time the army returned. The king was surprised at the progress we had made and Count Striguil was delighted. It would give him a secure base should the Irish try to take back Leinster. When the bulk of the knights returned to England he would have to use the castle as a base with which to hold the land. The only one who appeared unhappy was Domhnall Caemanach mac Murchada. I think he saw it as a means of making the Count's claim to Leinster a little more solid. It was the first time I had met the king's son and I did not like him. He was a huge beast of a man but he was sulky and petulant. He had been a hostage for a long time and it showed. He had run to fat. Instead of keeping himself as fit as he should, he had brooded and now it showed. His father was getting on in years. Domhnall Caemanach mac Murchada saw himself as king.

When we feasted, two days later, it was Domhnall who brought up the plan to attack Dyflin. He spoke not to me but his words were intended for my ears, "So brother Richard, when do you begin your attack on the Vikings, who have claimed my father's land?"

The Count had been busy speaking with his bride and he looked around guiltily. He had not spoken to me of it yet. "I am sorry, Earl Marshal, I should have mentioned this before. I have promised the King that we will take Dyflin from the Vikings."

I played it as though I was ignorant of the plans. "And how many of the King's men do we take?"

Domhnall Caemanach mac Murchada took great delight in saying, "None, for Count Striguil believes that he can do so with Normans only."

I nodded, "I believe the Count is right." I had taken all but Sir Raymond by surprise. "If the Vikings at Wexford are typical Vikings then the treasure we find will make us all rich!"

The King nodded but his son said, "The treasure belongs to the King."

I shook my head, "To the victor goes the spoils. If you were a warrior then you would know that."

Some of the Irish lords laughed at his discomfort. I knew that I had made an enemy. It did not worry me. He glowered and glared at me.

We did not leave straight away as the King was waiting for reparations from the High King. Had we chosen, we could have taken the whole kingdom for they appeared incapable of achieving anything on their own. I had seen their warriors fight. They were courageous but there appeared to be no leadership. Men fought for chiefs and chieftains. What they would do when the chief died appeared to be totally unpredictable. Sometimes they would go on a rampage and fight on until dead or exhausted. At other times they would simply go home. When the reparations arrived, we left. We did not take all of our men. I did not trust Prince Domhnall Caemanach mac Murchada. I feared he might do something to damage the masons or the work on the castle. We left Sir Raymond's uncle, Meiler FitzHenry, in command. He had three knights and thirty men at arms. It also gave us a reserve in case we needed it.

Dyflin was the centre of the Viking world in Ireland. It had been Norse for over two hundred years. I had learned, from Padraig, that the King of Leinster had rarely ruled there. If there was no strong Viking leader then the King was tolerated. If there was then he was ignored. It explained the reluctance of the Irish to take on the wild Norse warriors. Having beaten them once I was confident that I could beat them again. This time they would have a strong wall behind which they could shelter. I was reluctant to try to defeat them as we had at Wexford. We had lost too many knights and men at arms. Until I saw the defences I would not make my decision.

I learned of the new King of Dyflin as we rode. Although we had not been given any warriors we did have some of the officials King Diarmait had used to collect port dues in Dyflin. There were three of them. "The King, Ascall mac Ragnaill meic Torcaill, is of Viking origin, although his mother was an Irish princess. That meant little. Every other noblewoman called herself a princess. In most cases, they were not. His origins meant he had support both from the Norse and the Irish. I was uncertain of the number of true Viking warriors he could command. With our losses and our garrison, we had just two hundred knights and squires, two hundred men at arms and our one hundred and twenty archers. We had also suffered losses in horses. Although I still had two war horses some knights had lost valuable and irreplaceable horses. If I could avoid wasting my horses in fruitless charges then I would do so.

We moved quickly and those who wished to avoid our rule raced towards the town of Dyflin. It was a rout. The road was clogged. Had I wished then I could have had my archers and men at arms ride down the refugees. I did not for one thing they were not warriors and secondly, they would have to be fed inside the town. I had Aelric and my archers ahead of me and they had a stroke of good fortune. The Vikings we driving a herd of cattle into the city in anticipation of a siege. The men who were driving them were not warriors and they fled for the safety of the town adding to the charge of people who headed for the town. The houses and farms just outside were abandoned as panic set in. When we arrived, Aelric and his men had a thousand head of cattle they had captured.

Count Striguil said, "We will eat well."

"And, more importantly, they will starve!" We halted half a mile from the town. The wall was substantial. I could see the masts of at least five dragon ships along the river. I saw one mast at an ungainly angle closer to the mouth of the river. That meant that there were at least two hundred warriors in the town. It would be nearer to three hundred. The number of men we would be fighting would be more than double that.

"Sir Raymond, take your men and seal off the approach from the north."

"Aye lord."

"Sir Gerald, take your men and cut off the approach from the south."

"Aye, lord."

Sir Gerald Fitzmaurice had shown himself to be a dependable leader. He was only young but other knights followed him.

I planned on keeping all of the archers with me. The two conroi on the flanks were just there to stop the Vikings fleeing and to stop reinforcements. I saw that the walls of Dyflin, or Dublin as we called it, were manned and this time, unlike Waterford, they were manned by mailed men. I viewed the enemy defences. They had a ditch and a wooden palisade. The gate through which the people had fled had two small towers. The bridge over the ditch was fixed. I suspected they would make it a killing zone if we tried to cross it. We needed something to break the gatehouse.

"Count, I think that we will need an onager. Have the men at arms cut down the wood to make one."

James pointed to an abandoned farm. The farmer and his family must have fled with the cattle herders. "Earl Marshal, there is a wagon there and timbers upon it. We could use that."

"You have sharp eyes. Then all we need is some rope." I saw the dragon ship whose mast was at a strange angle. Now that I was closer I could see that they had been trying to make the quay but had run aground. She was hard and fast. They would only be able to refloat her at high tide. "Roger of Bath, bring the men at arms. "Aelric, I need ten archers. Come, Count. We will see if we can capture a ship!"

I dismounted and we ran towards the ship. There were just twelve or so men on board her. They were not in mail but they were Norse. I would not underestimate them. As we ran arrows were sent in our direction from the town walls. I hefted my shield but it was not necessary. They fell short. The crew also had bows and they began to send hurried arrows at us. I switched my shield to the front. Two arrows thudded into it. Then Aelric and his archers began to release from behind us. I heard cries from ahead. Roger of Bath and Harry Lightfoot raced aboard the ship and the arrows stopped. I lowered my shield just as the last two crew members jumped into the river and began to swim upstream.

"Put the bodies in the river. Aelric, you and the archers take every coil of rope you can find. We will use them to make an onager."

"Aye lord."

"Harry, do you know how to furl a sail?"

"It can't be that hard, lord." He turned to Wilson of Bristol. "Come with me and we will try to furl the sail."

"What is on your mind, Earl Marshal?"

"Simple, Count Striguil, when the tide rises and frees this ship I intend to lower her sail and set her alight. The rising tide and the wind from the south-east will take her into the town. At best she will set alight the other ships and perhaps the walls and, at the worst, she will sink in the river and block the channel."

"I will get men to bring oil and kindling."

"Roger, stay here and guard the ship. I intend to make it a fire ship."

I saw that the Vikings were curious. Would they sally forth to stop whatever we were doing? I hoped so for then we could catch them in the open. We moved our horses further away from the walls. I did not want them as targets for their archers. At the same time, I had my servants watch the cattle. We had already taken two and slaughtered them for our meal. It would feed us and, just as importantly, annoy those within who would see us eating the cattle intended for them.

Roger of Bath sent a runner for me when the tide was on the turn. It was sunset and the sky above the town was an orange-tinged with pink and blue. By the time I had reached the ship Harry and Wilson had managed to lower the sail and the wind was already tugging at it. Count Striguil had filled the ship with kindling. "How do you intend to ignite it, Count?"

"We have pots filled with hot, burning coals. We throw them aboard." I saw that he had ten of his largest men at arms with the pots.

Harry Lightfoot leapt from the ship. "Lord she is moving."

I nodded to the Count who shouted, "Throw them!" He must have instructed them where to send the burning missiles for they were not sent to one place but spread along the length of the ship. The ship moved with the incoming tide. It was the wind which would do the most damage. It suddenly caught the sail full on and the dragon ship seemed to race towards the narrowing river mouth. James pointed to the quay. The light tower at the end of the quay obscured our view somewhat but we could see the frantic activity as men ran to the ships.

The stricken ship moved inexorably towards the end two dragon ships. I saw the masts of the end two. They were silhouetted against the setting sun. Then the flames leapt up the sail and the mast of the fire ship. Sparks flew through the air and, even before it struck, the end ship caught fire. Men tried to douse the flames but more sparks flew and then there was a grinding crash as it struck. At that moment the flames raced across not only the first ship but the second and the third. The evening became daylight as the three ships burned. I saw flames moving upstream. They had moved another of the dragon ships. They might save her but she would not sail again without repairs.

"Let us go back to the camp. We may have angered them. If so they might seek retribution."

Harry laughed, "Lord I can guarantee that we have angered them!"

Most of our men were watching the fire. All men were fascinated by such events. The flames had spread across the quay to the nearest buildings. It was a fierce fire, fed by the winds from the south-east. They had an adequate supply of water and I heard the screams, shouts and orders in equal measure as they fought the fire. Finally, the flames reached the end of the wooden palisade. This was more than we might have hoped. They had saved two, perhaps three of their ships but they had lost houses and part of the palisade.

I rubbed my hands together. "Come, the fire has given me an appetite. I will enjoy the beef."

We ate well but I was not foolish enough to relax. We had a good watch set. We had moved the horses further away from the walls as the smell of smoke and fire unsettled them. All night we saw sparks fly through the air and we had the smell of burning in our nostrils. Some of the sparks set fire to one of the tents belonging to one of Count Striguil's knights. I gave the order for our tents to be soaked with water. I retired, tired but happy. We had had a good day.

Something woke me but I knew not what it was. I could hear no sound. I rose. As I was awake I would make water. When I stepped over James' sleeping body and opened the tent flap I saw the reassuring figure of John son of John on sentry duty.

"You are awake early, my lord. Dawn is not due for a while yet."

"I know. I have to make water." He nodded sympathetically. I went to the rear of the tent. When I had finished and returned I said, "Have you heard anything?"

He rubbed his chin. "Funny you should say that, lord. They were making all manner of noise for what seemed like an age. Then the flames went out and there was just a murmur. Then there was some shouting and then silence. Strange."

I was awake. I said, "I will go and put on my mail. Wake Roger and my men at arms; Aelric too."

"Something amiss, lord?"

"Let us just say that I was awoken by something." When I entered the tent I said, "James, awake and help me dress."

"Trouble, lord?"

"Perhaps nothing."

Padraig had woken, "Is there danger?"

I sighed, "There may be but it is as well to be prepared." By the time I had dressed in my mail my men had arrived. "Come let us take a walk by the enemy defences." Smoke still drifted towards us as we walked the five hundred paces towards the ditch. The ditch was five paces wide and there was a further five paces until the wall. We reached the line of sentries.

"Earl Marshal."

"Any movement?"

"Not movement as such but we heard the jangling of metal not long since."

"Metal?"

"Like a spear catching mail." The sentry shrugged, "Sorry, Earl Marshal, you asked."

I looked to the east. Dawn was some way off. Suddenly I heard a creak as the gate opened and the Vikings erupted from it. They made no sound but they ran at us. "Back to the camp. Sound the alarm!"

They had taken us unawares. The twenty or so sentries would not stop them. I ran back with my men. "Aelric, Roger, come with me. James and Padraig, rouse the Count. I want a shield wall at the camp." It would take some time for my men to arm themselves. If they did not then the Vikings would butcher them. I had one idea but it was a ridiculous one. I glanced over my shoulder. They were ignoring us. They thought we were fleeing. We were not. The Vikings began to form into a wedge. It made sense for it would take some time for them all to pass through the gate and they still had enough time to reach our camp before our men were mailed.

We reached the cattle. I shouted to the men with me, "We are going to stampede these cattle through the Vikings. At the very least it will disorder them and it may thwart their attack. Get around the rear and keep driving them. Aelric, once we get close to the Vikings you and your archers pick off as many of their leaders as you can."

Harry Lightfoot laughed, "If we survive this morning I will enjoy telling this tale over a flagon of ale."

We hurried to the rear of the herd. I shouted to the cattle guards, "Drive them towards the sea. Make them stampede!"

We began to scream and shout. We slapped their rumps with the flats of our swords. At first, they were slow but as panic spread amongst them they ran. They would keep running so long as there was a threat behind. We were that threat. The cattle made an awful noise as they raced towards the Vikings. The sun was still below the horizon and I could not make out the warband but I knew where they were from the occasional flash of white as a face turned towards us. It was when I heard the first scream that I knew the cattle had reached the Vikings.

"Roger, keep them stampeding until we get to the gate." I had to shout over the noise of the animals. I saw Roger nod. As we neared the place where the cattle had struck I saw the first bodies. There were trampled warriors. One cow had had its head hacked by a Viking. The dead warrior lay with his hands around the haft of the axe which was embedded in the cow's skull. A horn was buried deep in the warrior's body.

I saw arms waving from my right. It was James. He was mouthing something but I could not hear. I patted Roger on the back as I ran towards him. I saw that there were thirty knights in mail. From the camp, I saw the rest of the knights and men at arms racing towards us. Had we not stampeded the cattle then our camp would have been a charnel house. If I had not awoken then I would be there with them.

Count Striguil ran up. His squire carried his helmet and shield. He put his mouth to my ear and shouted above the noise of hooves and dying warriors. "What happened?"

I put my mouth to his ear. "The Vikings thought to surprise us with a night attack. I stampeded the cattle. I have bought us time, that is all."

He nodded and shouted to me again, "It is fortunate that the horses are far from here. The stampeding cattle might have made them run too."

The noise began to recede as the cattle turned and moved south. Roger of Bath led my men back to us. I saw two hundred paces from us, the remnants of the Vikings forming a shield wall. I saw many bodies before us, for the sky was growing lighter but they still had a formidable shield wall.

"James, fetch spears!"

Aelric was organising the archers. They had no mail to don and they had joined their captain. He had his men sending arrows into the ranks of the Vikings as they tried to form a shield wall. Until they had shields locked then they were vulnerable. We needed the other two parts of our army but Sir Gerald and Sir Maurice were too far away. They would have heard the noise and might even have thought to come to our aid but by the time they did so then battle would be joined. We would have to fight them with the men I had with me now.

James handed me a spear. I looked down the line and saw that we had a mix of knights and men at arms. We were opposite their gate and, therefore opposite the Vikings. I saw them reorganising a shield wall. Aelric had kept my archers to the left of our line. It meant he could loose directly into their flank. I took the decision. "Two deep line." As men began to move I said, "James, behind me."

He said, "I have Padraig behind me, lord. He has your banner."

James would be able to fight but the young Irish boy would be in danger.

I shouted, "We hold them. Do not move forward until I give the word."

"Aye, lord!"

The light was better now. The Viking leader, I saw that it was not the king, was waiting for better light now that we were prepared. I saw why. The ground was littered with bodies. There was a danger of falling. I counted fifty shields in the front rank. There were three ranks. They had a hundred and fifty men. I could not see if they were mailed but I did see helmets and I saw that at least half had spears. They began banging their shields and chanting.

I shouted, "Padraig, is this the song about the warrior with the sword?"

"No lord, it is one about a young warrior fighting an Irish champion."

Next to me, de Clare asked, "Why is that important?"

"Each clan will have their own songs and chants. Padraig told me. These are not the men we fought before. I was worried that Waterford's men might have joined and that we would have to fight them again."

The sun rose and the Vikings, still chanting, began to move. Since they had formed their line Aelric had conserved his arrows. Now our archers began to pick men off as they stepped over bodies and gaps appeared. I saw one warrior who was close to the centre of the line stumbled as his seal skin boot caught on the shield strap of a man whose body he stepped over. Although he was mailed he had no coif and I watched an arrow hit him in the neck. He stood briefly transfixed and then he fell forward. As he did so the four men behind stumbled and two more were hit. The leader shouted something and they halted to dress their lines. In those few moments, three more men were slain. The ones at the back would have even more bodies to negotiate.

They were forty paces from us and I saw my archers' arrows targeting the men at the rear who were climbing over dead Vikings. We would still have the same number to face but they would have less support. When they were twenty paces from us I shouted, "Brace!" I put my right foot behind me and felt James' shield in my back. We would be pushed but it would be back and not off our feet. I placed the haft of the spear against my right foot and James slid his spear over my head and rested it on my shoulder.

The Vikings ran the last ten paces. They could not keep the same tight shape and I saw men in the second and third ranks disappear as our arrows hit them. Then they struck us. The warrior I was facing had a spear and he rammed it at my head. I bent my head forward slightly and the spear hit the reinforced strip on my helmet. My ears rang and my head was forced back but, as I looked up I saw that he had run into the spearhead of James' weapon. The press of men behind forced the spear into his skull. His body went limp. It was held there by the men behind. I was forced back a hand span but no more. Then I felt something hit my spear as a Viking hand tore the dead warrior from James' spear. It slurped as it came out of his eye. Eye, brains and gore hung from it.

Freed I was able to pull my own spear back and ram it again, blindly into the mass of men before me. I saw a sword come down from above me. I lifted my shield and took the blow. I saw a Viking face and I pulled back my head to butt it. Something struck my spear but I could not see what then I felt a crack in my hand as someone sliced through the spear. I lifted the broke shaft and raised my head. I had hit the Viking in the mouth. His teeth were broken and bloody. He spat some at me and cursed. I plunged the broken end into the man's open screaming mouth. I punched hard. He began to gag and choke. A spear came over my left shoulder and sliced across his neck. Dropping my broken spear, I was able to draw my sword as the man before me slipped to the ground. I saw that there was just one man behind him. We had hope.

"Hold them! Hold them!"

A spear was thrust at me and I felt it hit me in the right shoulder. It pierced the mail and stuck in my arm. I felt blood trickling down. A hand reached forward from behind me and pulled the spear away. I heard a Norse voice shout something and Padraig shouted, "Lord, they are coming for you and the standard!"

James shouted, "Close ranks around the Earl!"

I felt de Clare press closely to me on one side and Harry Lightfoot on the other. The Vikings filled the gaps behind the men facing me. There were three ranks again and they lurched at us. This time it was just a wall of shields with a few spears. They were trying to push us from our feet. With three ranks against our two they would succeed.

I felt us being pushed. I tried to recollect what was behind us. Just then I heard a horn sound and then a second. The pressure from the shields seemed to diminish slightly. "Push back!" I felt James' shield in my back and I pushed off my right foot against the shield before me. It did not move but, then again, we were no longer going backwards. I could see little for there was a wall of shields before me and my helmet limited my peripheral vision but I heard to my right and left, the clash of metal on metal and the wail of men.

A voice shouted, "It is Le Gros! It is our men."

Irish War

I pushed my sword at the shields and hit wood. I moved it down until there was no resistance and I swung it. I hit something. It was a leg. Where there was a leg there was a foot. I moved the sword down and pushed hard. As I did so I leaned into the shield with all my weight. "Push!"

Suddenly my sword went through flesh and then struck the ground. Before me a man screamed before falling backwards. It was as though a dam had burst. Where there had been a dark wall of shields, the falling man had punched a hole in his own line. I lifted my sword and lunged at the mail byrnie before me. The Viking's shield had been held above the man I had just wounded. My sword drove into the man's chest and he fell backwards. I barely kept my feet as I stumbled over the wounded man. I heard a grunt as James ended his life and then we were in the open. I saw that we had breached their line. The Vikings were running for the gate.

Even as I blocked a blow from my right I saw arrows felling those who fled. The man who had struck at me had his life ended by Harry Lightfoot's sword.

"Get the gates! Do not let them bar it!"

I saw Roger of Bath leading my men at arms to race through the gap we had created. I felt warm and sticky blood in my hand. I had forgotten about the wound. James saw it and shouted, "You are wounded! Padraig, fetch a healer. Arne Arneson, come and protect the Earl."

I shook my head, "I am fine!"

James shook his head, "What kind of squire would I be if I let you die of your wounds after such a victory."

"Victory?"

"Aye lord. They have surrendered, look!"

I turned and looked at the gatehouse. My men stood on the top and were banging their shields. He was right. We had won.

Chapter 15

King Ascall mac Ragnaill meic Torcaill had escaped. Two drekar had managed to leave Dyflin when Raymond Le Gros and Sir Maurice had brought their men to our aid. We had slaughtered more than a hundred Vikings and many more were wounded. More than half of the wounded would die of their wounds and the other half would never be warriors again. It was the end of the Viking threat at least on the east coast. There were still Vikings in the far west but they would not threaten Leinster. I was told all of this for the priest who tended me would not let me leave my bed.

"The wound came close to the bone lord. I will need to cleanse and then stitch it. Count Striguil is in command and he will do all that is needed."

James said, "He is right lord. We have had a great victory and done all that was needed. We can go home now."

"Perhaps. We will see."

By the time my wound had been attended to the town was completely in our hands. As I had been stitched and eaten food, the priest allowed me to walk into Dyflin. I was greeted by cheers and shouts from my men. I was flanked by my men at arms as we marched into the heart of this powerful Norse kingdom. Count Striguil and Raymond le Gros walked towards me. Both were still covered in our enemies' blood but both appeared whole. They saw my right arm in a sling.

"You have an honourable wound, Earl Marshal."

"It is nothing. I understand the king escaped."

"He did but he only took two boatloads. We will make this a stronger place than he left it. I will have Sir Raymond begin a castle here. He will be my constable in this town. This is a good site for a castle. The harbour is a good one and it is the border to the kingdoms north of here."

Irish War

I nodded, "Soon it will be Christmas and war will cease. I think I will take my men home. We have done enough and fulfilled our promise to the King of Leinster."

Count Striguil came closer and spoke quietly, "Earl Marshal the Irish do not stop making war in the winter. Here the winters are wet rather than cold. I would that you wait until we have the two castles defensible."

I looked at Padraig, "Is it true about the winters?"

"Yes lord. If we get snow it is on the high peaks but it does rain. The roads become slithery tracks."

"Then they cannot make war."

Sir Raymond said, "Not true Earl Marshal. It is not war as we fight it but they come in the night to slit throats and steal livestock. Your men and your archers have proved to be the equal of many knights. I beg you to stay until Spring."

I wanted to return home. I was desperate to see Ruth and Samuel but I had in me a sense of honour that would not allow me to think of myself if others needed me. I nodded, "Very well. Until the Spring."

We spent a week in the port. During that time the wet weather of winter swept in from the west. Padraig told me that the winds from the south and west were the wet ones. He happily prophesied that we would have this weather for months. After we had helped Sir Raymond lay the groundwork for the castle, we left with most of the army to return to Ferns. Sir Maurice and his men stayed with Sir Raymond. The castle would be well garrisoned. Already we had repaired the burned section of wall but Sir Raymond intended to build in stone. We had the coin to send to England and buy good stone. We had found gold and silver in the hall of the king. He had fled so quickly that he had not had time to take it. I knew that Prince Domhnall Caemanach mac Murchada would be less than happy.

I let Count Striguil ride ahead of me. The glory would be his and we both knew that it would help made his position in the king's household even stronger. As we headed back I spoke with Padraig about the Prince. "He has brothers lord. Conchobar is the next in line. He was not taken hostage and he and his father are close. If his father could choose an heir then it would be Conchobar."

"And he cannot choose?"

"Oh yes lord. It is often done like that but here in Ireland it often results in murder. The High King's brother was blinded by a rival brother when he was proposed as king."

"And what of Count Striguil? How does he stand? He is married to the King's daughter. Does that give him a claim to the throne?"

He looked thoughtful, "I believe so lord but I am not certain."

James asked, "How do you know so much about this?"

"When I was the Bishop's slave I was often present when these matters were discussed. I was a slave and I was like the table on which they placed their wine. I was not seen."

James looked at me, "But Count Striguil is Norman. What would the effect be for him? Would King Henry be happy?"

"You are clever, James and you are right in your assumption. The King would not like a Norman ruling what he saw as a potential rival kingdom. Ireland is close to Chester and Carlisle. Besides Sir Richard has a claim to the Dukedom of Normandy. I do not think that he would choose to exercise that claim but King Henry will be aware of it." We were just five miles from Ferns. "I will speak with Sir Richard when time allows. Now is not the time. The prospect of needing a new king is not even close. King Diarmait may not be a fighting warrior but he has some years ahead of him."

The Count was accoladed as a hero for having driven the Vikings from the jewel that was Dyflin. The richest port in the whole of Hibernia, it gave money and power to whoever held it. When we arrived, I saw the Count's wife and her father, along with Conchobar praising the Count. The exception to the praise and adulation was Prince Domhnall and his coterie of followers. They scowled, grumbled and mumbled. He would bear watching. I feared he might try to do the Count harm. I had no worries on a battlefield but, until we had a castle built, then he was in danger for he would be sleeping in the King's hall. I could not leave him; not just yet.

They had worked hard on the castle. You could now see its shape. The ditch and the foundations had been the first elements to be built. You could see the shape of the four towers and the gatehouse. The mason had worked well. Then again, he and his men were being well paid. The Vikings we had slain had been rich. We now had even more treasure coming thanks to the capture of Dyflin. They had laid the first course of the outer and inner walls. Men were using wheelbarrows to infill them with smaller stones. Other men were building the treadmill crane for soon we would need it. We had the wagon, timber and rope we had taken from Dyflin. They would prove useful in the hauling of stones and the building of a second treadmill crane.

My men were unhappy about the prospect of staying in the Irish warrior hall. Roger of Bath asked if they could make a hall at the castle site. I was more than happy to agree. We had our own servants and the nearby woods teemed with game. Until Count Striguil was secure we would be there to protect his castle while avoiding any of the problems which arose by sharing a warrior hall.

Before we had taken Dyflin we had experienced them. Warriors who had no war to fight drank, gambled and whored. Those three activities invariably led to violence. One Leinsterman had been killed in a fight with one of Raymond Fitzgerald's men. Now that Raymond Le Gros was the constable at Dyflin there was no issue but the Irishmen carried on blood feuds. Being separate helped us avoid such problems.

My men were hard working and the first use of the wagon was to fetch freshly cut trees. They were adept at splitting them into planks. After digging eight post holes, the frame went up in one day. Stones were packed around the timbers and the smaller branches used to tie in the larger pieces of wood. The roof was made up of the shorter lengths of split wood. They would not be watertight but we had seen how the locals built and copied them. Instead of wattle and daub, they used a technique used by the Vikings and adapted by the Irish. They cut turf. It worked not only for walls but also the roof. In three days we had our own hall. The floor was covered in rushes we collected from the river and we used the remains of the trees for tables and chairs. Once built we did not need to be in contact with the Leinstermen and their plots. Count Striguil, his knights and his men at arms were. We saw the effects when two of Count Striguil's men were hanged for murder following a vicious fight in the warrior hall. As it was around the Christmas feast it was particularly unwelcome. We knew nothing of it, at the time, for we celebrated in our own hall with our own food. We had started to brew our own beer. The soft water made for a particularly pleasant tasting ale. We had even built a bread oven so that we could bake our own bread. The waste from the brewery gave that a distinctive taste too. I began to enjoy my life while planning for my return to England.

My wound healed and I took to riding the countryside with James, Padraig, Aelric and Harry Lightfoot. We hunted and we explored. We spoke, through Padraig, to the people. What I discovered surprised me.

Since our arrival, they had had more peace than they had known for some years. We had captured three towns and fought half a dozen battles! It told me much about this violent land. It was Theophany and we were heading back across a frosty land when I broached a subject which had been on my mind for some time. Padraig and James were riding next to me. Aelric and Harry led the two sumpters with the wild pig we had killed.

"Padraig, soon, probably in the next couple of months or so, I will be returning to England. I release you from my service and I will give you coin so that you can start life anew. What I wish to know is where do you wish this life? Here or on Man?"

He was silent and when he spoke it was in a low earnest voice, "Lord, I would not leave your service. I know that you will not need me to translate and I am not a particularly useful warrior but I could watch your horses. I could help you dress. I could…"

I held up my hand, "Padraig, I am more than happy for you to continue in my service but know you that it means leaving your home and going to a strange land."

He shook his head, "This is not my home, lord. This has unhappy memories for me. The Bishop was not a pleasant master. Some of his priests," he shuddered, "I will put those memories from my head. Therein lies madness. As for Man. I am no Viking. I was taken too young. A Viking starts to become a warrior when he is seven summers old. He can fight with bow, sling, spear and sword by the time he has seen ten summers and by twelve summers he will be taking an oar and raiding. I would be mocked and I would find myself being a thrall if I returned hence. You, lord, are the only person who has treated me with kindness. I would serve you."

"Then I accept your offer."

From that day forth Padraig never stopped smiling! He and James got on well together and my men all had a soft spot for him. The castle grew. The lack of snow meant they could work even longer than in England and it was already as high as Padraig. My new servant also proved to be a useful source of information. It was he who told us that Conchobar, the King's favourite son had gone missing. He had been at the King's hall delivering a message from me to Count Striguil asking when I could return to England. He rushed back, "Lord Prince Conchobar has disappeared."

"Disappeared?"

"He has not been seen for three days. There is a rumour that he has fled north to join the High King."

"And whence do the rumours emanate?"

"His brother, Prince Domhnall."

"Then I do not believe it. Fetch Aelric and my archers. James, come with me and we will speak with Count Striguil."

We found the Count and his wife in the church on the opposite side of the cathedral. I could see that she was with child. "Earl Marshal! Why do you keep apart? My husband has told me great things about you and yet you and your men are like monks in your little hall by the new castle."

"You should visit it, Count. It is almost as tall as me now and when the longer days come it will be defensible."

"That is good. As you can see, I am going to be a father."

"Excellent. Is your father pleased, Princess?"

"He was but since my brother disappeared…"

I nodded, "What do you think happened to him?"

They looked at each other. The Count said, "My wife fears that Prince Domhnall has something to do with it. Her father had been speaking about leaving his kingdom to Conchobar."

Aoife put her hand on mine, "We have no proof, Earl Marshal and my brother," She shook her head, "he is a very cruel man but I cannot think he hurt my little brother."

I nodded, "I will take my men and look for him."

"Where will you look? He could have gone anywhere."

"Did he take a horse or servants?"

"No, he went alone."

"My men and I have been hunting in many of the woods around here for the past seven days. We have not seen any sign of him. Where we have not hunted is in the woods by the stream which leads to the Slaney River. We will try there. We can ride as far as Ballycarney. If he is not there…"

Count Striguil rose, "I should come with you."

I shook my head, "Stay close to your wife and keep guards around you."

"Surely I am safe."

I did not answer.

I took Padraig with us in case we met any locals who might be questioned. The stream in question was so small that it had no name. We did not hunt there for it was difficult to cross the undergrowth and there were easier places to hunt. James and I would not be of much use. Aelric and my archers were the finest scouts and trackers I had. Aiden, Edward and Edgar were better but they were an ocean and mountain divide away in Stockton.

We were almost at Ballycarney when Tomas ap Tomas shouted us over. The stream twisted and turned. The rains must have eroded the soil around a sapling and it had fallen across the stream making a small dam. There we found Prince Conchobar. His throat had been cut. Had the sapling not fallen then his body would have made its way, eventually, to the Slaney and thence the sea. His disappearance would have remained a mystery. We put his body on Padraig's horse and he rode double with James. I sent Will Green Leg back to warn Count Striguil. Treachery was afoot.

Aelric said, "That body has been in the water for at least two days, lord."

"Thank you Aelric. We need to keep a close watch on our hall."

Aetheling said, "If you are worried about Prince Domhnall then I can end his threat easily."

I smiled; Aetheling was deadly with a knife, "Thank you but I fear that would do the Count's cause no good at all." That set me to thinking about the Count and his position. Now that Conchobar was dead it made it more likely that Sir Richard would be the next King of Leinster. I wondered just what the Count planned. If he became King of Leinster would he try to become High King? From what I had seen that would be relatively easy. He would need more men than he had at present but there were many landless young knights who would flock to his banner. That, of course, would not please King Henry.

Count Striguil had some of his men awaiting us when we arrived at the King's hall. I think his daughter must have given her father the news for she supported his arm as they came out of the hall. He looked ancient. "It is true then. He is dead. How did he die? Did he fall in the stream and drown?"

His voice told me that he did not believe it was an accident and he hoped I would lie. I could not do that; not even for his peace of mind. I shook my head. "He was murdered, your majesty."

Just then Prince Domhnall came out. He must have heard my words, "And you were the murderer, Earl Marshal. For it is very convenient that you discovered his body."

I dismounted and walked over to him, "You may be upset about the death of your brother but if you call me a liar or a murderer then you and I will settle this by trial by combat! We will let God decide who is a liar and a murderer." He backed off and I saw absolute terror in his eyes.

Aoife said firmly, "Apologise brother! If the Earl Marshal was the murderer then the body would have remained hidden. Are you such a fool that you cannot see that? He was not murdered by a Norman but by an Irishman!"

The Prince remained silent.

The King said, "Apologize or I shall banish you!"

He jabbed his finger in the direction of the King. "You take her side against me as you did with my brother. He deserved to die." He pointed at his sister. "And you will have to watch your back now!" Just then four men galloped up with a fifth horse and the Prince threw himself on its back. "This is not over! I will have Leinster, one way or another!"

We would have followed him had the King not keeled over and fallen to the ground. We all ran to him and the five men galloped away. The King was taken to his chambers where the Bishop of Ferns brought healers to him. After giving him restoratives he came to. Count Striguil, his daughter and the Bishop were permitted to see him. I had the guards doubled.

I sent Padraig, with James and Harry Lightfoot as bodyguards to question his servants who remained. Most of his men had fled with him. When they returned after interrogating the remaining men he said, "I believe he has gone north to the land of the Southern Uí Neill. His men said that he struck up a friendship with a young chief from just over the border when he was a hostage with the High King."

"Thank you. We will see what the Count wishes to do about this."

"That is simple," said Harry, "go and kill the bastard. If he murdered once he will do so again."

"Perhaps."

It was many hours later when the Count came to speak with us. "The King lives but he is shocked and shaken. He has named me and his daughter as joint heirs before the Bishop."

"Then I would watch yourself. The Prince is a murderer. You now stand in his path to the throne."

"I know."

"I discovered where we think he has gone. He has probably gone to the land of the Southern Uí Neill."

"That is what my wife believes. We have more men coming from England. We will gather a large force and go and capture him. We will bring him back for trial."

"Better we just kill him."

"He is still the King's son." I thought back to King Henry and what he had done to prevent his brothers from claiming the throne. He had been ruthless. Count Striguil would need to learn.

For the next month, as we gathered our forces I watched the castle rise layer of stones by layer of stones. By Easter, it would be finished and I could go home. I had one more task to perform first. I had to persuade Count Striguil to kill Domhnall rather than take him prisoner. Taking the Prince prisoner might cost more of our men their lives. In the end, I did not need to persuade him. His wife did. When the King died, his daughter said because of a broken heart for her brother Conchobar, she told her husband that if he did not kill him then he would try to take the throne from them. She was now heavily pregnant and her words had an effect on Count Striguil.

Our departure was delayed by the funeral of the King. It was a solemn affair and the cathedral was packed. After he had been laid in his tomb then every Irishman drank himself into a stupor as did many of the women. Queen Aoife told us that it was the custom. The Bishop affirmed, the next day, that Richard was King of Leinster. He anointed the King and the Queen's heads with oil but the crown would not be placed on his head in the cathedral until the only other potential heir, Domhnall, was dead.

Two weeks later we left Ferns having been blessed by the Bishop. He made it seem like a holy crusade. Irish scouts, eager for vengeance, had discovered the exact whereabouts of Prince Domhnall. He was with a local chief, Turloch Mór Ó Conor at Athlone, on the Shannon. There had always been a ford there but there was now a bridge. The scouts told us that they had recently built a fort to protect the bridge. When questioned closer they told us that it was a series of ditches with two concentric palisades. There was no keep. Our exact plans would have to wait until we were closer.

We went first to Dyflin. Members of the Fitzgerald family had come to help their brother and, as the garrison was large enough, we took Sir Maurice and his men with us. They had already proved to be both reliable and skilled. The journey from Dyflin was almost seventy miles. Our scouts told us that there were members of the Ó Conor clan at

Tullamore. It was roughly halfway to our destination. There was no fort there and Sir Maurice came up with the clever idea of taking Tullamore. It would give us a base and we would be reducing the number of men we would have to eventually fight. As we had to pass through the town to get to Athlone it made sense to me. Another factor was that by taking it we would be enlarging the Count's new kingdom. I did not call him king. He was not yet crowned. The main reason I did not use the title was because I was King Henry's Earl Marshal. If I called him king then it made it legitimate.

We spoke about the coronation as we headed towards Tullamore. "King Henry may not be happy, Richard."

"I know. You are his friend and mentor, Earl Marshal. I beg you to speak to him. Although I was unhappy and disappointed not to be given the title, Earl of Pembroke, I am King Henry's man. I would not vie for the crown of England nor the Dukedom of Normandy."

"Let us be honest with one another. We both know that Leinster is just the start. You could become King of Ireland. That would seem a threat to King Henry."

"Then tell him I pay homage to him. I will be his King of Leinster."

"You know that I will never lie to my king. I need to know that you mean what you say. When you are crowned we will speak again and then we will seek your wife's advice."

"My wife?"

"You may have no desire to be High King of Ireland but she may wish to be High Queen."

For the next ten miles, he was quiet. It was only when the scouts rode in to say that Tullamore was eight miles ahead that he roused himself. "We need to make camp in five miles or so lest we alert them."

"Agreed. I will send our archers around the village to camp on the far side. Our purpose here is to prevent warning of our arrival reaching Domhnall."

I could not get over how flat and featureless the land hereabouts was. It made a secretive approach much harder. We had a cold camp with one man in three, knights included, on guard. The Count, Sir Maurice and I sat and discussed our plan.

The Count had spoken with the men who knew Tullamore. "The scouts have said there are no defences. We can simply ride in and slay or capture every man. With Tullamore safe, we can march and reach Athlone by dark."

"I favour a night crossing of the Shannon."

Count Striguil said, "That is risky is it not? There are dangers."

"There are more dangers in trying to cross a river with arrows and stones showering us. They have a fort. That will make a difference." They both nodded. "We ride in three conroi. We approach from southeast and west. Aelric has the north. He will shut the door on any escape to warn Athlone. We will need twenty men to guard our prisoners. Choose them from amongst the older knights and men at arms. We will ride with the sun behind us."

Sir Maurice shook his head, "It has been so long since I saw the sun that I wondered if it has not abandoned us. What you mean, Earl Marshal is that we ride in with the rain clouds behind us."

I laughed, "I confess that it is a wet country."

"You do not wish to go in at night?"

"There may not be a river but there may be obstacles in our way. Besides my archers need daylight to get into position."

Padraig now had his own position. He carried the banner and rode behind and amongst my men at arms with James. The fact that he carried the banner freed up James to protect my back. I had twelve men at arms and I was flanked by three on each side. Count Striguil had offered me some of his knights but I had declined. I knew my men at arms and what they lacked in breeding they made up for in experience. They knew one end of a sword from another and knew how to win in a fight. Unconcerned with glory they had two purposes in life: one was to protect me and the other was to kill the enemy and take whatever they carried.

Leaving our spare equipment and horses with our servants, they would follow when they heard four blasts on the horn, we mounted and headed into the lightening sky. I had knights on my two flanks. All had now fought alongside me in enough battles for me to be confident that they would obey orders. We walked in the grey light until we saw the huts ahead and we smelled the smoke from their fires. I began to see that we were crossing fields. They had been cleared of their winter crops and lay bare. They were not flat but there were neither crops nor plough marks yet. We had a direct route to the huts. As soon as we were seen a cry went off and I said, "Forward!"

I spurred Storm Bringer so that he was cantering. It was an easy gait and would not strain him. It meant that when I put my spurs in again he would be able to gallop very quickly. Horns sounded in the settlement. I heard the wail of women. They were used to raids by men. They normally resulted in life as a slave. The sound of our hooves added the threat of the unknown. Full daylight had arrived and Sir Maurice had been correct, it was a grey day. The rain had not yet begun and that was a mercy.

I glanced to my left and right. I could see the other two conroi of knights and men at arms. The huts were surrounded. The Clan Ó Conor came to meet us. They made a couple of long lines. They were not continuous and they were not supporting each other. I had time, as we headed towards them to see that they fought in little knots of men. I guessed they were families. There were a few helmets and a few shields. This time some of the shields were square ones I had not seen before.

When we were a hundred paces from them I spurred Storm Bringer and shouted, "Charge!" I held my spear to the side and I held it overhand. I did not need a couched spear. I would be striking down.

This time we were together. We were not exactly boot to boot; the slightly uneven ground did not suit that but we were tight enough and the Irish would have a wall of spears and snapping horses to face. My men at arms and I had about thirty men before us. There were a group of eight who stood together and tried to make a shield wall. It was not a Viking shield wall. It was just men who held a hopeful shield before them. The shields did not overlap. They were in a single rank and there were only five spears facing us. As we neared them I raised my spear and thrust down over the top of the shield and down into the man's chest. He thrust at me with his spear at the same time. It was fire-hardened and it did no damage to my mail. My padded gambeson meant it did not even hurt overmuch. I allowed his body to be dragged from my spear and I raised it ready to strike again.

I saw that the next knot of men was slightly to my left. "Wheel left!" This time there were fifteen or so of them. One of them looked to be a leader of some kind. He had a fancy helmet which was adorned with some sort of animal's skull. He was bare-chested and held a long axe. These were singing as we approached. I observed that all along our line our men had swept through the opposition. "Close ranks!" I reined Storm Bringer in slightly so that my men at arms could get closer to me. If we could sweep through this group then we might have broken the resistance of the clan.

Suddenly they broke ranks and ran at us! It was unexpected. Instead of fifteen men in two ranks, they ran to try to surround us. One ran and leapt in the air at me. He held a two-handed sword in his hands. With limed hair and a heavily tattooed chest, he looked like some wild beast. I pulled back my arm and my spear plucked his body from the air. My horse's speed and his jump mean that the spear came through his body and the weight of it snapped the spear in two.

I saw Davy of Ingleby pitched from his horse as the chief hacked into the leg of his mount. He landed heavily and did not move. The sudden attack had broken our ranks. I wheeled Storm Bringer around as I drew my sword. The chief ran to Davy's recumbent body. He raised his axe to take his head. I spurred Storm Bringer and he leapt, almost into the air. Even as the sword was slicing down I leaned from the saddle and swung my sword in a wide sweep. As the axe descended my sword hacked into his side and then his spine. My arm was jarred and numbed by the force of the blow. His arms were thrown up and then my sword was pulled from the dying man's body and he fell to the ground.

I reined in Storm Bringer and glanced around. I saw my men at arms had also stopped and were finishing off the men who had charged us. I risked taking off my helmet so that I could have a better view of the battle. We had won. I saw riderless horses and I saw men at arms and knights walking but the chief and his men had been the last opposition. I turned Storm Bringer and rode back to Davy. Peter Strong Arm was kneeling next to him.

I dismounted. James was at my side and I handed my reins to him. "How is he?"

Peter had taken Davy's helmet from him. "He lives." He pointed to Davy's left arm which lay at an unnatural angle. "I know not what other wounds there are but he has a broken arm and he has a blow to the head."

"James, signal the healers and the servants."

"Aye lord."

I turned to Peter, "You and the rest of my men at arms stay here with Davy until the healers come." I pointed to the body of the dead chief. "If there is treasure then it will be about him." He nodded. With an injured comrade, treasure was the least of his concern. "Come, James and Padraig. We will ride into the settlement."

"Be careful lord."

"Do not worry Peter Strong Arm. Their chief is dead. They will either flee or surrender. We have won but I wonder at the cost."

"They fought well lord."

"They did, James, and I think I made the right decision to cross the river at night. I will have to give much thought to how we defeat men such as this inside a fort."

Chapter 16

Aelric and his archers had stopped the villagers from fleeing. We slaughtered some of their animals for food. While our wounded warriors were tended to I allowed them to collect and bury their dead. I spoke with Sir Maurice and Count Striguil. "They were brave men and wild!"

The Count was shaken, "Aye, Earl Marshal. I thought to just ride through them. It cost us eight horses and five men. The men we can replace but not the horses."

I nodded, "And that confirms my plan. We do not risk our horses when we attack Athlone. Have the men get as much rest as they can. We leave the wounded and the healers here. Padraig tells me that it is twenty-three miles or so to Athlone. We leave in the dark of night." I spied the Irish families returning from burying their dead. "Come, Count, it is time that you became king. Padraig, we will speak to these people."

Gathering them around us I spoke to them through Padraig. The women appeared to have many children each and they gathered them protectively around their feet. Padraig had told me that they feared they would be enslaved.

"First, you will not be enslaved." After Padraig had spoken I allowed some moments for that to sink in and for them to be less fearful. "There is a new King of Leinster, King Richard." I pointed to the Count. "He will build a castle here. You can continue to farm your fields. There will be a stone church and a priest so that you can worship. You will have protection from other Irish warriors who may wish to do you harm."

Again, I allowed them to take that in and then there was a hubbub of noise. Eventually one woman came forward. She looked to be better dressed than the rest and had a bronze torc around her neck. I guessed that she was the wife of the chief.

She spoke and Padraig translated, "Morag, the wife of the chief, asked what about men? They have women who have needs. There are children who need a father."

I nodded, "Tell her that there will be men here who will wish to take wives. There will be more men coming."

When Padraig had told her, she came over and bowed to Count Striguil. She spoke, "She accepts you as her lord, Count Striguil."

As we headed into the dark night I felt happier. We had not needed to leave as many guards as I had expected. The women had all helped to prepare food and to care for the wounded. Davy of Ingleby and the others would be safe. This was not England. Here rulers changed quickly. The old would be swept away in a sea of blood and the new would sweep in until they, too, were removed. That had been the Irish way. It would now change. Norman rule meant order.

Although the ground was relatively flat it did descend, slowly towards the Shannon. The road was not built by the Romans. It twisted and turned. Aelric and his men, along with the Irish scouts, kept us on the right route. Our horses smelled the water. They began to move faster to reach it. Dawn was still some time away. If they had a fort then any sentries would hear us as we splashed through the river. That could not be helped. It was vital that they could not see us. We could have ridden across the bridge but I did not see the point in risking armed sentries who would raise the alarm. By the time any sentries in the fort realised that a Norman army was approaching my archers would be across and they would not be able to contest the crossing. We waited at the river's edge while the rear elements arrived. I wanted us all to cross in one movement. The scouts would go first for they knew the ford. They would be followed by the archers and then I would come next with my men at arms. I had been told that the ford was wide enough for ten men. We were eight men wide. As soon as the last man arrived I waved my standard and the scouts, followed by Aelric, headed across.

I soon realised why they had built the bridge. The river was just a hundred paces wide but, when we reached the deepest part the water lapped up to our girths. The current tried to pull us downstream. I heard the clamour from inside the fort as we splashed ashore. The fort was four hundred paces away. It was a large black shadow by the river and the bridge. We had been told that it had only been recently built.

Aelric and his men dismounted and unslung their bows. I did not think that the Ó Conor would do anything immediately but this was not the time to take chances. We were as far into the territory of the High King as we had yet been. Until now we had been in Leinster or the borderlands. Now we were isolated. We would have a long ride back to Tullamore and even that was not secure.

By the time the last knights and men at arms, along with the little baggage we had brought had arrived, then dawn was breaking. We had seen burning brands on the walls of the fort and at both ends of the bridge. I heard hooves as a horse galloped across the bridge heading towards the east. They would be riding to Tullamore to summon help. They would not see much of us. We would be shadows; moving shadows but shadows nonetheless. I had no doubt that Domhnall knew who we were and he would have told Chief Ó Conor. What would they do? I dismounted and handed my reins to James. He and Padraig also dismounted. I was not wearing my helmet. When Count Striguil and Sir Maurice appeared, I gestured for them to accompany me closer to the fort. We stopped at what I estimated to be two hundred and fifty paces from the walls. Had they been Vikings then I might have stopped further away but the bows of the Irish could rarely, even from elevation, reach more than a hundred and fifty paces. We were safe.

I waved a hand around. "This is flat. It looks like the water floods over here when there are heavy rains. If we need to we can threaten them with mounted knights."

"But we are not risking our horses are we, Earl Marshal?"

Sir Maurice's men had lost horses. He intended to lose no more.

"No. First, we will try to talk to them and ask for them to hand over Domhnall. They will, of course, refuse. After a couple of days, when their rider from Tullamore has not returned they might be more willing to negotiate but once we have seen the scale of the defences we will begin our attack."

"On foot."

Count Striguil knew how to fight now, "Yes, Sir Maurice, the Earl Marshal and I have fought like this before. Unless they have well-constructed walls and defences then we have the upper hand for we have mail."

We stood and I assessed the ground as the sun came up from our right. I saw that they had used a natural bank and the spoil from the bridge foundations to make a series of ditches and ramparts. They were neither deep ditches nor high ramparts. The ditches looked to be no more than a couple of paces deep and the ramparts were the same height. The wooden palisade was perhaps a little higher. I guessed they had a fighting step rather than a fighting platform. The town wall, which was also wooden was behind the fort. The fort was there to guard the town and the bridge. If you attacked either the bridge or the town then both could be reinforced from the fort.

I saw men on the ramparts. Two standards flew: that of the Ó Conor family and that of the Kingdom of Leinster. Domhnall was staking his claim to his father's kingdom, albeit from a distance. The men who lined the two concentric lines of wooden walls varied from warriors with helmets and shields to those with limed hair and tattoos. In my experience, neither of them was particularly effective at stopping an arrow or a sword!

"How would we gain entry, Earl Marshal?"

Sir Maurice had wondered at my extended silence. I was examining the entrance to the fort. They had made it hard for a ram to attack it. One bridge led across the first ditch and there was a gate with two small towers. The second gate was offset by about thirty paces. An attacker would be subject to missiles as they turned and made their way to the second one. I assumed that, on the town side, there would be another bridge both as a means of reinforcement and as an escape route. The fort's position meant that you either had to take the bridge or take the fort to get to the town.

I had seen enough. "Come Count Striguil. Let us go and greet your brother in law!"

"I doubt it will be a pleasant meeting, Earl Marshal."

We mounted our horses and, with our squires and standards, we rode, bare-headed towards the gates. Padraig rode directly behind me. Behind us, Aelric and ten archers followed just twenty paces behind. Any attempt at treachery would be quickly quashed. We halted twenty paces from the first ditch which meant we were fifty paces from the gate where the standards flew.

I waited until someone spoke. He had a helmet with a metal animal on the top and I guessed it was the chief. That was confirmed when he spoke and Padraig translated, "I am Lord Turloch Mór Ó Conor. Why are you in my land and dressed for war?"

I spoke and Padraig translated, "We are here to secure a murderer, Prince Domhnall Caemanach mac Murchada. He killed Prince Conchobar mac Murchada and fled before his father could impose justice."

The chief flashed a look at Prince Domhnall. I assumed that the story he had heard was not the one I had given. The chief returned his gaze to me, "His father is dead and the Prince is now King of Leinster."

"This is Richard de Clare, Count of Striguil and now, through his marriage to Princess Aoife mac Murchada, the rightful ruler of Leinster. The Bishop of Ferns has anointed him as king. When we return, he will be crowned in Ferns Cathedral. All was done well and in accordance with both the King's wishes and the King's will."

When Padraig had finished translating there was a heated discussion and I saw Prince Domhnall gesturing towards us and remonstrating. After some time, the chief turned. "You may be right, Norman, but the High King is coming. He does not wish a foreigner to rule any part of Ireland. You will be driven into the sea."

"If we attack, chief, then you will lose many men."

He pointed to the east, "Already we have allies coming. You will not take our walls so easily."

I took out the torc my men had taken from the chieftain of Tullamore, "Were your allies led by a man who wore this torc?"

Even before Padraig had finished translating the men on the walls began banging their shields in anger and shouting. I turned to the Count of Striguil. "I think there will be little point in delaying an attack." He nodded. "Padraig tell him that he has until noon to surrender. After that time, we will attack!"

After the ultimatum had been given we rode back. "Sir Maurice have your men begin to build an onager."

"Lord that will take days. We have neither rope nor wood."

I pointed to a stand of trees. "Have your men cut those trees down. This is a ruse. I have no intention of building an onager. I want them to think that they have more time than they do. The Prince knows how effective an onager can be."

"Aye, Earl Marshal."

As he went off I said, "And you Count Striguil, I would have you make a defensive camp. We may not need it but if the High King is foolish enough to come a third time we will give him a warm welcome."

"But he gave hostages!"

Padraig said, "Aye lord and he has, in the past, blinded his own brothers because they offended him. I would not gamble that the hostages are of any value to the High King."

"Padraig may be right but I do not think that the High King will let them die without good reason. If he comes then it will be because he thinks he can win."

As he went off I said, "Aelric, fetch my men at arms and your archers. While they are debating what they wish to do I will give them something else to think about. Bring kindling, oil and flint." I had no intention of waiting until noon. I would not break my word but I had said nothing about the bridge.

James asked, "What are we to do then, lord?"

I pointed to the bridge. "That is valuable to them but it is made of wood. I will threaten it. By doing so it will stop them interfering with the building of the camp. Padraig, you stay here in case Count Striguil needs you."

"Lord, why do you not call him King? He is King of Leinster."

"True but if I call him that then, as King Henry's representative I am acknowledging him as such. King Henry may not wish the Count to be king." I saw that Padraig was confused. "If Count Striguil is to be called King it must be by King Henry first. King Henry will only do that if Count Striguil acknowledges King Henry's position as his liege lord."

When my men arrived, we headed back across the ford. The Irish, despite the truce, sent arrows in our direction. They fell woefully short and told Aelric and me that they had poor bows and were not skilled archers. Once we had crossed the river we headed south and when we were out of sight, we headed back inland to the road. As we headed towards the road I saw a rider galloping west. I assumed it was the messenger they had sent to Tullamore. He must have seen our standards from afar and returned to his chief.

Once we reached the road I explained what I intended. "We will charge the guards at the eastern end of the bridge and then Aelric and his archers will clear the far end. I intend to set fire to the bridge."

Roger of Bath said, "They will douse the flames, lord."

"To do so they will have to leave their fort and chase us hence. They will manage to do that but Aelric and his archers will thin their numbers first. Then, on the morrow, we ride to the town wall and attempt to set fire to the town walls."

"And they will have to come to drive us off and douse the flames."

"Exactly and when they do then the Count of Striguil and myself will lead the attack on the gate. We are making them spread their large numbers of men to both extremes of their defensive line and we attack with the majority of our men at the gate; their weak spot."

They knew what to do and, with me leading my men at arms, we galloped down the road towards the bridge. We did not take spears and we did not wear helmets. We would not need them. We could see the town in the distance but the trees and the undergrowth, as well as the bend in the road, meant that we could not see the bridge itself. The road turned and we saw the river and the bridge. It looked to be about ninety paces long. They had no towers there. It was just a dozen or so men armed with spears. They must have been gathered to talk of the news the rider had brought for they were slow to turn and in that delay, we were thirty paces closer.

Two had bows and when they saw us they sent arrows in our direction. One hit the shield of Roger of Bath. Then they ran. They were fleet of foot but no man alive can outrun a horse. John son of John clattered across the bridge and, as we reached the middle his sword swung first at one side of his horse's head and then the other. The two archers had paid for their courage with their lives. I saw that men were gathering on the other side of the bridge. Men were coming from a gate on the northern side of the fort.

"Enough. Let us go back and start the fires."

As we turned we passed Aelric and his archers. They were dismounted and had an arrow nocked ready to loose. We dismounted at the eastern end of the bridge and Roger and my men at arms took the kindling to pack beneath the timbers which supported the bridge at the river bank. Aelric and his archers had reached the middle and were sending arrows into the Ó Conor clan who were slowly advancing towards them. The Irishmen had learned, probably from Domhnall, of our skill, and they were protected by shields. Their slow pace meant that they were not making much progress.

Roger of Bath shouted, "Ready to fire, Earl Marshal." He held the flint in this hand. The kindling had been dry and wrapped around some hay. They had then been doused in oil to help the burning. It would burn quickly.

"Then fire the bridge!" I smelled the wood burning and heard it crackling. On the far side of the bridge, more men were approaching my archers who were still falling back. "Aelric! Fall back!"

My archers sent another flight of arrows and then ran. Smoke began to drift up from below the bridge. Aelric and his archers turned at the end of the bridge and sent a penultimate flight towards the far end of the bridge. The Irish were racing towards us and the last flight hit six of them.

"I would move, lord. The oil we used is helping the fire to catch quickly."

"One last flight Aelric."

The last one was the most effective. Twelve Irishmen fell to the deadly arrows. They were less than thirty paces from us. As we turned and ran to our horses, the mob picked up the shields that the dead men were carrying and ran after us. Once on their horses Aelric and his men sent a few more arrows towards the Irish. They were not as effective from the back of a horse but it made the Irish halt.

I shouted, "Charge!" I led my twelve men at the Irish who were advancing down the road. There were thirty of them and more were coming. I do not think they thought that we would charge. We had the element of surprise, mail and better weapons. They had no shield wall and when we hit them our horses knocked some of them to the ground before they could even think of fighting. I hacked and slashed over the top of their shields. My sword ripped open an arm and laid open a skull. Arne Arneson was using his axe and he split the shield and chest of one Irishman. Aelric loosed another flight over our heads to kill five more advancing men.

"Fall back!"

We had done enough. They had lost a number of men and we had lost none. The bridge was ablaze and, although they would be able to put the fire out it would take time. I led my victorious men back down the road, across the fields and then back over the ford. The men building the camp cheered.

Instead of heading back to the camp, I rode close to the gate. I stopped beyond the range of bows. I knew that Prince Domhnall would understand my words, "Are you ready to come and be tried for murder, Prince Domhnall?"

My answer was a shower of a dozen arrows. All landed forty paces from me.

"Then we will take you by force!"

That night I discussed my plan with the other leaders. We had two hundred and fifty horsemen. Eighty of them were knights. We also had a hundred and twenty archers. I had Aelric divide the archers into three. One third would go with Sir Maurice and attack and fire the western end of the town wall. Sir Maurice would lead ten knights and twenty men at arms. Sir Jocelyn would take another third of the archers and five knights with ten men at arms and they would do as we had done and attack the bridge. Leaving just ten men to guard the camp, Count Striguil and I would lead the rest to attack the fort. I think my men and I were the only ones confident of our success. The others wondered at the wisdom, or as they saw it, the folly of dividing our limited numbers by three.

We kept a good watch that night for I worried that the Irishmen might try to get to our horses or the structure we had begun to build. Sir Maurice and his men had cut lengths of wood and laid them out as though they were going to assemble an onager. From what I had seen of Prince Domhnall in Kerns he would try to outwit us. He would think that we were building an onager and our attack would come once it was built.

We ate well; my men had laid nets across the river and we had its bounty to break our fast. We drank the last of the ale. We would have to use water when that was gone. My two raiding parties prepared to move. I had the rest of the army gather to wave them off. We cheered as though they were bound on some mighty quest. I wanted them to think that the two flank attacks were our only ones. Our waving drew the Irish to their walls. They had the upper wall manned by large numbers of men. The lower wall was sparsely manned. My knights, bareheaded, then gathered in, what I hoped would look like groups of men chatting. We were less than two hundred paces from the walls. Shields and helmets lay scattered around.

When Sir Jocelyn and his men were seen crossing the ford, a trumpet sounded and I saw men leaving the main wall to head to the north gate and the bridge. Not long after the men had begun to move I heard a shout from the town wall as they saw Sir Maurice's intent. Another trumpet sounded and more men left the upper walls. Surreptitiously picking up helmets and shields we moved a little closer.

I said, "Begin to taunt them, Roger of Bath!"

"Aye, lord!" He and my men had been looking forward to this. I asked my men at arms to begin taunting as Padraig had taught them a little crude Irish. They began to curse their forebears and suggest that their mothers slept with swine. The others did the same but in English. Crude gestures were made and the Irish responded. The two archers with my raiding parties began to send their arrows towards the bridge and the town walls. I saw more men leave the main wall. Sir Maurice used a shield wall to allow his men with fire to get closer to the walls. At the bridge, I heard the clash of arms. Another trumpet sounded and more men left to stop the fires. Now it was time. There were less than half the men on the upper walls than there had been before.

"Form ranks." I joined Count Striguil and six carefully chosen knights. They had all attacked a wall before and they all had a full helmet such as I wore. I used knights for the first six ranks. Three of them, the three largest, bore axes. Roger of Bath held my men at arms and the other men at arms as a reserve. The squires fell in behind the knights. We did not chant we just hefted our shields and, with helmets donned, began to hurry towards the bridge. I heard a shout and knew that we had been spotted. They had large numbers of men trying to put out the fires. They had learned their lesson the previous day. Arrows and slingshot were sent in our direction. With our shields high and our full helmets on our heads, we were immune from damage by their missiles. I heard an arrow clang off my helmet. The Irish used hunting arrows. The stones were more dangerous but we were lucky, they struck shields.

We reached the bridge and crossed to the first gate. Aelric and his archers had followed up behind. The Irish archers were at the bridge and the town wall trying to deter our two attacks. Our archers could release with impunity. A body crashed down before us as we reached the gate.

"Shields and axes!" I lifted my shield as did the Count and Sir Ranulf. Beneath the three shields, three other knights began to swing their axes at the gate. Another body fell from the wall and almost knocked me from my feet. I angled the shield and the Irish warrior slid into the ditch. I heard shouts from within as they tried to reinforce this wall. That was a mistake. Had I been in command I would have abandoned the gate and retired to the second wall. They did not and, when the gate was burst asunder, we raced in and butchered the men who were running along the ditch to reach the second gate.

As we ran I saw another flaw in their plan. We were able to have our shields on our left arms for the path went to our right. We could run and we were still protected. They had brought more archers back. Stones and arrows hit our shields but we were not knocked to the ground. We were not trying to run in one column. It would have been fruitless. Knights were catching Irish warriors and slaying them. As soon as Aelric and his archers got through the gate they began to pick off the enemy archers. At the same time, Roger of Bath brought our men at arms to clamber up the ditch and using the short ladders they had made. They would ascend the walls. I risked looking up and saw the Chief and the Prince were at the gate.

There were no Irish left alive before us and I shouted, "Halt and reform!" As soon as we turned to cross the bridge and attack the second gate then the men on our right would be in danger of being struck. "Rear rank! Shields!" The last line of knights ran to stand with their backs to our column, holding their shields before them.

Once again, my knights with axes began to hack at the gate. This time they poured boiling water upon us. They had not prepared large enough quantities and although it was painful our surcoats and mail prevented serious damage. If they had used oil then we would have been in trouble. I heard a shout from our left. Then James, who led the squires, shouted, "Roger of Bath is inside the fort!"

The shout spurred on our knights and four mighty strokes later the gates burst open and we were inside. This time there were men waiting for us. I used my shield to block the axe which swung down at me and I slashed across the middle of the warrior. I saw his entrails as my sword came away. I passed the dead man to allow the other knights to enter. A sword came from nowhere towards my head. The helmet did not help with peripheral vision. The sword rang off my helmet I turned my head and saw a surprised Irishman with a bent sword in his hand. I backhanded my sword across his neck and he died with the same surprised look on his face.

"Shields!"

Now was not the time to become reckless. We needed to drive the Irishmen before us and suffer as few casualties as possible. Count Striguil appeared on my right and other knights joined to his right.

"March!"

We stepped forward with swords held above our shields. The knights with axes moved down the palisade. The three of them hacked and chopped all those who ran at them. With our right flank secure and our men at arms piling down to our left we moved towards the centre of the fort. Inside it was largely empty save for a hall which looked as though it was their barracks. I heard Irish voices. I had no doubt that they were exhorting their men to great deeds. Without Padraig to interpret it was just a strident cacophony of cries.

The Irish way of war appeared to be to throw yourself high in the air and land upon your opponent. Perhaps it worked if your enemy was without mail and as poorly armed as you. We were not. Three young warriors with limed hair and a crudely made tattoo of a bear on their chest ran at our line and jumped high into the air. Their swords were above their heads. If they had struck down with them then we would have been knocked from our feet. As it was we swung our swords and the men were disembowelled as they fell. Their swords fell from lifeless hands and we stepped over their bodies.

Having seen that those tactics did not work the next one was to race at us in such numbers that they would overwhelm us. We now had thirty knights within the walls. They might have numbers but no longer enough to surround us. Our two flank attacks, which were still going on, had drawn a large number of Irish warriors away. We now had to drive them from the fort.

It was when Aelric and his archers entered the main gates that the tide really turned. Once the arrows flew to take the ones at the rear of the line we were able to force back the press of men before us. They had battered our shields and our helmets but done us no damage. Our blades found flesh whenever they struck for they had no armour. This was not like fighting a Viking. As I swept my sword before me to slash two men at the same time I realised why the Vikings had been able to hold on to such large towns as they had. The Irish, no matter how brave and how numerous, could not defeat mailed men.

I saw Prince Domhnall and his five oathsworn. They were desperately trying to find a way out of the trap they were in. I shouted, "Count, there is our target!"

The two of us led six knights towards them. The squires had caught up with us and they were able to take over our drive towards the north gate of the fort. Prince Domhnall was trying to get to the west gate. I guessed he had horses waiting. The problem was that Roger of Bath and the men at arms had cut off their escape.

Two oathsworn stepped before their Prince. Count Striguil said to me, "Take these two and I will try to take him alive!"

It was a mistake but I admired his courage and his noble intent. "Sir William, these two are ours."

The young knight, delighted to be fighting alongside the Earl Marshal roared, "Aye lord!"

My aim was to move them from before their Prince. Both had shields and swords. I swung my sword backhanded across my shield. It had the effect of making him turn his body to take the blow, aimed at his sword, on his shield. Sir William was even more direct. He punched his opponent in the face with his shield and the Irishman tumbled over. He was agile and leapt to his feet but there was now a gap into which Count

Striguil stepped. As I brought my sword over my head to slice into the helmet and skull of the oathsworn I fought I heard Count Striguil's sword clash with Prince Domhnall.

"You cannot win. Come back and stand trial!"

There was another clash of steel and I heard the Prince's voice, "So that I may be paraded before you Normans and kept a prisoner for the rest of my life? I would rather die."

I took my sword from the skull of the dead Irishman and turned. The other oathsworn were dead, dying or so badly wounded that they would not survive the night. I glanced to my right and saw that Lord Turloch Mór Ó Conor had been knocked to the ground by Sir Jocelyn and the Irish were surrendering. I took off my helmet.

There were just two men left fighting. Count Striguil could have killed the Prince of Leinster any time he chose. He was being too honourable. The blows struck by Prince Domhnall grew weaker and weaker. Count Striguil was going to wear him down. The Count might have succeeded if one of the badly wounded oathsworn not reached up to stab the Count in the calf. Instinct took over. The Count stabbed down to kill the man as Prince Domhnall tried to sweep his sword across the Count's body. The blow was blocked and the Count could not help himself. He reacted as any well-trained warrior would do. He just lunged forward and his sword ended the life of Prince Domhnall mac Murchada.

For Sir Richard, this was no victory. He felt that he had lost. He would now be crowned King but it was not the way he wished it to be.

Our knights, men at arms and archers were cheering and banging their shields. Count Striguil had his head hung down. I put my arm around his shoulders, "You did your best. Conchobar is avenged and, I think, his father. I do not think his father would have died so soon had not his favourite been murdered."

He stood. "Perhaps you are right. And now what do we do?"

I pointed to the five dead knights and three men at arms who lay close to us. "We have lost too many men to let this jewel go. Take it for your kingdom. Build a real castle here. You have the makings of a motte."

"But what of King Henry?"

"You still have that bridge to cross but if you control the Shannon then you have more to bargain with should there be a problem. The King will recognise that he has a good chance for us to subdue Ireland. He can obey the papal bull and make England and Wales safer from the slave raiders. Build the castle."

"Then I will give it to Sir Maurice. He has done well."

"And you had best get the wound seen to. You do not want to lose the leg because of a dirty wound."

We spent the rest of the day clearing the dead and moving our men into the fort. We moved the horses closer to the fort and they grazed happily on the lush grass. Lord Turloch Mór Ó Conor had survived. He was held in the hall with his oathsworn. They would be our prisoners. The Count had not decided what to do with them yet. The rest of his men had disappeared.

As we ate that night I said, "On the morrow, I will take my men at arms and archers. We will return to Dyflin and I will take ship for England. You need me no longer."

The Count nodded, "You are right although I am reluctant to see you go. Will you return?"

I could not lie to the Count. We had stood together in a shield wall. We were brothers in arms. "The King may be unhappy with your gains. I will make your case for you but I am King Henry's man. I cannot promise that this will end well."

"I could not fight you."

"Let us not make problems which do not exist. The King may not be unhappy with your gains."

"I do not want to be king!"

"I smiled, "I think in your heart you do. What you really mean is that you do not wish to antagonise King Henry and that I can understand. Know you that I will plead your case as best I can."

"Then I am hopeful. You are honest and your word is trusted. If you cannot persuade the King then no man can."

I did not depart the next day. Count Striguil had sent men out early to seek any survivors who might be waiting to do harm. They rode back within a short time of leaving. "Count, the High King. He is approaching from the south-west. He has an army."

"I thought he had paid reparations and given hostages?" The Count was visibly shocked.

I pointed to Padraig, "As my servant said, that means nothing. I fear we must fight him again and this time the hostage we take and hold must be the High King and his family."

"You are right. How do we fight him?"

"The land to the west is flat. He may think his ally still holds the crossing. We have the archers in the fort and we charge them."

"That sounds simple."

"Sometimes the best ideas are. There are no woods in which they can hide. Our horses have been rested for three days and our men are exultant. Men fight better when they have won a battle. These men have yet to lose one." I looked at his leg. "How is the wound?"

"It will not stop me."

"Then lead them Count. I will ride behind your banner."

We made out three lines. The difference this time was that the Count placed the men at arms in the second rank. He said they had earned the right. Padraig, reluctantly, stayed in the fort. We saw the horde approach. There was no order whatsoever. The High King had taken any man he could to wrest the land back from us and he had large numbers. I saw half-naked wild men. There were some mailed men. I even saw a few Vikings fighting for the High King. Apart from the Vikings and the chiefs around the High King, I saw few shields. There was no order to their approach. Men looked to be fighting in clans or family groups. They were knotted around one warrior. The High King rode at the fore and they spread out over a large area.

The Count waited until they were just three hundred paces from us and then he gave the command, "Charge!"

This time we rode boot to boot. We rode in straight lines. Our horses were puissant beasts and they ate up the ground. They thundered across it and they made it shake. The High King had met us before and he led his mounted men towards the fort. Perhaps he thought it was still in his hands for we had no banners flying. The horde was slow to turn. The men he led were confused and they slowed. We ploughed into them. They had aided us for when they turned they presented their right sides to us. There were few shields amongst them but the ones they did possess were on the wrong side.

I pulled back my arm and thrust into flesh four times, killing each time I did so. On the fourth my spear broke and, as I pulled my sword out, I glanced to my right and the fort. The mounted men had reached the outer ditch. The High King had discovered that we held it. My archers slew half of the chiefs and oathsworn. Then my sword was out and I had no opportunity to see what went on anywhere but in front of me. I leaned forward to hack across the side of a Viking who was fighting with Sir Stephen. He had good mail. I had a better sword.

We were no longer boot to boot. Richard de Clare led the horsemen as a true leader should, from the front. His sword slashed left and right. We found ourselves deep in the heart of them. The folly of fighting in family groups was clearly shown. When a leader fell then his men fled. As more and more were slain so the flood of men fleeing grew. The enemy had broken. It had begun when the High King turned for the fort and speeded up when we struck. Now that we were in the heart of them, panic had set in and men tripped and fell in their efforts to escape. Horses trampled those that did so. My sword became an iron bar. I was not hitting mail but skulls and spines and bone and my blade became blunted. It was when Warrior stumbled that I halted. De Clare and I were alone. The rest of the army was behind us slaughtering all who still stood. Ahead of us more than a thousand men were still running.

    The High King tried to join it but I watched as Count Striguil, Sir Maurice and Sir Stephen surrounded him with their men. The High King was no warrior nor was he a fool. I saw his standard cast to the ground and his helmet removed. We had won. This time the campaign was really over. The High King would be kept a prisoner. Castles would be built and Count Striguil would become King of Leinster. Someday he might become King of Ireland. That was for the future. For myself, I was going home. It might be a long journey for first I would have to find King Henry. With my men at arms and archers along with our share of the treasure we had won, I headed for Dyflin and the *'Maid of Portishead'*.

Epilogue

My journey home took longer than I either expected or hoped. I took ship and we rode, first to Chester, then Lincoln and finally London. The King and Queen were not there. They were in Chinon. I had sent my ship to London and we waited for five days for it to arrive. Then we sailed for Anjou. I reached Chinon almost four months after we defeated the High King. I had outridden the news. None knew of our success. There were rumours that we had defeated an Irish army and two Viking ones but details were vague. That heartened me. The King would hear what had happened from the lips of someone he trusted; me.

I found him and the Queen, once again pregnant, in the Great Hall. Every head turned as we were announced and entered. "Earl Marshal! We have missed you! How went the campaign?"

We were in the full court. I did not want the King to hear my news that way. "My liege I am weary after many months travelling. I would speak with you and the Queen privately."

He frowned, "Why? What are you hiding?"

Eleanor had ever been my friend and she put her hand on her husband's, "My lord I think that Alfraed has earned the right to speak to us privately." She cocked her head on one side and gave him a winning smile.

He nodded, "You are right. I am sorry Earl Marshal. You are never one to make a fuss. Come we will go to my solar."

Once in the private room, I told him all that had happened. At first, his face was dark and he stood as though angry. He went to the window and looked west. "Tell me this, Earl Marshal. Did he go there to win a kingdom?"

I sighed, "Your majesty it was you who encouraged him to go the aid of the Irish King. You were there when the matter of matrimony was introduced. Did you not think he might be in line for the throne?"

He threw me a sharp look and then smiled, "I did not think he would be so successful! He defeated the Irish and the Vikings?" He shook his head and then gave me a shrewd look. "Of course, it was you defeated them."

"He could have done it without me."

"That I doubt. Do not forget, Earl Marshal, that I have seen you fight and know that when you fight you win."

Eleanor sipped her wine, "Is the land valuable?"

"It could be. The land looks to be perfect for farming. They have rain but little snow. The ground is largely flat and they have many rivers. The Irish fight amongst themselves. That has been their problem. They rarely have peace. England was the same when we had the civil war. Now that we have peace then prosperity brings a bounty to the land. The Irish are brave but we took more than a third of the country with just a thousand men."

The King looked up, suddenly interested, "Then the other two thirds could be conquered easily?"

Eleanor said, "Do not forget the French, husband. If you were to go and take the rest then you might lose Normandy and Anjou too."

He nodded, "Damned French." He sat and sipped his wine. I could see his mind working as he devised a way to take the island whilst holding on to power in Normandy and Anjou. "Then here is what you can tell de Clare. He can have his titles returned and the lands he holds in Wales, England Normandy and Anjou. I will recognise him as King of Leinster."

"That is generous your majesty."

The King nodded, "Aye, I know. He must publicly acknowledge me as his liege lord. He will make obeisance to me."

I was relieved. That was what Richard wished. "I know that he will do that, your majesty."

"And…I will have his fortresses including Waterford, Wexford and Dyflin given over to me as Royal fortresses. I will let him keep Ferns. I believe you when you say he does not wish to challenge me but if I hold his mighty castles then he cannot, can he? In addition, he will bring men to support me in the war with France."

I admired my son, Henry the King. He was ruthless and he was ambitious. Without lifting a finger, save send me to fight for De Clare, he had gained another kingdom to add to his Empire. He had also gained large numbers of experienced men to fight in his French wars. What worried me was that if he wanted de Clare then he would want me. When would I get home?

I smiled and bowed, "I am certain he will agree."

"If he does not then he will lose more than his lands." He smiled and put his arm around my shoulder, "Stay awhile but I need you to return with my message by the end of the week. I would have this in writing."

"Of course, your majesty."

"Thank you, Earl Marshal, you are still my mother's faithful knight and mine too. What would we do without you?"

Eleanor smiled, "Let us hope that we never have to, my husband."

There was little to say. I would have to take another three-week voyage to Dyflin. After I had spoken with Count Striguil I would have to take his answer and the agreement back to King Henry. I would not be home for another four months. It might be longer if he wished me to begin war against the French. I served my king and I served my country. When would I be able to serve myself?

The End

Glossary

Akolouthos – the leader of the Guard
Aldeneby - Alston (Cumbria)
Al-Andalus- Spain
Angevin- the people of Anjou, mainly the ruling family
Arthuret -Longtown in Cumbria (This is the Brythionic name)
Bannau Brycheiniog – Brecon Beacons
Battle- a formation in war (a modern battalion)
Booth Castle – Bewcastle north of Hadrian's Wall
Bachelor knight- an unattached knight
Banneret- a single knight
Burn- stream (Scottish)
Butts- targets for archers
Cadge- the frame upon which hunting birds are carried (by a codger- hence the phrase old codger being the old man who carries the frame)
Caerdyf- Cardiff
Caparison- a surcoat for a horse; often padded for protection
Captain- a leader of archers
Chausses - mail leggings. (They were separate- imagine lady's stockings rather than tights!)
Coningestun- Coniston
Conroi- A group of knights fighting together. The smallest unit of the period
Corebricg – Corbridge
Cuneceastra- Chester-Le-Street
Demesne- estate
Destrier- war horse
Doxy- prostitute
Dyflin- Dublin
Fissebourne- Fishburn County Durham
Fess- a horizontal line in heraldry
Galloglass- Irish mercenaries
Gambeson- a padded tunic worn underneath mail. When worn by an archer they came to the waist. It was more of a quilted jacket but I have used the term freely
Gonfanon- A standard used in medieval times (Also known as a Gonfalon in Italy)

Hartness- the manor which became Hartlepool
Hautwesel- Haltwhistle
Hulle- Rhyl (North Wales)
Liedeberge- Ledbury
Lusitania- Portugal
Mansio- staging houses along Roman Roads
Maredudd ap Bleddyn- King of Powys
Martinmas- 11th November
Mêlée- a medieval fight between knights
Morthpath- Morpeth (Northumbria)
Moravians- the men of Moray
Mormaer- A Scottish lord and leader
Mummer- an actor from a medieval tableau
Musselmen- Muslims
Nithing- A man without honour (Saxon)
Nomismata- a gold coin equivalent to an aureus
Novo Burgus -Newport (Gwent)
Outremer- the kingdoms of the Holy Land
Owain ap Gruffudd- Son of Gruffudd ap Cynan and King of Gwynedd from 1137
Palfrey- a riding horse
Poitevin- the language of Aquitaine
Prestetone- Prestatyn- North Wales
Pyx- a box containing a holy relic (Shakespeare's Pax from Henry V)
Refuge- a safe area for squires and captives (tournaments)
Sauve qui peut – Every man for himself (French)
Serengford- Shellingford Oxfordshire
Sergeant-a leader of a company of men at arms
Striguil- Chepstow (Gwent)
Surcoat- a tunic worn over mail or armour
Sumpter- pack horse
Theophany- the feast which is on the 6th of January
Ventail – a piece of mail which covered the neck and the lower face Al-Andalus- Spain
Veðrafjǫrðr -Waterford (Ireland)
Veisafjǫrðr- Wexford (Ireland)
Wulfestun- Wolviston (Durham)

Historical Notes

Alfraed is not a real person. He is based upon a number of people, most notably William Marshal. The title of Earl marshal was a real one. Earl Marshal (alternatively Marschal, Marischal or Marshall) is a hereditary royal officeholder and chivalric title under the sovereign of the United Kingdom used in England. He is the eighth of the Great Officers of State in the United Kingdom, ranking beneath the Lord High Constable and above the Lord High Admiral. The Earl Marshal has among his responsibilities the organisation of major ceremonial state occasions like the monarch's coronation in Westminster Abbey and state funerals. He is also a leading officer of arms and oversees the College of Arms.

Especial thanks are due to Rich Sankovich. He allowed me to use his crossbow. I now understand how hard it is to fire one. The end is very heavy. You have to be kneeling or resting to use one. Its accuracy is also not as good as that of a bow despite the mechanical nature of the beast. Pulling back the cord to fire it is also a challenge. I would defy anyone to send more than a couple of bolts in a four-minute period. I am also indebted to the Essex re-enactors who told me of a competition held between muskets and war bows. Even tap firing the muskets (apparently an unsafe procedure) the war bow sent more arrows further and at a greater rate than the musket. Wellington, it is alleged, wondered about having a battalion of archers!

The leaders and kings were, in the main real people. William de Beauchamp was the Sherriff of both Hereford and Gloucester. I have changed some of the dates slightly to make a tighter novel- this is fiction but the events concerning King Henry really happened. In North Wales, he barely escaped with his life. His cousin did die when his knights disobeyed their orders. The story will continue for the Scots have yet to be brought to heel. Of course, that may well involve his son William. The saga is of a family and not a man.

Strongbow (Richard de Clare) in Ireland

Diarmait Mac Murchada (Dermot MacMurrough) was deprived of the Kingdom of Leinster by the High King of Ireland – Ruaidrí Ua Conchobair. The grounds for the dispossession were that Mac Murchada had, in 1152, abducted Derbforgaill, the wife of the King of Breifne, Tiernan O'Rourke (Irish: Tighearnán Ua Ruairc). To recover his kingdom, Mac Murchada solicited help from the King of England – Henry II. The deposed king embarked for Bristol from near Bannow. Henry could not help him at this time but provided a letter of comfort for willing supporters of Mac Murchada's cause in his kingdom. However, after his return to Wales, he failed to rally any forces to his standard. He eventually met the count of Striguil (nicknamed "Strongbow") and other barons of the Welsh Marches. Mac Murchada came to an agreement with Richard de Clare: for the Earl's assistance with an army the following spring, he could have Aoife, Mac Murchada's eldest daughter in marriage and the succession to Leinster. As Henry's approval or license to Mac Murchada was a general one, the count of Striguil thought it prudent to obtain Henry's specific consent to travel to Ireland: he waited two years to do this. The license he got was to aid Mac Murchada in the recovery of his kingdom of Leinster.

Mac Murchada and Richard de Clare raised a large army, which included Welsh archers and arranged for Raymond FitzGerald (also known as Raymond le Gros) to lead it. The force took the Ostman towns of Wexford, Waterford, and Dublin in rapid succession.

The events around the invasion of Ireland all happened. However, I have shortened the time to make a more exciting story and brought it forward by a year or two to allow the Warlord to participate. The Pope was English and he did order a papal bull. The Irish clung on to slavery for longer than anywhere else in Western Europe. Of course, its replacement was little better. Serfdom still tied men and their families to lords where they worked for a pittance but they had rights; a slave had none.

The Vikings ruled Man (Mann) and the westerns islands until the thirteenth century. The Vikings in Ireland were only defeated when the Normans arrived. They ruled five towns, Dublin, Limerick, Cork, Wexford and Waterford. They still raided but they traded more. At the time of the Normans they were past their best. It should be remembered that the Normans were descended from the Vikings who settled along the lower Seine.

The incident with the cattle actually happened. It was Raymond Le Gros. He found himself facing a thousand Irishmen and he had ten knights and ninety others. Nearby was a huge herd of cattle. They drove the cattle through the Irishmen and defeated them.

I have used the Warlord to be the instrument which delivered King Henry's judgement to de Clare. In reality it was Hervey de

Montmorency. King Henry gained the island of Ireland with just a handful of knights.

The Warlord and William will return. Their story and that of King Henry II will continue.

Books used in the research:

- The Varangian Guard- 988-1453 Raffael D'Amato
- Saxon Viking and Norman- Terence Wise
- The Walls of Constantinople AD 324-1453-Stephen Turnbull
- Byzantine Armies- 886-1118- Ian Heath
- The Age of Charlemagne-David Nicolle
- The Normans- David Nicolle
- Norman Knight AD 950-1204- Christopher Gravett
- The Norman Conquest of the North- William A Kappelle
- The Knight in History- Francis Gies
- The Norman Achievement- Richard F Cassady
- Knights- Constance Brittain Bouchard
- Knight Templar 1120-1312 -Helen Nicholson
- Feudal England: Historical Studies on the Eleventh and Twelfth Centuries- J. H. Round
- Armies of the Crusades- Helen Nicholson
- Knight of Outremer 1187- 1344 - David Nicholle
- Crusader Castles in the Holy Land- David Nicholle
- The Crusades- David Nicholle
- Bamburgh Castle Heritage group
- Warkworth Castle- English Heritage Guide
- The Times Atlas of World History
- Old Series Ordnance Survey Maps #93 Middlesbrough
- Old Series Ordnance Survey Maps #81 Alnwick and Morpeth
- Old Series Ordnance Survey Maps #92 Barnard Castle

For those who like authentic maps the last two maps are part of a series now available. They are the first Government produced maps of the British Isles. Great Britain, apart from the larger conurbations, was the same as it had been 800 years earlier.

I also discovered a good website http://orbis.stanford.edu/. This allows a reader to plot any two places in the Roman world and if you input the mode of transport you wish to use and the time of year it will calculate how long it would take you to travel the route. I have used it for all of my books up to the eighteenth century as the transportation system was roughly the same. The Romans would have been quicker!

Griff Hosker
October 2017

Irish War

Other books by Griff Hosker

If you enjoyed reading this book, then why not read another one by the author?

Ancient History

The Sword of Cartimandua Series
(Germania and Britannia 50 A.D. – 128 A.D.)
Ulpius Felix- Roman Warrior (prequel)
The Sword of Cartimandua
The Horse Warriors
Invasion Caledonia
Roman Retreat
Revolt of the Red Witch
Druid's Gold
Trajan's Hunters
The Last Frontier
Hero of Rome
Roman Hawk
Roman Treachery
Roman Wall
Roman Courage

The Wolf Warrior series
(Britain in the late 6th Century)
Saxon Dawn
Saxon Revenge
Saxon England
Saxon Blood
Saxon Slayer
Saxon Slaughter
Saxon Bane
Saxon Fall: Rise of the Warlord
Saxon Throne
Saxon Sword

Irish War

Medieval History

The Dragon Heart Series
Viking Slave
Viking Warrior
Viking Jarl
Viking Kingdom
Viking Wolf
Viking War
Viking Sword
Viking Wrath
Viking Raid
Viking Legend
Viking Vengeance
Viking Dragon
Viking Treasure
Viking Enemy
Viking Witch
Viking Blood
Viking Weregeld
Viking Storm
Viking Warband
Viking Shadow
Viking Legacy
Viking Clan
Viking Bravery

The Norman Genesis Series
Hrolf the Viking
Horseman
The Battle for a Home
Revenge of the Franks
The Land of the Northmen
Ragnvald Hrolfsson
Brothers in Blood
Lord of Rouen
Drekar in the Seine
Duke of Normandy
The Duke and the King

Irish War

Danelaw
(England and Denmark in the 11th Century)
Dragon Sword
Oathsword

New World Series
Blood on the Blade
Across the Seas
The Savage Wilderness
The Bear and the Wolf
Erik The Navigator

The Vengeance Trail

The Reconquista Chronicles
Castilian Knight
El Campeador
The Lord of Valencia

The Aelfraed Series
(Britain and Byzantium 1050 A.D. - 1085 A.D.)
Housecarl
Outlaw
Varangian

The Anarchy Series England 1120-1180
English Knight
Knight of the Empress
Northern Knight
Baron of the North
Earl
King Henry's Champion
The King is Dead
Warlord of the North
Enemy at the Gate
The Fallen Crown
Warlord's War

Irish War

Kingmaker
Henry II
Crusader
The Welsh Marches
Irish War
Poisonous Plots
The Princes' Revolt
Earl Marshal
The Perfect Knight

**Border Knight
1182-1300**
Sword for Hire
Return of the Knight
Baron's War
Magna Carta
Welsh Wars
Henry III
The Bloody Border
Baron's Crusade
Sentinel of the North
War in the West
Debt of Honour
The Blood of the Warlord (Feb 2022)

**Sir John Hawkwood Series
France and Italy 1339- 1387**
Crécy: The Age of the Archer
Man At Arms
The White Company

Lord Edward's Archer
Lord Edward's Archer
King in Waiting
An Archer's Crusade
Targets of Treachery
The Great Cause (April 2022)

Struggle for a Crown

Irish War

1360- 1485
Blood on the Crown
To Murder a King
The Throne
King Henry IV
The Road to Agincourt
St Crispin's Day
The Battle For France
The Last Knight
Queen's Knight

Tales from the Sword I
(Short stories from the Medieval period)

Tudor Warrior series
England and Scotland in the late 14th and early 15th century
Tudor Warrior

Conquistador
England and America in the 16th Century
Conquistador

Modern History

The Napoleonic Horseman Series
Chasseur à Cheval
Napoleon's Guard
British Light Dragoon
Soldier Spy
1808: The Road to Coruña
Talavera
The Lines of Torres Vedras
Bloody Badajoz
The Road to France
Waterloo

The Lucky Jack American Civil War series
Rebel Raiders
Confederate Rangers

Irish War

The Road to Gettysburg

The British Ace Series
1914
1915 Fokker Scourge
1916 Angels over the Somme
1917 Eagles Fall
1918 We will remember them
From Arctic Snow to Desert Sand
Wings over Persia

Combined Operations series
1940-1945
Commando
Raider
Behind Enemy Lines
Dieppe
Toehold in Europe
Sword Beach
Breakout
The Battle for Antwerp
King Tiger
Beyond the Rhine
Korea
Korean Winter

Tales from the Sword II
(Short stories from the Modern period)

Other Books
Great Granny's Ghost (Aimed at 9-14-year-old young people)

For more information on all of the books then please visit the author's website at www.griffhosker.com where there is a link to contact him or visit his Facebook page: GriffHosker at Sword Books

Printed in Dunstable, United Kingdom